A KINGDOM FALLS

THE FIVE REALMS VOLUME 1

M.L. DARLOW

Second Printing, 2024

CONTENTS

To Gramma, thank you for never failing to support me. This one is for you.

Molly J. Carpenter
July 24, 1941 - March 23, 2019

The Safe Haven
Saloris City
The Forest of Fools
The Skyward Range
Blackbay
The Kingdom of Elves
Lakelands
Ardon Lake
The Strip
Golden City
Cohmdhail
Mayfire
Graystone Ruins
Death Valley
Aren

The Idonian Kingdom
Galactic Gates
The Idonian Forest
Endurion Lake
Witherow
Redding
Crane
Dracus
Olaigon
Lorcan
Dairth
N
W
E
S
The Regal Mountains
The Edge of the Underworld

PROLOGUE

Gideon VanCamp's world was falling apart right before his eyes. As he stared at the barrier that now surrounded Idona's Galactic Gates, tears pricked at his eyes, but this was no time to shed them. As High King, he'd sworn to protect the Five Realms of Si Realtra. And right now, that meant preventing the Pandora from invading the other four Realms. He refused to subject the rest of the Galaxy to their vicious nature. He wouldn't allow it. He *couldn't* allow it.

In the beginning, the Pandora seemed to be nothing more passing day. Now, Gideon was forced to face the largest enemy to walk upon Idona's soil.

The Realm Prophetess, Valentina Gold, had seen this coming. Without her, Gideon wouldn't have been able to shut the Galactic Gates in time, and the Pandora forces, along with their nefarious leader — Malachai, would have escaped into the other than a thorn in a lion's paw, but their numbers tripled with every four Realms.

"We need to leave," the Prophetess plead, her golden eyes shimmering with tears.

"No," Gideon choked, shaking his head. His heart broke for his kingdom, for his people, and his Realm. He had failed them so far, but he wouldn't continue to do so. He would stand and fight until his very last breath emptied from his lungs. He wouldn't run and hide from the red eyes illuminating the rolling hills that surrounded Idona's Galactic Gates. He wouldn't cower from the snarls and hisses echoing in the dark.

"We'll die. I stole this with the intent of using it to ensure our survival." Valentina's lip trembled as she held out the chrome teleportation sphere wrapped tightly in her grip.

"You'll survive," Gideon insisted. "Use it. Go back to Dracus. Without you, there's no way Idona will withstand this war. Especially, now that it won't have the aid of the other four Realms. By shutting these Gates, we might have kept the Pandora at bay, but we've also shut ourselves inside with the enemy."

Valentina shook her head, the lump in her throat bobbing. "You can't die. What about Meera? Penelope? The twins?"

"Valentina." Gideon reached for her, placing a shaking hand on her shoulder. He hung his head, trying to hide the tears now rolling down his cheek. "He's here. I would be a fool not to take this opportunity to defeat him. To end this, here and now, for the sake of my people."

"How sweet," a hauntingly familiar voice mocked in the distance. Valentina blanched, her eyes narrowing in the direction from which the voice had come. "You should listen to him, Valentina. He's your King. For now, anyway."

"Malachai," she growled, her fingers curling into white-knuckled fists.

Gideon wove his fingers in with Valentina's, squeezing her hand gently in reassurance before he pried the sphere from her hands and tossed it onto the ground. A portal to Dracus appeared as Valentina's screams of protest echoed into the night. "Watch out for them," Gideon said as he pushed her, sending her stumbling through the shimmering wall. His chest tightened as he gazed upon the Draconian Kingdom for the last time before the portal evaporated, leaving nothing but the chrome sphere in its wake.

Pulling in a deep, shaky breath, Gideon turned his attention to the army of Pandora lingering in the distance. "Come out, come out, wherever you are," he said, his hand reaching for the hilt of his sword.

Malachai emerged from the shadows, his lips spread into a menacing smirk. The Pandora Prince had changed significantly since the last time Gideon had set his sights upon him. His dark hair had grown long, falling down his back in sheets of silk. What were once a pleasant shade of emerald eyes, were now an unnerving shade of red, blazing in the night around him.

Gideon watched as the prince's gaze slid to the Galactic Gates, which had once hummed with eternal life. Now, they sat lifeless at the end of the crystal bridge, blocked by the translucent barrier Gideon had enabled. No one would ever set foot upon that bridge again unless he, or one of his kin, willed it.

"You've made a grave mistake," Malachai snarled, venom dripping from every word.

"I wouldn't call it a mistake," Gideon replied through clenched teeth. "I'd call it divine intervention. You can play your little game with Idona, assuming that you live through this encounter — and I sincerely hope that you don't. However, if it is *I* that dies this evening, at least I'll die knowing neither you nor your demented father will lay a hand on the other four Realms."

Gideon watched as Malachai's body trembled with rage and waited for him to transition into the savage beast that he knew waited beneath his Mortal facade.

"Your fight isn't with me, Gideon," Malachai snapped. "It's with Xavier. You're wasting your time on me when you should be focusing on *him*. My defeat will do nothing for this Realm if he still breathes."

"You're wrong," Gideon replied, unsheathing his sword. "It would do *everything* for this Realm."

A guttural growl erupted from the Pandoran Prince as his jet-black pupils transitioned into dragon-like slits. "When I said that you'd made a mistake, I wasn't referring to the Gates. I was referring to the fact that you were idiotic enough to face *me* when you might have been able to face my father and live. Now, you'll die."

PART I

RUMORS

1

Marcus Bonaventure had evolved to be the man he'd always dreamed of becoming throughout his entire twenty-one years of life. As a child, he aspired to be one of the elites — a Black Knight. Unfortunately, those aspirations were pushed aside at the age of ten, when he'd awoken to find that his entire family had vanished. He'd been abandoned, and because of that, he'd needed to focus more on surviving each day in the bustling city of Solaris instead of becoming a knight.

By some unexpected miracle, he'd managed to become precisely what he'd wanted to be. Humphrey Adams, a Draconian representative, had found young Marcus starving on the streets eleven years ago. It was then that his future was decided for him. From that day forward, Marcus had worked incredibly hard to become what he was today.

Becoming a Black Knight had been more than good enough, but last year, he had learned that he was meant for more. He remembered the day as if it were yesterday. Solaris had been filled to the brim with people eager to watch the Realm Prophetess announce who the three Moons' had chosen to be the High Queen's Guardian — an honor unlike any other. Marcus could still hear Valentina's voice ringing in his ears as his name passed her lips. The thought of the entire ordeal gave him chills, even now, bringing a proud smile to his face.

Over the last year, Marcus had grown accustomed to being a Guardian. The position came with the unique sword sheathed down his spine —Whitefire—and it was with that sword that he was meant to protect High Queen Meera VanCamp.

However, he wasn't sure that he could do that now.

His gut twisted into knots as he recalled how he'd left Meera yesterday morning. He'd made her a promise to keep her heir, Penelope, safe. As directed, he'd deliver her to the Kingdom of Elves, where she'd remain until further notice. It was crucial that the VanCamps' survived.

At the moment, the four-year-old Princess was asleep, slumped against Marcus's torso as his horse trekked toward the Elves' historic Golden City. She seemed so sweet and peaceful, with no clue as to what was transpiring around her.

They weren't far off from the golden walls surrounding the Elven Kingdom when she began to stir. Marcus glanced down at her and smiled as she looked up at him with innocent hazel eyes.

"Where are we going?" she asked, tilting her head curiously, scanning their surroundings.

"To visit Queen Esmeralda and King Thaddeus," Marcus replied.

"Why?" The princess's brow furrowed.

Marcus pursed his lips. He had hoped Penelope wouldn't ask too many questions because he couldn't bear to give the answers. He fought to come up with a response she wouldn't analyze. "Princess Mika of the Elves is going to be having a birthday party, and you're invited."

Penelope's eyes narrowed accusingly. "Mika's birthday was in Autumn Solstice."

"Nanny Dessa will be joining you." Marcus hurried to change the subject. "She just needed to help your mother with a few things for the Fire and Ice Ball."

"I thought Mother wasn't going to have the ball this year because Father died," Penelope replied quizzically.

Marcus swallowed hard. He wished their conversation hadn't taken such a difficult turn. He peered ahead, hoping to catch sight of the golden walls. "We're nearly there. Aren't you excited?"

Penelope failed to answer. Instead, she stared silently down at her hands. Before long, the golden gate leading into the Kingdom of Elves appeared. Marcus briefly closed his eyes, drawing in a deep breath through his nose, and slowly exhaled before opening his eyes and starting forward. The gatekeeper allowed them to enter, and as Marcus led the horse through the cobblestone streets toward the alabaster castle looming off in the distance, he could feel gazes overcome with pity upon his back. Elves lined the streets, holding their right hands over their hearts, a symbol of respect. Marcus's eyes became misty, causing the young princess to believe that something was terribly wrong.

Marcus knew that at just four years old, Penelope wasn't blind to the harsh reality Idona was now facing. She saw the hurt in the eyes of those around her, as well as the pity. A crack seared through his heart as he set his palm on top of her head, smoothing her soft brown hair.

"Take me back," Penelope whimpered as the horse stopped in front of the castle.

A painful lump developed in Marcus's throat as he helped her to the ground. "I can't," he admitted, his voice no higher than a whisper.

"Why?" Penelope demanded. Tears began to spill from her

eyes. The doors to the castle opened, and King Thaddeus and Queen Esmeralda gracefully stepped through, their own eyes reflecting the pain that the entire Idonian Council felt.

Esmeralda, a mother of two herself, reached out to comfort the princess, but Penelope slapped her hand away and turned toward Marcus, wrapping her arms around his leg and weeping into his armor.

"Just take me back, *please!*" She clenched her little fists around Marcus's silver cape, squinting her eyes shut. "Don't leave me. Don't leave me here. Take me with you."

Marcus fought to keep his composure. Feelings of his own abandonment were still fresh, even eleven years later. While abandoning Penelope with the Elves hadn't been his intent, he worried about how she might feel or if she might grow to hate him. This moment was the one he'd feared most, and it was coming to life, breaking him, sinking painfully to his very core.

Tears threatening his own eyes, Marcus averted his gaze from the small princess and turned it toward the castle steps. One of the most powerful men in the Realms stood before him, and as a Black Knight, Marcus hated for Thaddeus to see him fall to such weakness. However, he could see understanding reflecting in the King's golden eyes.

"I have to help your mother and the twins." Marcus struggled to keep his voice from wavering.

"Why didn't you bring them with us?" Penelope wept. "Then you wouldn't have to leave. We could all be safe right now."

Marcus grimaced, having never understood the High Queen's plan to begin with. "You'll all be safe. I'll make sure of it. I promise." He knew he shouldn't have, but deep down, he felt like it was a promise he could keep. He *needed* to keep it because if he couldn't, he might not be able to live with himself come the morning.

"That's a lie!" Penelope screamed, tightening her grip around Marcus's cape. "If you leave this place, you'll die; you and I both know it! Don't leave me."

Marcus looked up at the Elven King and Queen, silently begging for their aid. "Penelope, dear," Esmeralda called softly. "You have to let Marcus go. He'll be right back. Before you know it, he'll walk right through those gates."

Penelope's cries were stifled. She slowly released his cape, taking a step back. She stared up at Marcus with swollen eyes and a quivering lip. "Is that true?"

A pit of dread settled in Marcus's stomach as he nodded. "I will come back through those gates," he assured her.

"You'll bring my mother and the twins?"

Marcus kneeled before her, his own green eyes staring directly into hers. "Do you remember when your cat went missing last year?"

Penelope nodded, her features softening. "You went to look for him, and you said you'd be right back. But you came back after a long time with the cat." Her brow creased. "So, you're trying to tell me it might take a while, but in the end, you'll make good on your promise?"

"Yes," Marcus nodded, clenching his fists. He pulled in a deep breath, exhaling slowly, fighting desperately to hide the storm of emotions raging within him. This was just the tip of the iceberg when it came to heartache, and he knew he would endure far more throughout the next few days. "I will," he told her, rising to his full height again. "King Thaddeus, would you be so kind as to show me to your Portal Room? I need to return quickly. I have a promise to keep."

The Elven King smiled faintly before leading Marcus into the castle. The Guardian walked silently behind him, holding his head high. He didn't dare look over his shoulder, unwilling to set his eyes on Penelope, fearing he would lose what was left of his composure at the sight of more tears streaming down her cheeks. Now was not the time to show weakness, for if he did in the days to come, it would surely cost him his life.

2

Three weeks had passed since Gideon VanCamp's disappearance, and now the fate of Idona was left in the hands of the High Queen, Meera VanCamp. While she'd fought to remain strong for the sake of the Idonian Kingdom, the city of Solaris, and the entire Realm around it, she wondered how much longer she could last. Her facade was fading, and before long, she felt as though she might fall apart.

"Just a few more hours," the queen whispered as she stared into the mirror, unable to recognize the person staring back at her. In the past, it was her husband that had done the fighting. Now, the weight of that horrid task fell upon Meera's shoulders. She could only pray that she was as fearless as her fellow Idonians needed her to be.

One of the queen's newborn twins began to stir in their bassinet, and Meera didn't need to look to know which one it was. Ash was always restless.

Sucking in a deep calming breath, Meera worked on composing herself. The armor that sat over her flesh felt so foreign. The impenetrable fabric felt stiff. Her sapphire cape felt like it might strangle her as it fluttered along with her movements.

A knock on the door startled the queen as she lifted the baby into her arms. She glanced over at Vincent, watching as a smile formed on his sleepy little face. "Come in," she called, her expression hardening once again. The last thing she needed was for anyone to know how afraid she truly was.

When Meera turned around, her heart sank. She gazed upon her Guardian, devastated, unable to miss the sorrow etched in every line of his face. She attempted to memorize those features while she still had the chance and couldn't help but notice the pain that had always haunted him, lurking in his bright green eyes. His short, chocolate locks were damp from the snow, causing drops of water to roll down to his chiseled jaw.

"Is she safe?" Meera asked, her voice trembled around the question. Deep down, she knew this would be the last time she saw the boy her husband had rescued eleven years ago. The boy who grew up to be her Guardian. The boy she considered her first son.

"She doesn't understand," Marcus replied solemnly, casting his gaze downward. "She wishes you were with her. And to be honest, I don't understand either, Meera."

The sound of her first name sailing past his lips caused the Queen's mouth to fall open. She shut it, her lips disappearing into a thin line. Instead of chastising him, she just stared, waiting for him to finish. She owed him that, at least. "You know you can't defeat Xavier. Only the Messenger can, and yet, you want to try? You filled our ballroom with Idona's best warriors, knowing there's a significant chance that they'll all die. What's the point?"

Meera's brows furrowed as she bounced Ash gingerly, happy that the newborn had no idea of the chaos around her. "I will not run away, Marcus," she replied. "I will not hand over my throne willingly. My people wouldn't expect that of me. I may not be a VanCamp by blood, but I carry the name proudly. I will not run off to the hills and wait. I will do my part. Here and now."

Meera knew that Marcus took his position as her Guardian seriously. Every day since Meera had revealed to him what her source had told her about Xavier's coming attack, he'd said that he couldn't fathom walking away from her, knowing she would never follow. The Moons had trusted him, and he would never willingly choose to betray that trust. "You expect me to disobey the Moons and fail to protect you on purpose!"

"No." Meera lowered Ash back into her bassinet. Her teary gaze lingered upon her daughter's peaceful, slumbering face for a few moments longer before she went on to say, "I expect you to carry on and protect my children instead. They will survive to see the Messenger succeed in ending this war."

Marcus set his jaw, nodding slowly, his eyes falling on the two bassinets. "As you wish."

"Lucinda and Humphrey will be here soon to aid you in taking the twins to the nearest transportation hatch." Meera changed the subject as she walked over to her desk, where she retrieved a few scrolls she'd prepared for the trio. "Here are the hatch exit locations and my will."

Marcus glared the second he'd heard her mention her will, but he was quick to place the scrolls in his satchel. "You're positive these locations are correct?" He glowered, lifting a single brow.

"I trust my source."

"And who *is* that source?" he pressed.

"Someone who's been around a long time and knows a great deal about not only this Realm but all five." Meera released an exaggerated sigh, placing her hands firmly on her hips as she shifted her gaze back to the bassinets. Her stomach churned at the idea of having to say goodbye to the two babies she'd barely had a chance to know.

Her hands rose to her neck, where the Idonian Sectra hung gracefully. Meera's breath shuddered as her fingers grazed the enchanted chain cradling the powerful amulet. "Do me one last favor," she instructed as she unclasped the chain, watching as Marcus's jaw fell open in shock.

"Have you gone mad?" he roared as she held the amulet out to him. "Put that back on your neck right now! It's your only form of defense!"

"I have the VanCamp family sword. Like Whitefire, it's one of Idona's four enchanted swords. It could be enough." Meera squared her shoulders. "If Xavier gets the best of me, I'd prefer this to be far out of his reach. Should `he gets his hands on it, this war is over. He wins. Whoever wears that amulet claims the Idonian throne and the position of High King or Queen. There would be no question. Our Kingdoms in Idona and all the others throughout Si Realtra would bow down to him. We can't allow that to happen."

Marcus stared at her silently. The Queen frowned, wishing that it didn't have to be this way. The Sectras were the five most powerful weapons in the Galaxy, one belonging to each Realm. As Sectra to the main Realm, the amulet provided its owner with a title unlike any other, and she couldn't allow Xavier to gain such political *and* physical power.

Meera forced the Sectra into her Guardian's hands, holding her own around his for a few moments longer. "Give it to Ash when she comes of age," she whispered.

"What about Penelope?"

"Penelope is the heir to the Idonian throne. Ash is no queen. You'll understand what I'm saying as you watch her grow. She's a warrior, just like her father and his father before him." Meera's gaze cut toward the sleeping baby. The sight of her caused heat to blossom within the Queen's chest. Her mind whirled with thoughts about who she might become. "There's no telling just how powerful she and Vincent will be. The Magic in their blood could cause them to grow to be the most powerful beings this Realm has ever seen."

"It could also turn them into Hybrids. They could be slaughtered," Marcus warned, gently placing the amulet in his satchel. "You shouldn't have used Magic during their birth. I'll admit I don't know much about it. I'm a Mortal Knight, but even I know that."

"They survived the harsh birth I endured because of that potion," Meera reminded him coolly. "And they won't be slaughtered because you'll be by their side." Marcus nodded, clenching his jaw. "And between you and me," she added, " Magic was already in their blood to begin with."

3

As planned, Idona's best warriors had arrived in Solaris to participate in the Queen's clever plot. As Meera walked into the ballroom, every soul inside quickly dropped to a knee out of respect for their Monarch, all while she attempted to hide her tear-stained cheeks from their curious gazes.

"I've asked far too great a favor from you all," she began, her voice wavering with an onslaught of emotions as her gaze danced from face to face. "I've asked you to risk your lives to protect this Kingdom. Some of you hail from the Kingdom of Elves, and some of you from the Fae's Safe Haven. Some of you are even from the Kingdom of Dracus. You kneel to your own Kings and Queens, and yet, you kneel before me now. I can only hope that it's not only out of respect for me but my late husband as well." Her sinuses burned with coming tears as she sucked in a deep, shaky breath. Her stony facade had gone away for good, and there was no stopping it.

"High King Gideon VanCamp ascended to the High Throne at just fifteen. He fought for Idona and Si Realtra until his dying breath." Tears dripped from Meera's eyes, but she forced a smile upon her lips despite them. Those who had offered to fight for her deserved the encouragement, and that was all she could truly offer them right now.

"What we are about to do tonight will go down in history. On this evening, on the sixth day of the third week of Winter Solstice in the year of one-thousand and twenty N.D., Xavier will lead his Dark Army into Solaris. He has already breached the Idonian Kingdom's borders, and that army will be upon us within the hour. The Pandora will expect to attack our Fire and Ice Ball's typical guests. They will not anticipate meeting the Realm's best warriors, dressed in ball gowns and tuxedos." The thought of how the Pandora might react caused the Queen to chuckle under her breath. "We may be outnumbered, but together, we are stronger than any force our Realm has ever seen. We will do whatever it takes to defend this castle, this city, *and* this kingdom. Idona will not fall to Darkness because *we won't allow it!*"

The entire Kingdom shook as the ballroom erupted with applause. Meera's heart soared. The sound of their cheering rattled in her ears. Xavier and his Dark Army could take their homes, their fortunes, and their loved ones. But, he could not take their hope.

Meera settled into her throne as the sirens began to wail outside. Her pulse thrummed in her ears while she pictured what the city looked like outside her castle walls. Xavier and his army had arrived, and it was only a matter of time before she would have to face him.

The Queen gripped the arms of her throne, her nerves beginning to get the best of her. Her mouth grew dry, her eyes falling on the entrance to the throne room as the lights started to flicker, signaling that not only had the Pandora swarmed the city, but they had entered the castle.

"Good luck," she whispered, knowing very well who was causing the castle's electricity to become so flawed.

The atmosphere around the Queen seemed to change in an instant. The temperature dropped, sending a chill through the room and a shiver down her spine. Every one of her muscles went rigid, her back as straight as a board. Meera may be falling apart on the inside, riddled with fear, but she wouldn't dare show it — no matter who was heading her way.

Meera's eyes narrowed in the direction of the throne room's ornate entrance, her nostrils flaring as she fought to keep hold of her courage. When a figure appeared, her breath caught in her throat. She didn't need him to announce himself to know who he was. She remembered Malachai quite well. Yet now, with long dark hair and eerie red eyes, she could hardly recognize the man she'd once called her friend. Her fear quickly transitioned into anger, rippling throughout her, boiling her blood. Had Xavier not seen her worthy enough to kill him?

Rising from her throne, Meera growled in response to the man who smirked in her direction. She wouldn't allow herself to die by the same hands who'd killed her husband. She couldn't.

Malachai crossed the room, each movement so smooth he might as well have been gliding across the marble floors. Arrogance practically seeped from his every pour. Yet, his smirk faltered as he drew near, shadows crossing over his ruby eyes. It was almost as if he hated for her to see him in such a way or to bear so much hate for him. She reached out and slapped him across the face as soon as he was within reach, her nails dragging against the flesh of his cheek and quickly drawing lines of scarlet blood.

Staggering back, Malachai gaped at the queen, his hand rising to his bleeding cheek.

"You were brilliant," Meera snarled, baring her teeth, clenched fists trembling at her sides. "You had all the potential in the Galaxy to be something great one day, yet you threw it all away so that your lying, cheating, bastard of a father could lead you down this path? You've allowed him to corrupt your once beautiful soul! Was becoming the Prince of Darkness more exciting than becoming a Black Knight?" she roared. "Where's your father? If you think that you're going to be my opponent this evening, you're even more moronic than I thought."

Hurt flashed in Malachai's haunting gaze. "You're right; I'm not your opponent, thankfully for you," he replied, whispering as if he were afraid the other Pandora in the castle might hear him. "I just came to give you a bit of advice."

Meera's brow wrinkled as she tried to make sense of the man before her. There was no hate-fueled passion behind his tone. Instead, it appeared that she'd been met with honesty. "What?"

"Aim for his heart."

Meera staggered back with surprise and watched as Malachai transitioned in the blink of an eye. He took the shape of a hawk, using his newfound jet-black wings to glide out of the Throne Room. She stared at the place he'd just been standing, wondering if she'd ever been so confused in all her life.

"Aim for his heart." Her heart rate began to quicken as she repeated his words.

From what Meera remembered of her husband's adviser, Xavier, was that he'd been nothing more than a Mortal — and a weak one, at that. He lacked all the skills required to be a soldier, so he'd taken to politics instead. She'd always imagined that he'd be far too easy to kill, which was why he made his son do all his dirty work for him. But after what Malachai had told her, it was clear that Xavier was something far more powerful than what he used to be. Even more powerful than the Pandora he commanded.

Manic laughter echoed through the halls, causing Meera's stomach to twist into knots. Her blood chilled to ice in her veins as she reached for Shadow Strike, the VanCamp family sword. Her clammy fingers wrapped around its shining silver hilt. As she lifted it, she took on the same weight the royal family had carried with them since before the New Dawn. No other sword within Idona could compare to its enchanted obsidian blade.

"I highly doubt that you're powerful enough to yield the notorious Shadow Strike," the Dark King cackled.

Many years had passed since the queen had heard his voice, but despite all that time, she recognized it instantly.

Meera's lips curled into a sinister smirk. Xavier wasn't the only one with secrets. "You don't know me one bit then," she sneered, raising the sword, pointing the tip of its blade in the direction from which his voice had come.

Xavier materialized in front of her, cloaked in black silk lined with red. A symbol of three intersecting swords glistened on his chest. The mere sight of it caused shivers to snake down her spine. She knew that symbol all too well.

"You haven't changed at all," Xavier mocked.

"You certainly have!" Meera took in his new appearance. She remembered Xavier to be an aging man in his forties, yet now, he appeared to be much younger. Power radiated off him like a waterfall, black mist spreading out from beneath his cloak.

Xavier sighed, cocking his head to the side, glaring in the sword's direction. "Why even bother to wield it? You certainly don't need it to fight. Not after all your mother has told me, and the amulet—" The second he noticed the

Sectra's absence, his eyes fixed on the queen's neck, rage consumed him. "Where is it?" he demanded, his eyes shifting from their usual, earthy brown shade to nothing but an unnerving black. His flesh paled, the veins on his neck blackening as the dark power within him visibly intensified.

"Far away from you," Meera hissed, lifting the sword and driving it into his chest in the time it took for her heart to manage a single beat. His painful scream echoed through the throne room as she felt his flesh cave beneath its black blade, the scent of blood flooding the air around her. Bones splintered and cracked. Meera cringed as she pushed further, aiming for the heart just as she was told.

Xavier's knees wobbled before he sank to the marble floor. His blood oozed down, staining his silk cloak. The poison that coated Shadow Strike's blade seeped into him, eating away at his Dark power, weakening him, and threatening to steal the life from his eyes.

With her might, Meera twisted the blade, determined to stop any more Darkness from tainting her Realm. She would prevent the Messenger Prophecy from ever needing to reach its fulfillment. She would stop this war, here and now. She felt Xavier's body weaken against her sword, a smile creeping across her face as he fell into a lifeless heap onto the floor.

Meera retracted Shadow Strike's blade, gazing down at the strange, tar-like blood that covered it before turning her attention to the enemy, her heart thrashing furiously against the walls of her chest.

"Amoria is dead," she hissed. "And so are you, motherfucker."

Just when the Queen was sure that the last of the Dark King's life had left him, a cough made her heart shudder. "You missed," Xavier croaked, pushing to his feet. Meera froze, shock riddling through her like an earthquake in Erim.

She had hit his heart. She was sure of it. Yet, he stood before her with pure Darkness reflecting in his eyes.

Xavier utilized the queen's fear to his advantage and lurched toward her. Before Meera could process what had happened, his hand had wrapped around her neck, crushing her airways. She gasped for air, her vision tunneling as he laughed. His dark gaze bore into her own, waiting for all signs of her life to disappear, but she would not give in to him. She had no choice but to live, if not for her kingdom, for her children.

Xavier's strength was impeccable, and Meera wondered if Shadow Strike had even affected him at all. She opened her mouth to scream. Perhaps if she could, someone might hear and come to her aid. Despite her effort, not a single sound reverberated from her. There was no escape. Soon, she would be lost to Idona and her children, never to see them or the Realm she'd sworn to protect again. But before she gave up, there was still at least one more thing that she could do.

Meera's hand crept up Xavier's torso, causing his brow to furrow with confusion. Her hand grazed the wound she had left, his blood staining her fingers before she pressed her palm against it. Xavier cried out in agony. Dusty golden rays flowed from her fingertips, seeping into his wound and invading his bloodstream.

"What did you just do?" Xavier roared, tightening his grip around her throat.

Meera's eyelids became leaden, her vision consumed by a cruel and unwelcome emptiness. Her body became limp, the light in her soul shrinking until it threatened to vanish, sending her into an unconscious state from which she would never emerge. With the last shreds of life that remained within her, she forced her lips into a vicious smile and said, "You'll never escape me now."

The scent of smoke filtered through the air, burning through Marcus's lungs as black clouds began to overtake the sky above Solaris. No matter how badly he wanted to, he refused to look over his shoulder. He couldn't bear to see the city he loved fall into the hands of the Dark King and his wicked, shape-shifting army.

At one time, Marcus may have believed that losing the Idonian Kingdom to the Dark King was the worst thing that could happen, but what of the other Kingdoms in Idona? What of the Kingdom of Elves or Dracus? Would they all suffer the same fate? Too many questions swarmed his tired mind. He shook his head, willing the thoughts away.

One battle at a time.

Lucinda and Humphrey traveled in front of the Guardian, each of them cradling one of Meera's newborn twins. The air around them was frigid, turning their breaths into icy plumes. Clouds swarmed the black velvet night sky above, threatening to shower them with snow at any moment.

"I don't like this plan," Lucinda Cross, the Realm Sorceress, admitted, her amber gaze darting nervously around them. "What if the other knights don't find the babies in time, and they freeze? How do we know for sure that this source of Meera's was correct about the exit locations?"

"Meera trusted this person," Humphrey reminded her. "And if she trusted them, so should we."

Marcus frowned at the thought of the Queen's mysterious source, knowing he could never trust a person when he didn't even know their name. "There are Black Knights stationed at every possible hatch exit. As soon as these babies are transported, they'll be found and brought to the nearest village, city, or Kingdom," he explained, his faith in his fellow knights unwavering.

"But what if we missed one?" Lucinda whispered, fear audible in her somber voice.

"We didn't," Marcus insisted, clenching his jaw. "Now, we're getting close, and this forest is overrun with Pandora. We need to get moving and get this over with before they interfere."

The cavern came into view just as Marcus began to feel the Pandora's eyes upon him. He wasted no time when it came to releasing Whitefire from its sheath. "We have company," he growled.

Humphrey rushed to the cavern's door, holding Ash tightly against his chest. Marcus watched as he attempted to open it but to no avail. "Lucinda, take this baby," he ordered, turning to set the newborn in the Sorceress's free arm.

Behind the Draconian, Lucinda stood, her gaze darting in every direction as Humphrey drove his foot into the old oak door over and over again. Every second, another pair of red eyes appeared in the shadows, low growls echoing throughout the night.

"Hurry up!" Marcus roared, Whitefire igniting in his grip. Burning white fire surrounded the enchanted blade, heating the forest around him and turning the snow around the Guardian into tendrils of rising steam. He held the edge out, casting its white-hot glow upon the shadows, revealing the enemy's deadly crouching forms.

Bears, wolves, lions, birds, snakes, and everything in between stood ready to tear the Guardian limb from limb. Marcus set his jaw, every one of his muscles tense with fear. His heart thundered with adrenaline as he rolled his shoulders, his grip tightening around Whitefire before the beasts sprang forward in a rush of snarls and razor-sharp teeth.

While the Guardian fought to keep the Pandora at bay, Humphrey took a step back and said a silent prayer to the Moons, the Sovereign, and whoever might listen, before he threw himself into the cavern.

The door burst free from its hinges, falling to the cavern's floor with a clatter, sending centuries' worth of dust billowing in the air. Lucinda rushed inside, blinking as she waited for her eyes to adjust to the darkness. One of the babies started to squirm and whimper in her arms, waking the other. If the Pandora hadn't known about the infants, they certainly did now.

Cursing under her breath, Lucinda's eyes fell on the hatch, just barely big enough to fit one twin at a time. She exhaled in a relieved rush and turned to Humphrey, taking in his appearance. The Draconian was covered in dust, his fangs gleaming in the moonlight spilling into the cavern.

"Go help Marcus; I'll handle this," she insisted. Humphrey gave her a curt nod and took a final look at everyone before heading back outside, He took up a stance in front of the entrance. Lucinda knew that stance. He would fight with everything he had. There was no way Humphrey would allow a single Pandora through.

Marcus's mind was whirling, his heart thrashing against his sternum. He'd never been so outnumbered. The beasts were everywhere, swarming the small clearing. With no other choice but to keep fighting, he swung his burning blade, driving it through flesh and bone. White flames caught on their fur, intensifying until they swallowed the Pandora whole. Their screams echoed throughout the forest, and the revolting scent of their charred flesh sailed through the air.

Some of the Pandora shrank back into the shadows in retreat, their glowing eyes fading. They were smart enough to avoid the Guardian after so many of their companions had perished right before their eyes. They would never be a match for Whitefire.

Roars of pure fury echoed in the night. Marcus whirled, watching in horror as the savage beasts rushed from the trees toward Humphrey, trying to push past him into the caverns.

To Lucinda and the Idonian heirs.

The Pandora were determined to not only take the Idonian Kingdom for themselves on this cold winter evening but to wipe the royal family off the face of the Realms. No matter how small and defenseless the newborn twins were, they would eventually grow to become full-fledged VanCamps, some of the strongest Mortals known throughout the history of Si Realtra. They would become a threat to the Dark King, and the Pandora were determined to prevent that threat from ever coming to fruition.

Humphrey's strength was comparable to the Berserkers that used to roam Idona. Therefore, the Pandora wouldn't have much luck when it came to getting past him. It was no wonder that the High Queen had chosen this group of people to defend her children. However, the savage beasts weren't going to give up just yet.

A Pandora latched itself to Humphrey's shoulder, its jaw locking in place, its teeth over an inch deep into the Draconian's flesh.

An agonizing scream ripped from Humphrey's lungs as his fingers gripped onto the beast's pitch-black fur. He couldn't reach the Pandora with his fangs and roared a slur of curse words. Marcus watched the Draconian surge with impossible speed and strength into the side of the cavern. The structure shook, littering dust and rock from the ceiling inside as bone crunched beneath Humphrey's body. He stood, watching as the Pandora fell onto the snow. A pool of crimson seeped out of its ruined form, staining the earth below.

Lucinda placed the babies into the hatch one at a time with tears streaming down her cheeks as she said silent goodbyes to them both before thrusting her hand into her boot. If the Pandora wanted to fight dirty, then they could fight her spells. With her diamond-encrusted wand in hand, she pulled in a deep, rickety breath and turned to look at the hatch one last time.

"I'll see you again one day," she promised before darting out of the cavern and into the fray.

Lucinda flew past Humphrey, rushing to aid Marcus, who was struggling to stay on his feet. Her eyes widened, watching as the Guardian slayed three Pandora with just one strike of his flaming sword. But as they fell, five more appeared in their place. Their numbers seemed to be never-ending, and it was time the Sorceress reminded them exactly who they were dealing with in order to save her ally.

Marcus fell to his knees, drenched in blood, as the weight of the four Pandora on his back pushed him down into the snow. His eyes shut as he cried out in agony, their claws ripping through his tender flesh, pinning him to the ground.

"No!" Lucinda shrieked, aiming her wand toward the sky. "Inceptstasis!" she roared, a bright, blinding light spewing from her wand.

Every Pandora within a mile radius froze in place, including the ones pinning the Guardian down. "Hurry up and help me get them off of him. This is a three-caliber spell, but it has its flaws. It doesn't last very long."

Humphrey nodded, hurrying over to where Marcus lay lifelessly in the snow. He kicked the beasts off of him as bile crept up his throat at the sight of what had become of him. The Guardian was nearly as pale as the snow, and Humphrey's sensitive ears could no longer hear his heartbeat. "Lucinda..." he trailed quietly as she leaned over the Guardian's body, staring down at him with tears dripping from her amber eyes.

"Breath Of Life," she whispered, her lips just barely grazing the Guardian's.

A strange, silver light began to spread from the Sorceress's lips, sailing past Marcus's. Humphrey swallowed his urge to gasp as the faint thrum of a heartbeat rattled in his ears.

"Impossible," he insisted as the Sorceress placed her palm against Marcus's chest.

"We need to get him to a healer, and we need to do it quickly. He won't live much longer. I've only managed to buy him a little time," she explained solemnly. She thrust her hand deep into the pockets of her hunter-green cloak, retrieving a chrome teleportation sphere.

"We need to take him to Dracus," Humphrey urged. "It's the only way."

"You want to... change him?" Lucinda asked, horror expanding across her face. Mortals could be changed, but to do it to someone in his condition could be dangerous. Marcus's body was already weak, and his heart was fading quickly. Draconian transitions were both extensive and painful, and she wasn't sure that the Guardian would survive it.

"It might kill him, but if we do nothing, we'll still lose him. We have to try, or he won't make good on the promise he made to Meera," Humphrey spat. "Open the damn portal."

Lucinda threw the sphere to the ground without uttering another word. She watched as the shimmering wall appeared, displaying a blurry image of Dracus. Humphrey moved, grunting as he threw Marcus's limp body over his shoulder. Blood stained the Draconian, seeping in steady crimson flows from the Guardian's wounds.

Without exchanging any words, Lucinda watched the pair pass through, disappearing from her view. She wanted to follow, but she couldn't. Her gut told her to wait. They were missing something. But what?

She turned to scan the area, her eyes falling on Marcus's leather satchel, gripped tightly in the frozen claws of a Pandora in the form of a bear. The color drained from Lucinda's face as she recalled the satchel's contents. She sucked in a breath, ignoring the rapid drum of her heart, and took a step toward the creature.

The Sorceress kneeled before the beast, holding out her hand, her eyes drifting shut. The weight of her scythe appeared in her grip. Her lips twitched into a devilish smirk at the sensation of the weapon's power coursing through her — power she'd sought for over a century to obtain. Her eyes fluttered open, glowing as orange as embers as she rose to her feet.

Lucinda trembled, raising the scythe above her head. The

Pandora began to twitch beneath her, the beast's grip tightening around the satchel's strap. An angry snarl sailed past her lips as she swung the scythe downward without a moment to spare, severing the Pandora's wrist. The beast's bloodcurdling scream seared throughout the night. Blood cascaded from the severed limb as she curled her fingers around the satchel's strap and returned to where her sphere sat on the ground. She picked it up, tossing it back down to reopen a portal to Dracus.

Another form emerged from the shadows as the portal manifested before Lucinda. Her eyes met his, and although she knew she'd be doing the Realm a favor if she were to stay and fight him, she needed to get back to Marcus and Humphrey.

"We'll meet one day again, *your Highness,*" the Sorceress purred as she disappeared into the portal.

Malachai watched as she disappeared, his lips twitching toward a smile. He hadn't anticipated running into the Realm Sorceress, of all people, and he was glad that she'd chosen to retreat. He stood there for another moment, watching the spell she'd placed on his Pandora begin to fade. They'd started to move, some transitioning into their Mortal forms, cursing loudly about their failed mission.

"Yes. We will," Malachai whispered his reply to the Sorceress, turning back toward the trees, his eyes falling on his subordinates. His smile vanished as his features twisted into a damning glare. They trembled at the sight, shrinking backward, their red eyes dancing with pure, undeniable fear. After all, he wasn't just the original Pandora. He was their creator. He had given them life, and he could so easily take it away.

5

THE KINGDOM OF ELVES

Sleep evaded ten-year-old Elven Princess Mika Chamberlain. After the nightmare she'd just experienced, she doubted she would ever sleep soundly again. Instead of trying to force herself into an unconscious state, she decided to abandon her bed and fasten her cloak around herself. She dipped her feet into her boots, preparing for the cold night that awaited her.

Moments later, she found herself in front of her brother's bedroom door, knocking lightly before she entered. Eight-year-old Beck sat at his window, staring out into the night. His skin was pale compared to its usual sun-kissed hue as Mika approached. Glancing outside, she saw what was troubling her younger brother so deeply. Smoke billowed into the sky from where Solaris glowed like an ember in the night. "The Idonian Kingdom is burning," Beck whispered.

"We need to go outside," Mika told him, her voice devoid of emotion as she waited for him to turn and face her. "I need fresh air."

Beck glanced over his shoulder, his eyes narrowing. "We're not allowed out after dark, especially without a guard," he reminded her, unwilling to disobey his parents' orders.

"That little princess is still screaming," Mika added softly. The sound of Penelope's cries had echoed throughout the castle's halls for hours. She wanted to cry for Penelope but was gripped with anxiety instead. She picked at her nails, casting her gaze on the floor. "I need to get away from her. Just for a little while. Please?"

Beck turned to face her, his arms crossed in front of his chest. His lips curved into a frown as he studied her face. "Fine," he huffed after too long of a silence.

Mika watched as her brother wrapped his gray wool cloak around himself and slipped into his boots. She moved to his side and grabbed his hand, intertwining her fingers with his. They opened the door together, greeted by another one of Penelope's wails.

Together, the pair fled into the complicated marble halls of the castle, running beneath green-and-gold banners reflecting the Chamberlain family symbol: the tree of life. The pair dipped into the dark servant's stairwell, hoping to avoid the watchful eyes of the guards that roamed the castle. Their way down the curving staircase was only lit by sconces perched upon the stony walls, casting warm orangey glows and causing their shadows to stretch out before them.

"I bet that most of the guards are on the wall, watching the smoke from Solaris," Mika said as they headed for the fields that sat behind the castle. The golden walls that surrounded the Kingdom were impossible to climb, especially for young Elves. Thankfully, the wall wrapped around a section of the forest, which provided a few trails to walk upon.

"They're fools," she snapped once her suspicions about the guards were confirmed. She could see them all, standing in silence, with her Elven eyes. "Just because most of the

Pandora are attacking that Kingdom doesn't mean there are none lurking here," she said, her tone coarse, her eyes falling on a particular forest trail.

"Where are we going?" Beck asked, glaring in his sister's direction. His body tensed, and a thin sheet of sweat gleamed from his skin as he looked toward the blackened forests. Mika stepped forward, silently beckoning him to follow. She heard her brother gulp before stepping into place beside her.

"I need to check something," Mika explained in a soft, low tone. "I had a nightmare, and I just want to make sure it wasn't real."

The princess stared at her brother, waiting for a reaction. She knew that he never believed her when she would tell him that her dreams had come true. Only Draconians had the ability to see the future. There were no Elven Prophetesses.

The night that surrounded the two children was eerily silent; no birds flew through the sky, no bugs buzzed in the air, and no frogs croaked their merry tunes. Mika shivered as she continued down the trail, scanning the forest around her; Beck walked silently at her side.

"D-do you smell that?" Mika stuttered, her breath catching in her throat.

"Blood. Mortal blood," he whispered, his expression grave. Mika knew that scent well; the coppery tang it carried as it spilled from its host. She stilled at the sound of a twig snapping in the distance, extending a hand out toward Beck, motioning for him to halt. Mika peered into the darkness, shrouding them. The branches wouldn't break on their own.

The cries of a baby pierced the silence. Mika took off running, her heart leaping into her throat.

"Mika, wait! It could be a trap!" Beck called as he raced after her, fighting to catch up. Mika pushed forward, her heart racing against what seemed like time itself. She skidded to a stop, sending plumes of dirt flying into the air, her stomach lurching at the sight of what lay before her.

"A... Black Knight," was all she said.

Mika stared at the mangled body, her stomach twisting into painful knots. She fought against the urge to retch, and she glanced toward her brother, who now stood beside her, his complexion ghastly. She knew that he expected to become the General one day, and in the future, he would likely see far worse things than this. However, she doubted he would ever forget the gruesome scene they had just stumbled upon.

The knight's body was torn into pieces, his face unrecognizable. The only feature of his that was left untouched was a mop of bloodied brown hair that reminded her of the shade the High Queen's Guardian had. Her heart began to race even more at the thought that it might very well be Marcus Bonaventure lying in a heap of blood, bone, and tissue before her. However, the body wasn't the most disturbing thing that Mika and her brother had stumbled upon; it was the baby wrapped in wool beside the corpse. It was crying, shivering in the cold.

Mika stepped over what was left of the Knight and dropped to a knee, reaching over pools of guts and blood to retrieve the baby. Gently, she lifted the sobbing bundle into her arms, wrapping her cloak around it so she could hold it close to her body to warm its freezing flesh.

"Tell me this isn't what your nightmare was about," Beck choked.

Mika nodded slowly, bouncing the baby. Soon enough, he quieted, and she looked up, peering into her younger brother's eyes. "If my nightmare was correct, this baby is Vincent VanCamp."

Esmeralda had worked all night to soothe Penelope. She'd held her through her screams, her sensitive Elven ears now ringing. She'd run her fingers through her long, soft brown hair and wiped away her tears. She'd sung soothing songs from her own childhood, watching as her teary hazel eyes filled with wonder before they finally drifted shut. Esmeralda breathed a tired sigh and slowly crept from the sleeping princess's bed, leaving her to sleep. She'd grown weary herself and, after hours of trying to calm the screaming child, craved a glass of fine wine.

She retreated to the kitchen to retrieve a glass when a knock sounded at the front door. Esmeralda made her way to the foyer to answer it, cursing under her breath. If whoever was at the door woke the child up, they could very well face the gallows come morning.

Esmeralda's heart skipped a beat as she opened the door, only to find her husband, Thaddeus, on the other side. She wondered if she'd ever seen him in such a way. His face was grave and angry, sending chills racing the queen's body. She knew that look. Something was wrong—horribly, inexplicably wrong. "What is it?" she asked, unsure of whether or not she wanted to know the answer.

"Mika and Beck left the castle this evening," Thaddeus told her bluntly, his golden eyes blazing. She flinched, nearly shaking with fear of what he would say next. She prayed that he wouldn't continue on to tell her that her children were gone... or worse. "When they returned, it was with a newborn baby."

Esmeralda's stomach dropped, her eyes growing wide. "Excuse me?"

"Beck said they went out onto one of the forest trails. It was there that they found the mangled body of a Black Knight and a newborn baby crying beside it," Thaddeus explained slowly. "The Black Knight's presence leads me to believe that this baby is one of the VanCamp twins."

Esmeralda's knees weakened, her heart shuddering. She leaned against the doorframe for support, her mind beginning to whirl. "If that baby is one of the VanCamp twins, then where is the other one?" she asked. "Where is Marcus?" She felt as if she was going to vomit all over the marble floors of her hall. "The Black Knight…" she croaked, lifting a trembling hand to her mouth.

"I sent out men to confirm the identity. I believe it may be him," Thaddeus replied, his tone just as grave as the expression upon his face.

Esmeralda imagined how Penelope would react to the news and wondered if they should even tell her. The poor thing had been through enough. She'd lost her father, her mother, her kingdom, and now this? Her heart crumbled all over again for the princess. The Guardian had promised her that one day, he would walk through the golden gates to meet her once again. Now, there was a strong possibility that that may never happen.

"What has our Realm come to, Thaddeus?" Esmeralda slowly shook her head in disbelief. "The Idonian Kingdom has fallen. I can smell the smoke, even this far west. I know it hasn't been confirmed, but I can feel that Gideon is dead. And Meera…" Her body shook violently, rage beginning to boil her blood, her heart beating so ferociously that she feared it might burst. "She sacrificed herself to stop Xavier. It was all for nothing, and now there are three children left without a mother and a Dark King sitting upon the most important throne in Si Realtra."

Thaddeus nodded slowly, shadows dancing in his eyes. "Don't fret, Esme," he said, placing two strong hands upon his wife's quivering shoulders. "I'm not sure when, and I'm not sure how, but we will take that Kingdom back. We will rid this Realm of the Darkness threatening to consume it. We will defeat Xavier, Malachai, and their blasted Dark Army," he assured her. Esmeralda swallowed, sucking down a large breath of air in an attempt to regain her composure as her husband wiped a tear from her cheek.

"I have to go meet the men," he said, pressing his lips to her forehead before turning on his heel. She watched him walk away, setting out to the forest where the Black Knight was found. It was time he found out if Marcus was truly dead and if Idona was truly lost.

6

Craven Amsterdam ran as fast as his body would allow him, fighting back the tears of both fear and rage as he escaped Solaris. His fist tightened around Shadow Strike's silver hilt, its black blade sparking with his electricity as it dripped Pandora ichor onto the snow that coated the Idonian Forest.

Blood pooled in his right eye, blocking his vision as he begged his body to continue. The Ballroom Battle had drained his energy, and he'd used far too much of it to cut the castle's electricity so that he could steal the enchanted sword from the Dark King. It was a miracle that the Draconian was still standing at all.

Every one of Craven's muscles screamed. His lungs burned, his hunger for blood intensifying with every dreaded second. He could hear snarls echoing in the night as the Pandora rushed after him, aiming to end his Immortal life. They wanted him dead after what he'd done, and they wouldn't stop their pursuit until they succeeded in painting the snowy Idonian Forest with his blood.

Craven had begged King Loren to let him fight for the High Queen on this night. He'd promised him that he would return to Dracus alive. He'd never broken a promise in the past, and he refused to start now.

In the distance, the sun began to rise over the snow-capped mountains belonging to The Strip. The sight of Idona's largest mountain range told him that he'd made it out of the Idonian Jurisdiction alive. He'd managed to outrun the Pandora, and now that dawn had arrived, he knew they'd be forced to return and report to their leaders, which meant the Draconian would live to see another day.

The Endurion River came into view, the raging water rushing toward the south. Craven followed it as his eyes fell on the black butterfly symbol carved into the trees on the other side. Hope flickered to life within him at the sight as he filled his lungs with a breath of relief. "Almost there," he said, exhaling.

The river started to widen, signaling that Craven was nearing the waterfalls that surrounded the Kingdom of Dracus. He was so close, and yet he could no longer run and resorted to limping slowly, dragging the sword alongside him, carving a line through ice and snow.

The Unity Bridge had never appeared to be so beautiful. Craven shuddered with relief as he approached, his heart skipping into an uneven beat as a rush of angry wind and chilling mist swept around him, blowing his damp, ebony locks into his violet eyes.

Despite the elements, Craven began to make his way across, his feet slipping upon the smooth, crystal bridge as he peered through the heavy mist, hoping to catch sight of Dracus's gates. His grip on the sword began to falter, the sound of the blade dragging against the bridge's surface screeching in his ears. He coughed, the taste of blood coating his mouth as it dripped down his lips.

Craven's bloodied vision prevented him from obtaining a clear view of the Kingdom beyond. His injured eye stung terribly in the salty mist rising from the waterfalls roaring around him. His dark hair dripped, sending freezing bits of water rolling down his cheeks and jaw, soaking his tattered tuxedo. He shivered, focusing on the bridge before him. Eventually, it would end, and he'd have made it home. He ground his teeth, concentrating on each and every wobbly step he took, willing his body not to stop.

The fog around the bridge dissipated, and the gate came into view at last. For the first time, Craven got a good look at what was waiting for him. Draconians had flooded the city square, surrounding the black butterfly fountain. Each of the council members stood up front, their hands over their hearts, a symbol of respect and unity.

Craven's feet left the crystal bridge and landed upon stone. He dropped to his knees, unable to stand a second longer. Valentina appeared in his blurry vision, a proud smile playing on her lips.

"I saw that you'd come, so we waited for you," Valentina said as she sank down onto the stone in front of him. He took her hand, feeling it just to make sure that she was real.

"I'm sorry that it took me so long to run here. But I brought you this." He set Shadow Strike down on her lap, his heart in his throat. "There was no way I was going to let him keep it."

A sound somewhere between a cry and a sigh of relief escaped Valentina before she said, "What you did was daring. I saw it all in a vision. I doubt anyone else would have dared to approach Xavier in such a way."

"If only I could have left that Throne Room with more than the sword," Craven whispered, swallowing the painful lump in his throat. "I went in there to rescue her, but she was already dead." Tears puddled in his eyes, mixing with blood and sweat as they rolled down his face.

Loren dropped to a knee beside the Prophetess. Craven

hung his head, afraid to look the King in the eye. "Your bravery is superior to any other warrior that I've known. What you did was both dangerous and idiotic, and by some miracle, you succeeded," he declared, placing a hand upon the Draconian's shoulder.

Craven bit back a sob, afraid to appear weak before all the other Draconians that had come to greet him. "I wouldn't say I succeeded," he replied. His stomach twisted as he recalled the events of last night. "I abandoned my allies."

"There's a reason you survived, Craven," Valentina whispered softly, reclaiming his hand, turning it gently so that his palm faced upward. When the Prophetess placed Shadow Strike back in his grip, his heart took a flying leap off a cliff. "Your journey has only just begun. Yes, many people died last night, and it's unfortunate that you're the only one to walk out of that battle alive, but all of this is for a reason." She took his face in her hands, forcing him to look up at her. "You did not abandon your allies last night, and you won't in the future."

Night had fallen in the Kingdom of Dracus, and Craven was getting the medical attention he needed while the news outlets across the Realm announced his survival. By the end of the day, the Electric Immortal was thought to be a hero. Mortals and Immortals across Idona raised a glass to the lone survivor in memory of all those who had fallen.

While King Loren wished he could do the same, he was too busy preparing for his trip to the Kingdom of Elves. His stomach churned at the thought of what the Idonian Council meeting would entail or how the sight of Meera and Gideon's empty seats would make him feel.

Loren had been busy putting the rest of his affairs in order when his adviser and second-in-command waltzed into his bedroom with a scroll wrapped tightly in his grip.

"What is it, Richard?" Loren grumbled, rubbing his tired eyes. He doubted he'd ever experienced a day as long as this one since the Five Realm War had ended nearly twenty years ago.

"We've received word from the Elves. One of Gideon's twins was found in a forest last night," Richard said flatly, his expression blank.

Loren's heart stumbled. Of course, he'd been expecting word of the twins to arrive at some point. However, he hadn't been anticipating one of them to wind up in the Kingdom of Elves. "What about the second one?" he whispered, unsure that he wanted to know the answer.

"Nothing yet, your Highness." Richard frowned. He was older than the other Immortals in Dracus, not just by his true age, which was little more than four hundred years, but his appearance as well. With his dark hair was speckled with silver and crow's feet wrinkled beside his pale eyes, he was likely one of the oldest appearing Immortals in all Five Realms. He'd been changed by Loren's father during the Age of Monsters after Richard had risked his life to save the former Draconian King. He had been a loyal servant to the crown ever since.

"It's been nearly a day. Any word on the other Black Knights Meera had stationed at the hatch exit locations?" Loren pressed.

Richard cleared his throat and shook his head. "The knight found with Vincent VanCamp appeared to be mangled. I fear the same has happened to the others, which leads me to suspect that the second twin likely faced the same fate."

Loren reached to brace himself on his bed, a wave of

nausea rippling through him."What monster would slaughter a newborn?" he snarled.

"The Pandora's cruelty knows no bounds," Richard replied softly.

"To slay a Black Knight so easily…." Loren gulped, his head spinning a mile a minute. "There's a reason those men were given such a title. Most of them were from Mayfire. Dragon's blood coursed through their veins."

Richard nodded in agreement, his expression solemn. "It's a true shame," he said. "I'll send word to the Elves to let them know we'll be using the portal rooms to arrive shortly," he explained, bowing elegantly before he turned his back on the King.

Loren watched as his adviser disappeared through his bedroom door, his hand rising to his aching chest. He could recall the day he and Gideon both rose to power in the wake of the Five Realm War as if it was just yesterday. Both of their fathers had been slain throughout the seven years it took for Raina, the former Queen of Erim, to tear the Galaxy apart in her search for power.

Now, Loren's heart felt that something was amiss. Idona felt incomplete without Gideon walking its luscious green fields or climbing its notorious mountain ranges. It felt sad without Meera's smile or her kindness. It felt empty without the VanCamps keeping the High Throne warm as the Grimms did before them and as the Cavanaghs did before them. He was sincerely beginning to doubt that this Realm would ever recover.

Esmeralda had yet to shut her eyes. How could she when the Realm around her was pure chaos? The entirety of her night was spent alongside her council, their gazes fixated on the screens displaying news from across Idona. Solaris had fallen. Queen Meera's plan had failed, and all the warriors sent to aid her had perished. All but one.

"One survivor," Esmeralda's adviser, Griffon, had breathed at her side. "*One*. Out of five hundred."

"How?" Camella, the Elven treasurer, whispered.

Esmeralda knew precisely how Craven Amsterdam had managed to survive. He had been unstoppable during the Five Realm War, and he was unstoppable now. Still, if he was the only one to walk out of Solaris alive, that meant…

"Most of the Calloway family is dead," Thaddeus said from where he paced in front of the nearby fire with newborn Vincent wrapped in his arms. "One of the most historic Elven families dwindled down to two on a single evening."

"What about Aveo?" General Rodrick Helevyre asked. "Shall he remain with Commander Halvar's wife?"

"We'll have to summon Lillian," Griffon murmured,

earning quite a scowl from both Esmeralda and Thaddeus. "She *is* his only surviving kin. Aveo's well-being is reason enough to put your bad blood aside."

The broadcast streaming on the screen quickly transitioned from a picture of Craven to Solaris' current condition, wiping all thoughts of Aveo and the Calloways from Esmeralda's mind. Her blood turned to ice, crawling in her veins as she surveyed the historic city. Rivers of blood ran through the cobblestone streets. Homes and shops were engulfed in flames. Pandora ran rampant in various forms, howling in victory. The front gate was congested with citizens attempting to flee, their cries echoing in the queen's ears. Tears welled in her eyes, spilling until they ran down her cheeks as she swallowed the sob creeping up her throat.

The drone capturing the horror zeroed in on the castle, where High Queen Meera's body had been tossed out onto the steps, pale and limp. Her neck was a deep shade of purple, bruised beyond belief, and her hazel eyes were open, gazing out in a way that made it seem as if she were staring straight into the camera hoving above her.

"Sovereign's sake," Thaddeus hissed as he arrived at Esmeralda's side with Vincent whimpering in his arms.

The feed cut a moment later, leaving a black screen in its wake. Esmeralda shivered from head to toe, her heart in her throat. She knew at that moment that she would never forget that image. For the rest of her Immortal days, it would sit at the forefront of her memory, reminding her of all that had happened that day, all they had lost, never to regain again.

In the day that had passed since Solaris fell, the city's surviving citizens had flocked east and west, seeking refuge in the Kingdom of Elves and Dracus. Esmeralda had spent her day preparing for their arrival, ensuring that her best Healers were on standby. Tents were set up in the city square, well stocked with all the supplies one could need. The residents of the Golden City had donated all they could, and some had even offered to open up their homes for displaced families until proper lodgings could be acquired.

While Esmeralda would prefer to be out in the city streets helping, she was contained in the castle. Penelope had yet to stop her tears, and Vincent hadn't taken well to his wet nurse. It was clear that he yearned for his other half, but his twin sister had yet to be located. Mangled bodies of Black Knights had been found at all the exit locations that Queen Meera had listed, but the newly-born princess, Ash, was nowhere to be found.

"Do you think that it's possible that the Pandora brought her back to Solaris?" Thaddeus asked Esmeralda as they prepared for the approaching Idonian Council meeting.

Refusing to believe that, Esmeralda banished the thought from her mind. "Xavier would have flaunted it by now. I suspect that someone heard the baby cry, the same way our children heard Vincent. No matter what, we know that she's alive. If the Pandora let Vincent be, they would have done the same for her."

"Why?" Thaddeus countered, pouring himself a glass of whiskey. "Why leave Vincent be? He may be a harmless newborn right now, but he won't be forever. Leaving them alive doesn't coincide with Xavier's agenda."

"No one knows what goes through that masochistic fool's head," Esmeralda retorted, her tone far harsher than she'd intended. "At the end of the day, by some miracle, Vincent is alive. We have to believe that Ash is as well. *I* have to believe that."

Thaddeus nodded, bringing his glass to his lips to take a sip.

"The Council has arrived," Griffon announced, slightly out of breath, from the threshold to the King's study. "I've told them all to head to the round table room. Nanny Dessa arrived as well. She's with Penelope and Vincent."

Esmeralda's lips spread into a faint smile for the first time in what felt like centuries. "That's good to hear." She sighed heavily, starting toward the threshold. "Let's go settle a few things."

The members of the Idonian Council each took their seats around the round table. Esmeralda was the last to lower into her chair, her eyes scanning the faces of those around her. Cleo of the Fae had finally come out of hiding. Her cheeks were stained with tears that streamed from her crystal blue eyes. Her translucent wings sparkled, hanging limply down her back while her dark hair fell around her like a midnight waterfall.

Valentina lowered into her usual seat beside King Loren Mason, her locks of gold falling around her face. Valentina's golden eyes were wet with her own tears — eyes that Esmeralda had only seen within the Elven community. However, it wasn't just their appearance that the Queen was concerned with, but what Valentina saw with those eyes.

King Loren sat emotionless beside the Prophetess, his stormy quarts gaze fixed on the hand-carved round table. Richard Anster sat on the other side of his kind with a blank expression, his hands folded neatly in front of him.

Lucinda Cross sat directly across from the Elven Queen,

her eyes nothing more than dead amber orbs. Esmeralda's heart sank at the sight of her, having heard about all that occurred in the Idonian Forest last night. She wondered how long it would take for the Sorceress to smile again if she could ever smile again at all.

"We must first discuss the matter of the VanCamp children," Esmeralda began, her voice soft and weary from exhaustion. "I believe Meera would have wanted for them to remain here. We can provide them with a good life. Much like the one they would have been given had the war not torn their family and the Idonian Kingdom apart."

Loren met the queen's gaze, and she watched as he slowly nodded, clearly exhausted himself. "I can't disagree with you," he replied, his eyes moving toward Cleo, awaiting a response.

The Fae Queen's lip quivered; her eyes cast downward. "I'm afraid all I could teach them is how to hide," she whispered. "While they'll always be welcome in the Safe Haven, they must be taught how to ascend to their parents' throne. That's not something I can help with."

"I agree," Aries, Cleo's adviser, spoke from beside her. While everyone else seated at the round table appeared to be devastated, the rare, black-winged Fae shook with rage. Esmeralda could see the fire burning in his burgundy eyes, as always. The history within those eyes...the power hiding behind them... they never failed to shake her to her core.

"Then it's settled," Richard declared. "But what of the Missing VanCamp? There is no word that she's been found. And all the men that I've sent out to locate the Black Knights came back with bodies." His nose wrinkled in disgust. "Should we be assuming that she's dead?"

Esmeralda shook her head, a shred of hope filling her heart. "No, we shouldn't. She's out there somewhere, living and breathing. I can feel it in my bones. We should continue to search for her."

"Meera's will...." Loren started, changing the subject.

Valentina went still in her seat. Esmeralda ground her teeth at the sight. Her eyes narrowed accusingly as she realized how deeply the Prophetess' distrust ran.

"What about her will?" Thaddeus asked in a dangerously low tone.

"Lucinda brought it to us," Loren revealed. "Meera altered it after the twins were born. It states that Penelope will remain her heir and that her Sectra will go to Ash. If Ash isn't found..." he trailed, shaking his head.

"Her Sectra?" Esmeralda's heart leaped into a gallop. How had she not thought of it before? How could something so substantial slip her mind?

Lucinda cleared her throat, drawing the Elven Queen's attention. "I brought it to Dracus last night. It's in their vault under constant surveillance."

"Which is where it should remain. We can't abandon the idea that Ash might be alive. The High Queen's will is absolute. That Sectra will go to Ash VanCamp when she comes of age in eighteen years," Valentina insisted sternly.

"I agree," Esmeralda replied. "But we must have a backup plan. The Sectra will undoubtedly be needed to rid the Realm of Xavier and his Dark Army. We can't leave it locked away for long."

"We'll cross that bridge eighteen years from now," Loren said, setting his jaw. "If we're to obey Meera, we must wait."

"How can we sit by and do nothing for eighteen years?" Thaddeus spat. "We don't know where the princess is or if she is even alive. And if she is, we have no idea how long it will take to find her. Just because Xavier won yesterday and sits on his stolen throne does not mean that he won't continue to torment this Realm. That amulet is the only thing that can steal that title back!"

"As horrible as it is, Xavier won the High Throne and, as a result, holds the title of High King," Richard stated matter-of-factly. "Appointing a Sectra Holder would do nothing of benefit right now. They could claim that title for themselves all they want, but at the end of the day, we're severely outnumbered. The Dark Army will continue to thrive, and Xavier will stop at nothing to acquire the amulet for himself. Bringing it out of that safe would put us at more risk than we already are."

The mere fact that the Sectra would remain in the Draconian vault stirred something in Esmeralda long forgotten. Her parents voices echoed in her mind, telling her that Draconians were no more than savage abominations. If they were alive today, they would insist that they were no better than the Pandora.

That was your war, not mine.

Aries cleared his throat, drawing the council's attention. "What Idona needs right now is for Dracus and the Kingdom of Elves to work together. The people will not accept Xavier as their High King and will look to both you and Loren for safety and direction," he said to Esmeralda.

"We cannot afford to continue on as separate entities," Lucinda added, her expression grave. "Even now, as the people flee east and west, they're picking a side. A Realm already divided is easier to conquer. Xavier may have won himself Solaris, but he won't stop there. In order to survive what's to come, we need to put our pasts aside and stand as one."

Loren offered Esmeralda a kind smile. "I agree," he said. "If the Kingdom of Elves is ever struck, consider Dracus struck as well."

Thaddeus huffed, his eyes narrowing skeptically, but he said nothing.

"I appreciate that from the bottom of my heart," Esmeralda replied honestly, returning Loren's smile. "The Kingdom of Elves will treat a threat to Dracus as a threat unto itself."

Tension dissipated from the room, and every soul around the round table visibly relaxed. Esmeralda felt as if, for the first time in days that, she could breathe easily. However, all that changed when another matter was brought to the round table.

"Now that we've settled that, there are a few more things that we need to discuss," Loren said slowly, glancing over to where Lucinda sat a few seats down. "Will you do the honors?"

Lucinda nodded, her lips disappearing into a thin line. "Last night, as Humphrey, Marcus, and I raced to get the twins to safety, we were attacked," she began, her voice wavering. "I was able to put both twins into the teleportation hatch seperately while Marcus and Humphrey fought the Pandora off, but by the time I was able to assist them, Marcus had been gravely injured."

"Marcus was there?" Thaddeus asked, the words barely more than a brush of air. "So, he wasn't the Black Knight that was found dead alongside Prince Vincent?"

"No, he wasn't," Lucinda replied, sniffling. "He died in the Idonian Forest, but I was able to perform the *Breath of Life* spell to buy him enough time to open a portal to Dracus."

Esmeralda went rigid all over again. Her eyes widened at the realization of what must have happened to the Guardian.

"I administered my venom," Loren said. "It was all we could do to help him, but as of right now, it's unclear whether his body is strong enough to complete the transition."

Aries groaned, falling back into his chair as he reached to

rake a hand through his dark, wavy locks. “Fuck,” he breathed, shaking his head.

Cleo’s lips quivered as she murmured in agreement. “Gideon and Meera loved that boy as their own. To think that he—”

“I wish I could tell you for certain that he’ll survive. If he does, he’ll be stronger now than he ever was before,” Valentina replied. “Meera wanted him to go on to protect her children. When he wakes, and I’m sure he will soon, he’ll likely proceed to finding the Missing VanCamp. He’s the best tracker in this Realm, so we know he’ll succeed.”

“If he’s alive, then who was the Black Knight Mika found last night?” Esmeralda asked, turning her gaze toward her husband.

“I suppose that we’ll find out once the blood tests come back,” Thaddeus replied. “We still need to discuss exactly what we’re going to do now. Guiding our people is one thing, but saving them is an entirely different animal. We have to destroy the Pandora, Xavier, and everything pertaining to them.”

The sound of wood against wood screeched as Valentina pushed her chair back. Esmeralda turned, tearing her attention away from her husband to the Prophetess, who was standing with a book held tightly against her chest. She set it on the table, sliding it into the middle so that the other council members could see the title. “I’m sure you’ve heard of this prophecy,” she began, placing both palms on the round table to brace herself. “This war is what it was referring to. We considered the idea before, but now I’m positive. If you don’t believe me, that’s your problem. If you recall, many of you didn’t believe me when I warned that a new species would be created. Look at us now,” she snapped.

“You truly think this war is the ‘Dark War’ the Messenger Prophecy refers to? That Xavier is the Evil being that the

Messenger is prophesied to slay?" Cleo asked, her eyes bulging with horror as her wings trembled at her back.

Valentina gave her a curt nod. "I'm positive. My predecessor is the one who predicted this prophecy, and before Amelia died during the Five Realm War, she warned me that the time of its fulfillment was nearing. She trusted me to aid the Messenger when she surfaced. I'll do just that, but I can assure you that nothing we do in the meantime will stop Xavier. We can kill the Pandora, but he'll just make more. The most we can do is protect our people, aid them where it's needed, and help guard the villages and the cities in our Realm. But we must wait because the only person capable of defeating Xavier is the woman this prophecy is talking about."

8

Thirteen years had passed since Penelope VanCamp was brought to the Kingdom of Elves, and she'd be lying to herself if she said that Queen Esmeralda and King Thaddeus Chamberlain hadn't provided her with the best life. On the contrary, they'd ensured she wanted nothing and had done the same for her younger brother, Vincent. Yet, despite their beautiful life, the siblings had been hidden behind the golden walls and gates of the Elven Kingdom, causing a cloud of depression to hang over Penelope's head that she couldn't escape.

The only familiar thing she had from her past life, as she liked to call it, was her Nanny, Dessa. The woman had aged but still spent every day by Penelope's side. She catered to, comforted, and had loved her dearly since the day she'd vacated her mother's womb, pink, healthy, and screaming.

Each morning, Penelope awoke to find a breakfast tray at her bedside and a note detailing her daily duties as an Idonian Princess. She may not be able to ascend to her parents' throne within the foreseeable future, but Esmeralda still expected the best of her. She would eat, dress, and move on with her day as if there wasn't a war raging around her.

Penelope absentmindedly changed out of her night dress and into a silken lavender dress, lacing the back on her own before putting on a matching set of slippers. It was then that she took the note off her nightstand and sat down to read it.

There wasn't much to do today, which was a pleasant surprise. Penelope wasn't required to appear or aid Princess Mika in her royal duties. Instead, only a single meeting was scheduled. Penelope stared down at the name, and her mouth fell open.

"Lucinda?" Penelope gasped. The note fell out of her hand as she shot to her feet, rushing toward her bedroom door. She threw it open and found Vincent in the hall, having just left his room. "Did you know the Realm Sorceress was coming today?"

Vincent lifted a brow in her direction. His mahogany curls were hardly tame, per usual, and he hadn't bothered to put on one of the elaborate tunics filling his closet. Instead, he was fumbling with the last few buttons of his simple white shirt, left untucked and hanging over his black slacks. "Nope. All I know is that they're assigning me a new tutor and that he won't be here until tomorrow. I have absolutely nothing to do today."

"You already know everything there is to know," Penelope said as they headed down the stairs into the rest of their suite. "What's the sense in forcing someone to teach you?"

Nanny Dessa appeared at the bottom of the stairs, her lips curving into a frown. "What's with all the fuss? I thought I heard an argument brewing between you two," she asked with her hands planted firmly upon her hips, her pale eyes narrowing. Her long silver hair was braided and wrapped into a neat bun atop her head, a black ribbon fastened around it that matched her signature wrinkle-free cotton dress. "I figured at seventeen and thirteen, the two of you would have grown out of bickering."

"Penelope doesn't think I need a tutor," Vincent said, shooting a damning glare in Penelope's direction. He stuck out his bottom lip in a pout. "I'm only thirteen. I'm not supposed to finish my schooling for three more years."

"You should learn for as long and often as you like, Vincent." Dessa rustled his mop of locks before ushering them toward the dining room, where their breakfast was waiting. "And Penelope, don't be so bothered by what your brother does with his time. What's it to you, anyway?"

Penelope rolled her eyes and followed the pair toward the dining room table, where tea was ready to be served. She watched Vincent take his seat, his expression the very epitome of smug. "He can do whatever he wants. I just don't see why he's wasting some poor soul's time when he's already a genius," she explained. "Dessa, did you know that Lucinda was coming today?"

The nanny's lips parted with surprise. "I did not. She hasn't visited in years. Most people say she's in hiding per the High Queen's direction. She's to aid the Messenger when they surface. It's rare for her to appear, but I suppose she'll likely be here for Beck's ceremony on Sunday."

"I have a meeting with her and Thaddeus today," Penelope said, her thoughts scrambling with ideas about what it could be.

Dessa grinned. "She'll be so glad to see you again."

Penelope found herself smiling at the few memories she had of Lucinda. She could easily recall her blood-red hair, porcelain complexion, and how full of life she always was.

"She used to take me horseback riding." She giggled lightly at the memory. "Marcus would always linger nearby, watching to ensure I didn't fall."

"I remember those days." Dessa smiled as she poured tea into the cup waiting in front of Vincent.

The thought of Marcus brought unpleasant memories to

the front of Penelope's mind, quickly ruining her mood. Her stomach churned with dread as she attempted to banish the image of his face, with all of the other terrible things she would prefer to forget. "I should go. I wouldn't want to be late," she said, abandoning the table and all thoughts of those she lost.

Penelope knocked lightly on King Thaddeus's study door and waited patiently for his reply. Instead, he quickly welcomed her, offering her a warm embrace before leading her into a room filled with people.

Although she'd expected a meeting with the King and the Realm Sorceress, Penelope hadn't anticipated finding many others in attendance as well. She bit back a snarl at the sight of Valentina Gold sitting on a leather sofa beside a man that Penelope knew to be the Draconian General, Axel Graves. The presence of the Draconian clad in full, black-and-red armor led to goosebumps pebbling along her flesh.

Penelope's thoughts about the Prophetess and General scattered once she was pulled into Lucinda's arms. Her heart melted as she buried her face in the Sorceress's shoulder, breathing in the scent of jasmine and fresh mountain air.

"I'm sorry," Lucinda told her. "I should have visited sooner, but I've been busy ensuring my league is ready."

"Your league of Sorcerers?" Penelope's brows raised.

Lucinda nodded, her lips spread into a prideful grin as she released the princess from her grasp. "Of course," she confirmed. "Every Realm Sorcerer or Sorceress has one. Mine is simply the only one trying to keep savage-shapeshifting beasts at bay."

Thaddeus stiffened at the mention of the Pandora,

shooting a warning glare in Lucinda's direction. "Penelope, do you know why we're having a meeting today?"

"My apologies, but I don't," she replied, her gaze drifting. "Why are the Draconians here?" Penelope asked as her eyes fell on a man who stood awkwardly in the corner. He wore black and had straight, shoulder-length brown hair dusted with streaks of gold. Penelope eyed him curiously, sure that they'd never met before.

"You're being provided with a Guardian," Valentina announced. The sound of her voice brought Penelope's blood to a quick boil. "Not the kind the Moons give the Queens, but someone to watch over you."

Penelope nodded slowly, having figured that she might receive one eventually. "Why now, though?" she asked, hoping her tone didn't betray her by revealing her evolving rage. Her mind whirled as she thought about how the entire Realm blamed Valentina for her father's death.

"The war is intensifying outside these walls," Axel stated, leaning forward in his seat, bracing his elbows on his knees. Thaddeus scowled at him, but the General paid him no mind. "And as if the Pandora weren't bad enough, we now have Rebels. Some Mortals think that Immortals are doing a shit job of protecting the Realm. They don't understand why we're waiting for the Messenger or to name a Sectra Holder. Right now, they seem harmless, but then again, that's how the Pandora appeared at first. We can't take our chances when it comes to your safety."

"Axel," Valentina snapped. "Watch your language."

"And what you say," Thaddeus warned.

The General frowned in the King's direction. "I apologize, Your Highness, but we can't shield her forever. She needs to know what's happening in the Realm that she will one day rule. Right now, the Pandora wouldn't dare issue an attack inside these walls. But that doesn't mean she shouldn't be prepared."

"And if the Rebels are Mortals, they could slip past the golden gates easily," Lucinda added, her expression grim. "They could be walking your streets as we speak, just waiting for the opportunity to make a statement."

"That's where the Guardian comes in." Valentina rose to her feet. "This way, you'll always have someone with you."

A muscle feathered in Penelope's jaw. "I don't need a babysitter."

"He's not a babysitter," Lucinda chimed with a smirk. "Abernathy." She gestured for the man standing in the corner to come forward.

"*This* is the Guardian you all chose?" Thaddeus asked, giving the black-clad man a long, skeptical look.

"Don't underestimate him," Lucinda warned with a glint of mischief shining in her eyes. "Not only is he the first in line to replace me one day, but Abernathy is also an Idonian Immortal and an impeccable Sorcerer."

Thaddeus's nose wrinkled with disapproval. "You mean to tell me this man will eventually become Idona's Realm Sorcerer?"

"I didn't believe it at first either," Axel admitted with a sigh as he reclined in his seat. "When you asked me to pick her a Guardian, I chose Craven. But honestly, without him, the Pandora would be doing far more damage every Red Winter. We need him in the field. There are more powerful Draconians, but none I'd trust enough for such a task. I reached out to Lucinda to ask for her aid in selecting someone."

"And I do trust him," Lucinda declared proudly. "He was trained in Ryiah like I was. I taught him myself."

The Sorcerer shifted uncomfortably beneath the gazes of

those around him as his blue eyes found Penelope's. He walked toward her and attempted a smile.

"I'm Matt Abernathy," he said as he held out his hand. Penelope took it without question, squeezing it tightly.

9

Relief washed over Matt Abernathy the moment he left King Thaddeus' study. In his three hundred years of Immortal life, he had never experienced something so uncomfortable. He was unsure how to conduct himself around Idona's most influential figures, having never been in the position until now.

Guardian to High Throne's heir. Abernathy shivered, following closely behind the princess as they navigated through the Kingdom of Elves' intricate streets. They were supposed to spend the rest of the day getting acquainted. So far, they hadn't shared more than two words, and Abernathy began to find the silence suffocating. Usually, his days were spent somewhere in the Realm, annihilating hoards of Pandora or completing tasks for Lucinda. He hardly had the time to make conversation…until now.

"How did I get here?" Abernathy mumbled aloud.

Penelope slowed and looked over her shoulder, meeting the Sorcerer's gaze. "You used the portal rooms, I would assume."

Abernathy felt a blush creep into his cheeks, painting them an embarrassing shade of pink. "No, that's not what I meant." He cleared his throat and cursed himself for not having more control of his tongue. "It seems that just yesterday, I finished my training in Ryiah, and now I'm here, guarding someone as important as you."

"I'm sure that's not the strangest thing to happen in recent years."A faint smile bloomed on Penelope's lips. "Xavier has turned this Realm upside down, but you'd know more about that than I do. I hardly have a clue as to what's happening outside of these golden walls."

You don't want to know. Abernathy frowned as he picked up the pace to walk beside her. "Where are we headed?"

"I deliver lunch to the gatekeepers every Wednesday," Penelope replied, her tone as delightful as tulips blossoming in spring. "It's a tradition that started when I first arrived here."

"Odd." Abernathy's mouth moved again without his permission, earning quite a scowl from Penelope. "I meant to say, that's oddly endearing," he amended hastily. "How did it start?"

The princess fixed her attention ahead. She swallowed audibly, shadows dancing in her hazel eyes. It was as if she had gone somewhere else, viewing the ghosts of her past. "I used to visit the gates daily and wait for someone to return. But they never did."

Abernathy opened his mouth and shut it quickly, choosing not to reply out of fear that he'd dampen the mood even further. He'd poked at an old wound that served as a reminder that while Penelope had lived an extraordinary, privileged life, it certainly hadn't been painless.

The pair continued their walk in silence, all while Abernathy wondered who Penelope might have been waiting for. There weren't many possibilities; unfortunately, most of the people she would have known back in Solaris were dead. Perhaps it was her lost sister, the Missing VanCamp. *If that's the case, she'll be waiting a long time...likely forever.* Most believed the newborn princess perished the night of the siege, and that she remains long since lost to Idona's harsh elements. Still, Abernathy had always wondered if she was out there somewhere, living unbeknownst to her true identity.

He pushed all thoughts of the Missing Vancamp from his mind and returned his focus to Penelope. As they moved through the city, he realized how much the citizens adored her. She smiled and waved at everyone that she passed. There was no sign of the haunted princess he had seen earlier as they stopped at a quaint café and purchased sandwiches and drinks, tipping all the workers a few gold coins each. They all cheered their thanks as Penelope bid them goodbye and headed back onto the cobblestone street, where a group of young girls was handing out flowers to celebrate the arrival of Spring Solstice.

The streets were decorated with lights meant to twinkle at night and fresh flowers woven into vines that wrapped around street lamps and draped from roofs of shops and homes. If one didn't know any better, they'd believe the great Golden City to be a vision of peace and perfection. Abernathy, however, knew better.

"Your Highness!" one girl shouted as she ran over. She was shorter than the rest, with dark ringlets and large blue eyes. "Would you like a flower?"

"Of course," Penelope replied, taking the daisy she was handed and sticking it behind her ear. "I love daisies. Thank you—"

"Lyla," the girl offered, dipping into a clumsy curtsy before turning her attention to an unsuspecting Abernathy. "Who are you? A prince?" she dropped her gaze to the basket. "Are you two having a picnic? That's a lot of sandwiches. Are you courting?"

Penelope laughed at the last question. "Moons, no! This is Matt Abernathy, my Guardian."

"Huh," Lyla huffed. "He doesn't look like a knight."

"I'm a Sorcerer," Abernathy scoffed.

"I thought Guardians were supposed to be knights and wear capes," Lyla countered, narrowing her eyes.

"Capes are flashy and unnecessary."

"You'd look scarier if you wore one," the girl insisted.

"They get in the way."

"Not all Guardians need to wear capes," Penelope intervened before the back-and-forth continued. "I'm sorry, Lyla, but I have to get these sandwiches to the gates." She grabbed Abernathy by his cloak and guided him away. "Thanks again for the flower!"

The rest of their journey to the gates was filled with similar questions from others they passed along the way. Everyone was curious about Penelope's new Guardian, and Abernathy couldn't blame them. His name wasn't known in every household, unlike prestigious warriors like Craven Amsterdam and Aveo Calloway. His face was never portrayed in the paper, and reporters never spoke about him on the screens. Sorcerers weren't meant for fame and fortune. Their sole purpose was to protect their Realms from harm.

"If I have to answer one more damn question, I might die," Abernathy complained as they approached their final destination.

Penelope snorted, her eyes twinkling with amusement.

"Well, that's a tad dramatic." She reached out and gave him a reassuring pat on the shoulder. "Don't worry, you'll get used to it, and by the time you do, your novelty will have worn off, and the people will obsess over something else."

Before Abernathy could reply and say "*good riddance*!" a massive, auburn-haired Elf slid down a ladder from his post in the above watchtower. "Well, if it isn't Princess Penelope!" he shouted as he approached, a broad smile upon his pale, freckled face. Abernathy quickly recognized him as Yuri 'Red' Beaumont, the Kingdom of Elves' head of security, having studied all necessary personnel at great lengths before his arrival. How was he supposed to adequately protect the princess if he didn't know the names and positions of those responsible for protecting the kingdom?

"Red!" Penelope chimed as she hurried to embrace the Elf. "I brought you lunch, per usual."

"We missed you last week," Red replied as he stared down at her with eyes like golden rings.

"Queen Esmeralda demanded I attend a dress fitting for Beck's ceremony."

"I suppose that's a good enough excuse to starve me," Red teased before his attention slid over to Abernathy and the basket of sandwiches. "So, this is who they chose for the important job of following you around." One of his brows lifted. "Doesn't look much like a knight, if you ask me."

"That's because he isn't a knight," Penelope stated for what was likely the tenth time in the last hour. "He's a Sorcerer and is first in line to succeed Lucinda when she decides to step down."

"Well, then," Red drawled, his hands landing on his hips. "Never judge a book by its cover."

Abernathy flinched with surprise at the comment. Exactly what had this Elf been thinking about him? He looked down at his attire and confirmed that he didn't *look* like a bum. He'd worn his best trousers cloak and had even gone as far as to shine his boots.

"Hey, Red!" another guard called down from the watchtower. "Someone's approaching!"

The golden gates creaked open, revealing a tall Elf with silver-shaded eyes and long raven-black hair braided at the temples in traditional Elven fashion. Abernathy assessed him before he made it close enough to initiate a conversation. He wore the typical garb that any Western noble would — black pants and a fitted high-collared coat the shade of emeralds, lined with silver embroidery. He walked gracefully, yet his every step demanded the power only a king should have.

As the man drew closer, Abernathy began to realize that he had met the Elf before, but where and what was his name? His brow wrinkled as he fought to invoke a memory. All the Elves nearby clearly knew the Elf's name, for all the men were gawking, and all the ladies were gaping at him and blushing as if he was some sort of eligible prince.

I bet he's not all that special, ladies; calm down.

"Well, I'll be...." Red trailed.

"Who is that?" Penelope asked in a whisper, stepping closer to where Abernathy stood. "Why is everyone staring at him like —"

"What's wrong, Yuri?" the man asked before Penelope could finish her sentence. "You look like you've seen a ghost."

Red bowed quickly before straightening his spine and squaring his shoulders. "Lord Cedric, we weren't expecting to welcome you until tomorrow morning. Forgive me, but I wasn't certain that you'd turn up at all."

"Well, why would I give up the chance to see my darling cousin become a prestigious Elven General?" Cedric asked, lifting a dark brow. "And, you don't have to be so formal, you know," he added, gesturing to Red's rigid posture. "It isn't as if we haven't been friends since we were in nappies."

The guard let loose an exasperated sigh and snatched the basket from Abernathy's grip. "Good, because I'm starved and don't feel like escorting you to the castle right now." He walked back to the ladder before climbing it, returning to his post on the watchtower and leaving Abernathy and Penelope alone with this supposed *Lord*.

"Cedric," Abernathy said, clicking his tongue. "As in Cedric Chamberlain?"

The Elf nodded, his gaze dancing between Penelope and her Guardian. "You're one of Lucinda's Sorcerers, aren't you? We met briefly before my estate burned down."

"You mean the *Grimm* estate, where you were residing," Abernathy corrected. "I heard that the Pandora decided that attacking Mortal villages was no longer enough, but I was shocked to find out that they'd attacked such a historical place well after the Red Winter ended. Strange times have certainly fallen upon us."

Cedric clenched his jaw, his nostrils flaring. "*'Strange times'* is an understatement. They didn't simply attack the estate. They destroyed most of it with Amorian Fire. It's uninhabitable now."

Abernathy's jaw dropped. Never before had the Pandora used such extreme measures. "What could they possibly gain from doing that? And *how* did they do it? Amorian fire hasn't been made since before the New Dawn."

"It was a message," Penelope concluded. "This war has been stagnant for too long. The Red Winters aren't working as well as Xavier assumed they would. No one is bowing down; instead, they've continued to retaliate yearly. This is likely his way of telling us that his precious Pandora aren't the only trick he has up his sleeve."

Cedric's brow perked as a smile played on his lips. "And to think all royals behind these walls are clueless," he said, holding out his hand. "We haven't met before."

Penelope took his hand, and Abernathy went rigid as Cedric lifted it to his lips, planting a gentle kiss on the top. "You're King Thaddeus's nephew," she said. A pink blush dusted her cheeks. "He and Queen Esmeralda took you in after your parents died during the Five Realm War. You left the Kingdom of Elves twenty-five years ago to travel the

Realms along with the Notorious Six shortly after your eighteenth birthday and haven't returned until now. You were the Elven heir until Princess Mika was born three years after you left, but King Thaddeus insists you never wanted to be. He says you prefer solitude and never liked to attend social gatherings, which is why you've stayed away so long. He also says that you're an accomplished scholar."

Abernathy's mouth fell open as he took in all Penelope had said. No part of him had expected her to recite so much about Cedric in such a short time. It was almost as if she'd read every detail about him straight from a textbook. Then, of course, there was the matter that she had so willingly shared all of that information in public with so many onlookers. Some might find such behavior unbecoming, but it somewhat captivated Abernathy. Penelope didn't care much for how others saw her, and that was an admirable trait, in his opinion.

Cedric began to laugh softly, and Aberanthy's shoulders slumped with relief. The former heir hadn't taken any offense. "I might recruit you to write my autobiography one day," he declared. "Unfortunately I must bid you both goodbye and report to the castle. Even so, I look forward to seeing more of you, Princess."

10

Cedric Chamberlain hated the constant bustling of the Kingdom of Elves and quickly fled to the castle's quiet atmosphere. Yet, as he walked through the front doors, he couldn't help but feel like he was stepping back in time.

The foyer hadn't changed. Everything was just as nostalgic as Cedric had expected it to be. The dome ceiling loomed above him, adorned in shimmering gold. The ivory marble floors shined, not a speck of dust or a footprint to be seen upon them. Statues of past kings and queens stood tall and proud in each corner. The green and gold Tree of Life banners hung from the walls, their golden tassels twitching in the gentle breeze blowing through the open door.

"You can't even walk in the place without *Chamberlain* screaming in your face," Cedric muttered beneath his breath, unaware of the maid approaching from the hall on his left. He was too busy drowning in memories of what it felt like as a child to run to this foyer to greet his Aunt Esmeralda and Uncle Thaddeus each time they returned from an Idonian Council meeting or an event. He could still hear the sound of his laughter. It echoed in his ears, taunting him.

The maid gasped and lost her grip on her silver tray. Glass shattered as it hit the ground, peppering his shoes and ripping Cedric from his reverie. The maid immediately dropped to her knees, trembling as she cleaned up her mess. Cedric kneeled to help her with the large puddle of what had once been tea, now coating the marble floors.

"I'm so sorry, m'lord," the maid said apologetically, using her white apron to clean up the tea. "We weren't expecting you until tomorrow."

"I'm sorry; I didn't mean to startle you," he replied as he piled shards of glass onto the tray.

The maid's cheeks burned red with an embarrassing blush. "That's quite alright. You don't have to help me. This certainly isn't your responsibility."

Cedric pushed to his feet and offered her a hand. She hesitantly took it, rising to her full height once more. "It's no trouble at all, I assure you," he replied, smoothing his silk tunic. "I decided to leave Mayfire a day sooner. I suppose I just couldn't wait to see my family again after so long," he explained. "You wouldn't happen to know where any relatives of mine are, would you?"

"Her Highness is in the Throne Room, hearing from the people and welcoming guests that have arrived for Prince Beck's ceremony," the maid replied, still failing to meet his gaze. Cedric thanked her and bid her farewell before setting off to find his Aunt Esmeralda.

He paused at the threshold for a moment, scanning his surroundings. The Throne Room hadn't changed, either. It was still as breathtaking as he remembered it to be. Much like the foyer, it was covered in white marble with silver and gold accents decorating extravagantly arched ceilings. Ladies in waiting, dressed in cream satin gowns, walked around carrying trays with refreshments. They swayed in unison as they made their way around the room, their gowns brushing against the marble floors. Red lipstick decorated their fake smiles as they offered drinks to the guests.

"It's Wednesday," Cedric murmured. "Esmeralda always hears from the people on Wednesdays."

Esmeralda sat tall on her throne, thrumming her fingers against the alabaster arms as she answered a Mortal's question about the Rebels while Cedric took his place in line. He exhaled slowly, taking in the faces of those around him. Far too many important people had arrived to watch Beck finally accept his position as the Elven General tomorrow. Therefore, the Kingdom was even busier than it usually was. All of this led Cedric to feel both nauseous and claustrophobic.

That girl was right. I can't stand this place.

His turn to ask the Queen a question had finally arrived, and Cedric approached her throne with sweaty palms. She had yet to look up from the rectangular, glass device she used to take notes on. Clearly, it was some sort of Draconian creation, likely designed by the renowned technical genius Benjamin Butler.

After a few long, painful moments, Cedric cleared his throat, causing her head to snap and her eyes to widen with shock.

"Cedric!" she gasped, leaping to her feet and dropping the device onto her throne.

"I just have a few questions." Cedric held up a hand to keep her from speaking any further. "Where's my suite, and who's this boy you want me to tutor?"

Later that evening, Cedric made himself at home in his new suite. Most of his things had all been delivered and unpacked, courtesy of the castle staff, but not in the way he preferred. He spent hours arranging his books and the various collections he'd acquired over the last few decades, placing everything exactly where he preferred it. He even went as far as to arrange his wardrobe in order of color and occasion.

Once he deemed his suite to his liking, Cedric went to his balcony and gazed out into the kingdom he detested. At this hour, the Elves and Mortals who resided here were leaving their jobs and either returning to their homes or stopping at the various shops and taverns. He watched them all, their laughter echoing in his ears. It was impossible not to wish for the same joy they were experiencing. Cedric was envious, no matter how hard he tried to convince himself otherwise. He wanted to feel how it felt to walk through those streets without being overcome with crippling anxiety. He wanted to feel as free as he had once felt, traveling throughout Si Realtra with the rest of Idona's Notorious six, surrounding himself with history and culture. Unfortunately, those days were long behind him, the remainder of the Six either dead or scattered beyond Idona's reach.

A knock on his door pulled Cedric from his thoughts, and although he preferred not to respond, he knew he'd better. His uncle Thaddeus had yet to visit him and likely would by the night's end. However, when Cedric opened the front door to his suite, he was surprised to find not only Thaddeus there but also his cousin Beck and the Draconian General.

Cedric jerked backward with surprise and opened his mouth to speak, but all the words he meant to say vanished from the tip of his tongue. All he could do was stare at the three of them.

"Are you going to let us in?" Thaddeus asked.

Cedric moved aside, allowing the trio to enter. His mind began to run rampant as he wondered why a Draconian would be accompanying the Elven King, but he figured he would find out soon enough.

"King Loren will be here soon," Thaddeus mentioned while Cedric shut the door, his heart dropping at his uncle's words. First the Draconian General, and now the king? Something was wrong, and Cedric couldn't help but imagine the worst. "But before he gets here, I must say it's nice to set my eyes upon you after all these years."

"It's nice to see you as well," Cedric said, hoping his tone didn't reveal his evolving nerves or that the impeccable hearing of his fellow Elves didn't pick up on his thundering heart. "I've heard rumors about all that happened while I was away. Supposedly, the VanCamp have fallen under your care?"

"The two of them have been for thirteen years," Beck informed him. "The third VanCamp is still… *missing*."

Cedric's lips dipped into a frown. He'd heard those rumors too — the ones about the Missing VanCamp and how the newborn girl's body had never been found. Many assumed that she was still alive somewhere. The Kingdom of Dracus was still searching ruthlessly for her. "So I've heard," he replied, his eyes falling on the General. "From what I've gathered, you're in charge of locating her."

"That's classified," Axel replied quickly. "But yes, Dracus is handling that mission. We have the best tracker in the Realm leading the search."

"So, why is Loren coming?" Cedric inquired.

Thaddeus' eyes narrowed. He set his jaw as Cedric watched a muscle feathering in it. "To discuss what really happened at the Grimm Estate."

Another knock on the door sounded, and Beck moved to

let the Draconian King into the suite. Many years had passed since Cedric last laid eyes on him, but he knew Loren was nearing his first century. Still, he hadn't changed at all. His short dark hair was groomed neatly, just as it had always been. His quartz eyes were smiling as their gazes met.

"Well, look who it is," Loren drawled. "You haven't changed one bit, Chamberlain."

Cedric waved him off. "Blame my Immortality."

The five men all moved toward the Great Room, pouring glasses of whiskey and taking their seats upon the comfortable white velvet sofas Esmeralda had picked out for her nephew. It took quite a few moments of awkward silence before Loren began the dreaded conversation.

"You stated in your letter that the estate was burned down using Amorian fire." Loren glowered. "An extinct form of fire that never ceases to extinguish. Not without the Ryhian Ice spell, that is."

Cedric kept his expression blank as he fought to form the right words to explain what had happened the night the Grimm Estate was attacked. "And if I told you I knew how to perform the Rhyian Ice spell?"

Thaddeus's mouth fell open, his eyes widening. "You practice sorcery?"

"I know everything, Uncle Thad," Cedric said with a shrug. "I've dabbled in sorcery here and there, although I'd hardly call myself a Sorcerer. I just know a spell or two."

"The Ryhian Ice spell is a five-caliber spell," Loren scoffed. "One does not simply whip out a wand and perform such a thing without years of training. *Centuries* of training," he clarified.

"I'm a quick learner," Cedric told him. "In case you forgot, my mother was an Eidetic Elf. I inherited this trait from her. I can memorize everything I see and record it in my autobiographical memory. I couldn't forget a thing if I tried. Once, when I was young and studying in the library here in the Kingdom of Elves, I came across the spell. The image is embedded in my memory. When I needed to use it, all the information required to do so flooded my mind. I hardly needed to think. Because of my actions, most of the Grimm Estate's stone exterior remains intact. You're welcome."

Loren stared at the Elf for a long, uncomfortable moment. When he finally looked at his fellow king, a snort escaped him. "Thank the Moons' he didn't take after you, I suppose."

Thaddeus' glower was response enough.

Axel shook his head in disbelief. "That still doesn't explain how the Pandora got their hands on Amorian fire."

Cedric chuckled under his breath, sipping his whiskey. "Do you think those beasts are just eyes and fur with no brains? Sure, some of them might be, but how do you think they were created?" He waited for a response, yet no one said a thing. "Malachai."

"You're saying Malachai created the fire?" Beck hissed, baring his teeth.

"I'd bet all my coin on it," Cedric replied, leaning back, crossing his feet at the ankles. "Xavier might be sitting on his stolen throne right now, but that's only thanks to his son. He may be powerful, sure. After all, his defeat requires a prophecy to reach its fulfillment and Moonlight, of all things. But I would go as far as to say that he's only half of the problem. Malachai's a force to be reckoned with."

Loren's gulp was heard around the room. "What are you trying to say?"

"Have you forgotten just how smart Malachai is?" Cedric scoffed, earning a scowl from his uncle. "Come on, Loren. It hasn't been *that* long since we've had that genius in our presence, blowing minds across Si Realtra. Obviously, he figured out how to make Amorian Fire, just like he found a way to do everything else he's done," Cedric said point-blank, unsure of any other way to put it. "He created a *species*. I doubt recreating the fire was much trouble."

"The ingredients to that fire were lost when Amoria was destroyed. We all know that," Axel argued, grunting frustratedly."So it would be impossible."

Cedric shook his head. "Nothing is impossible when it comes to that man. *Nothing*."

11

Compared to Dracus, the Kingdom of Elves was an entirely new Realm. Dracus was majestic, surrounded by waterfalls, and separate from the rest of Idona, only accessible via the Unity Bridge. While it was a busy kingdom, it was still far more peaceful than the one Valentina was currently in. As the day dragged on, she missed it more and more.

There was a long and complicated history between the Elves and the Draconians. Although the two species were at peace now, Valentina couldn't escape the festering feeling within her while she was inside their borders. She couldn't keep herself from looking over her shoulder or allowing her hand to hover above her thigh, where she kept a dagger hidden beneath her skirts.

While Valentina hadn't been alive during the Scarlet Era, she knew the history well enough. Draconian hunters traveled in groups, hunting down her species' originals to drive them extinct. But, unfortunately, they could not control their thirst for blood, and for a while, became Idona's apex predators. All it took was a single drop of Elven blood on a Draconian tongue to thrust Idona into another war.

At the time, Esmeralda's parents occupied the Elven Throne and were at fault for countless Draconian deaths. Unspeakable acts were committed against Valentina's people, even after they learned to control their bloodlust and became docile.

The Scarlet Era occurred centuries ago, and now, Dracus produced its blood. No one else in the Realm was at risk, even as their race grew and flourished. But, unfortunately, that didn't mean that hate had vanished entirely. As Valentina walked through the city streets alongside Richard, she could see it reflecting in plenty of Elven eyes.

"They act like all we do is drink blood," Valentina snarled, unafraid of who heard her. "Should I stop and tell them about all the eggs and bacon I had for breakfast this morning? Or remind them how my visions have helped keep this war from completely destroying our Realm?"

Richard let loose a long, mournful sigh. "Pay them no mind. We're here to celebrate Prince Beck, and that's all," he said as they turned a corner, heading back toward the castle.

"She's the one to blame," a female Elf told her friend as Valentina walked by. "She's the reason the High King is dead. She's the reason Xavier still sits on the throne. If she were out of the way, King Thaddeus and King Loren would likely combine their armies and take Solaris back."

Valentina paused mid-step and whirled around to face the Elf. "Gideon died protecting the rest of Si Realtra from facing the same fate Idona currently faces. If it weren't for him, the Prince of Darkness would have gone to each Realm and torn it to shreds, creating hundreds of thousands more of those masochistic beasts along the way," she explained in the sweetest tone could conjure. "And if you'd like to attempt to defeat Xavier yourself, by all means.

"There's only one person powerful enough to face him. And even that person must retrieve the Sovereign's Scepter from the Forest of Fools. Good luck getting that, considering how many traps Queen Cleo has laid out for you. Maybe you'll be suffocated by quicksand, drown, or fall through some crack in the earth. But, let's say by some miracle, you make it to the cavern the Scepter was placed in. The beast Xavier planted there will surely pick you apart like a roasted chicken and use your bones to pick its teeth."

The Elves gaped at the Prophetess, their faces contorting with horror. "Or," she continued, taking a step closer. "You defeat the beast and realize that you're *not* the one worthy of breaking the spell binding the Scepter to the soil. Your blood is useless, and you did all that work for nothing."

Richard cleared his throat, causing the Elf and her friend to jump. They turned their attention to him, the lumps in their throats bobbing. "In case you've forgotten, Valentina Gold is the Realm Prophetess and a member of the Idonian Council. She may not be an Elf, king, or queen, but she still resides far higher than you do on the *food* chain." He emphasized the word, his eyes flashing with mischief. "What you just said about her would have been cause for the High King you worship to put your head on a spike and leave it to rot. Consider yourself lucky we don't have King Loren do that on his behalf."

The two Elves bowed quickly and apologized before running off into the city. Valentina watched them disappear, shaking with clenched fists as her rage gripped her like a vice.

"We're going to need to report this to the others," Richard said as he turned to continue his journey toward the castle.

Valentina followed him, sucking in a deep breath to cool her temper. "I just thought you said you *wouldn't* have Loren put their heads on spikes?"

"I'm not," Richard replied over his shoulder. "They were speaking just like the Rebels, spreading like an infection across the Realm. But, unfortunately, we must tell Thaddeus that some might lurk in his streets."

Valentina watched Thaddeus's facial expressions change from shock to anger, to confusion, and then back to anger. "I want those women held accountable for their actions!" he hissed in the direction of his guards, who then left his side off to follow their orders.

"They're not the first people to hate me, Your Highness. Many people blame me for Gideon's death. After all, I was the one who stormed into his bedroom late that night and demanded he shut the Gates," she reminded, sorrow sinking into her, dragging her down like a Minorian ship's anchor.

Thaddeus nodded slowly. "I understand, but if this isn't just hate, Valentina, those women must be screened. If they're Rebels, we might have a much larger problem on our hands."

It was well into the later part of the evening, and everyone in the King's study had grown tired throughout their eventful days. Even Richard yawned silently from his place beside Loren. However, some matters simply couldn't wait.

"This Rebel problem seems larger than we initially thought it was. Their numbers are multiplying," Loren said. "We must extinguish them before we find ourselves fighting two wars instead of one."

Valentina hadn't received many visions about the Rebels, but she was sure that she eventually would. It was only a matter of time. "Not to mention what happened with the Grimm Estate. The Pandora haven't made that big of a statement since they leveled Ironhaven three years ago," she reminded everyone. "Do you think that attack was more of a message from Malachai to the Rebels?"

"I know who we could ask," Axel chimed in. "Cedric. He's lived outside these walls for two decades. He knows the inner workings of Idona better than we do. I bet he's also heard a thing or two about the Rebels."

"Wouldn't that be convenient?" Richard sighed, rubbing at his tired eyes. "Perhaps we should hold a Council meeting before we all head back to our Kingdoms and invite him to it?"

Thaddeus shifted in his seat, lips dipping into a frown as if he were uncomfortable with his nephew participating in such politics. "I'll tell him about it tomorrow. We'll be in the Round Table Room Monday morning. You're all dismissed for now. Rest before the festivities tomorrow."

Valentina watched as Loren nodded before leaving the study. She and Richard followed him to the hall where all their rooms had been assigned. As they walked, the Prophetess could feel Loren's eyes upon her, and she knew that he was reading her as he always did with concern and scrutiny.

"You know, Val, one day, people will understand what you've done for this Realm." He placed a comforting hand on her shoulder, giving it a gentle squeeze. "They may hate you, but that's because everyone needs someone to blame."

"Why blame me? I've done nothing other than using the visions the Moons blessed me with to protect them," Valentina snapped as they arrived before the door to her assigned suite while Richard retired to his own. "Oh well." She shrugged, feigning disinterest. "They'll see. The Messenger is coming, and soon. It's only a matter of time before everyone who has disagreed with me is proven wrong."

Loren's eyes narrowed at her words. Valentina sucked in a breath, a poor attempt to calm her raging nerves.

"You sound like you know something I don't," he said, leaning against her door to keep her from entering.

"I didn't want to say anything," Valentina admitted—the fewer people who knew what she would say, the better. "I saw a woman approaching the beast in the Forest of Fools," she disclosed. "And not just any woman. While I couldn't see her face, I could tell she was powerful. A Draconian with abilities unlike any other."

Loren's eyes bulged as the words left her mouth. "And when were you planning on saying something?"

"You know that when I see a vision, it could take up to five years to come true. Benjamin is constantly reminding me of that fact," Valentina replied coolly. "What's the point of warning everyone now? They'd get excited, only to find out they had half a decade to wait before their saving grace finally arrived."

She watched as Loren's lips pursed. "I know," he sighed, "but still, this is something to celebrate."

"We'll silently celebrate when we arrive back in Dracus. Moons know I need an entire bottle of wine to myself."

12

Penelope was trying to get used to the fact that there was always someone at her side. Not a moment had passed since she and Abernathy had left Thaddeus's study yesterday morning that he hadn't been near her. He'd been given a room in the VanCamp family suite so that he could remain close, and so far, he and Vincent had grown quite fond of each other. They were seated at the dining room table, where the Sorcerer told Vincent exciting stories about his past in Ryiah over a game of cards.

While Penelope would have loved to hear more stories about Abernathy's adventures, she longed for her bedroom's solitude. She bid goodbye to the pair, though they didn't bother to look her way as she turned toward the steps leading upstairs. The second she closed her door behind her, she slipped into her washroom, where Nanny Dessa had already run a bath, and threw off her dress before slipping in. She sighed with relief as the steaming, rose-scented water enveloped her. Although she tried to remain thoughtless as she watched bubbles swirl and pop about the water's surface, Penelope couldn't manage to get her mind off the man she'd met yesterday.

Cedric had seemed so different from the other Chamberlains she'd come to know. She wondered what made him that way, and oddly, she wished she'd had the life he'd had… until today. Oh, what she would give for a life of solitude. The idea seemed so peaceful that once Penelope reluctantly left her bath, she collapsed onto her bed and lulled into a deep sleep.

In all of her years, Penelope had never worn such a beautiful gown. It was made of smooth, shimmering plum silk that cascaded to the marble floors, its lengthy train spanning out behind her. The bodice clung to her torso, silver embellishments adorning the swooping neckline, dripping cap sleeves, and hem. She could hardly recognize the woman staring back as she gazed upon herself in the full-length mirror in her dressing room.

"All I've done is blink," Nanny Dessa said sadly as she inspected Penellope's waist-length chestnut curls. "I blinked, and now here you are, all grown up. Before I know it, I'll sob on your wedding day."

Penelope snorted at that. "We have plenty of time before we have to worry about *that*," she insisted, turning around to face Nanny Dessa, patting her withered cheek.

"Not as much as you think," Dessa replied as she straightened Penelope's shining silver circlet. "I must say, you wear the Grimm family colors well. It's a shame that there are none left to pair you with."

"A shame, indeed," Penelope murmured, running her fingers along the silky gown. She had long since developed a slight obsession with the infamous royal family that ruled Si Realtra before the VanCamp ascended to the High Throne four centuries ago.

High King Seamus Grimm and Queen Iyana had eleven

sons and one daughter, all of whom were formidable warriors. Well, all but young Lucan, who was a mere toddler when the family was wiped off the face of the Realms during the Age of Monsters. Alexi Grimm, the seventh son, was perhaps the most notable, for he was sixth in line to the throne and had yet managed to surpass all his brothers in strength and power. To this day, Some even said that he'd kept a phoenix, the Grimm Family symbol, as a pet. Songs of his bravery and courage were still often sung, especially during the dark period Idona had currently fallen within.

Penelope had read every book and article about the Grimms that she could get her hands on. One, in particular, was kept in her suite, *The Age Of Alexi*. She considered it her comfort read and often flipped through its pages on rainy days. She lost herself in how a single Mortal man roared in the face of monsters straight from the Underworld's fiery depths, keeping an invasion at bay that would have led to Idona's destruction.

Later, Penelope found herself lost in a daydream about the Grimm family as she walked down to the Throne Room alongside her Guardian and brother. Upon their arrival, they found Beck radiating with joy from across the room. He was in deep conversation with his best friend, Commander Aveo Calloway.

Penelope steered clear of them, having never been fond of Aveo. While they'd grown up alongside each other, him being seven years older, they'd never gotten along. He considered her a spoiled princess, and she thought he was nothing more than a pompous jerk. He'd become even more insufferable after being named a Commander. The title had gone straight to his head.

While the Throne Room was massive, it felt miniscule with all the people looming about. Penelope's stomach twisted with nerves as she scanned all the faces, stopping when her gaze fell on the man who had swarmed her thoughts last night. She gathered up all her courage and approached him; his face was stuck in a book as he leaned against one of the pillars scattered about the Throne Room. How he could read amidst so much chaos was beyond the limits of her imagination.

"Cedric!" Penelope chimed, causing his gaze to lift from his tome. He snapped it shut and looked her over in a way that made her feel as though he were trying to figure out who she was. Wearing the wrong family colors probably wasn't helping.

"I never got your name yesterday," he said, tucking his book beneath his arm. "But if you're standing in this Throne Room right now and a part of this ceremony, you must be a VanCamp."

"Yes," Penelope confirmed. "Penelope VanCamp."

Cedric reached for her hand, kissing it politely as he had the day before. Penelope's stomach dropped as she felt the heat on her cheeks, hoping Nanny Dessa had applied enough powder to hide her blush. "I should have known yesterday. Your Guardian should have served as a dead giveaway."

"That's quite alright," Penelope replied, waving him off. "Now that you're here, I imagine we'll see quite a lot of each other."

"I'd assume so. I'll be tutoring your brother."

Penelope blinked. Of all the people Thaddeus and Esmeralda could have chosen, they'd picked their own nephew? "*You're* his replacement tutor? Why?"

"Why not? I was invited back to stay when I contacted my aunt and uncle after the attack on the Grimm Estate. They mentioned that they'd like me to tutor someone while I was here. And, to be quite honest, there isn't much else for me to do with my time. So, when I found out that Vincent VaCamp would be my student, I just couldn't help myself," Cedric admitted with a shrug. Penelope's eyes fell on where her brother and Guardian were talking nearby. She smiled at the sight of them laughing.

"That must be Vincent," Cedric said, following her gaze.

"Yes," Penelope told him. "It appears both he and my new Guardian have taken a liking to one another."

"From what I hear, Vincent is easy to like," Cedric said. "My aunt described him as a young prodigy who likes to play piano and read any book he can get his hands on. She also mentioned that Aveo is helping him to learn his way around a sword."

"I see you two have met." Mika's shrill voice caused Penelope to startle, nearly leaping out of her skin. She scowled at the Princess, who offered her a smirk in response. "That's great. Really," she assured them. "But, Penelope, if I were you, I'd spend your time getting acquainted with the other royals in this room."

Penelope scanned the room once more. She fought to stifle a gasp when she spotted King Loren Mason, a man she had yet to meet. "That black crown," she whispered, eyes wide with awe.

"The Draconian King," Mika confirmed as she wedged between Penelope and her cousin. "Handsome, isn't he?" She sighed dreamily and slumped against the pillar, golden eyes sparkling.

Penelope's eyes narrowed into accusing slits. "Don't get any ideas," she warned. With long golden hair, sun-kissed skin, and gold-flaked eyes, Mika was breathtaking. However, she was also an Elf, and her attraction to Draconians would only lead her down a road of trouble in the future.

"I know. I'm just stating a simple fact."

Thaddeus had an elaborate dais constructed in the Golden City's square for the occasion. Penelope and the others gathered beneath a nearby tent that shielded them from the thousands of guests who'd arrived to witness the historic event. The princess sucked in a shaky breath as she slightly moved the thick fabric aside, peeping through to view the crowd. She swallowed as a chill crept down her spine at seeing them all. A wave of nausea rolled over her, and sweat peppered her brow.

Once the ceremony began, each Idonian Council member was called individually. While Loren and the others were used to standing in front of thousands of people, Penelope and Vincent were not. As she glanced at her younger brother, she doubted she'd ever seen him so pale.

Valentina and Richard had both been announced and were gracefully climbing the steps to the dais while Penelope awaited her turn. She stood beside her Guardian, who attempted to distract her with jokes, to no avail. Cedric stood nearby with his gaze glued to the floor. Penelope wondered if he was panicking just as she was beneath his stoic facade.

Vincent and Mika were both announced, and Penelope watched her brother freeze in place. He was trembling, his eyes wide with fright as Mika took him by the hand, whispering something in his ear that the princess couldn't hear. But, whatever it was, it worked, and Vincent approached the dais, his posture as rigid as a marble statue.

Penelope smiled at seeing her brother's success but knew she and Cedric would be next. Her stomach dropped as she listened to the Kingdom erupt with applause at the sight of Gideon and Meera VanCamp's only son, aware that they'd likely do the same thing for her. Fear seized her as the cheering continued, and Penelope couldn't help but wonder how far she'd make it if she decided to run.

"Is this your first time?" Cedric asked, one brow arched.

Penelope pressed her lips together, fixing her gaze on the dais. "I've never made such a public appearance," whispered, voice wavering around the words. "I suppose I'll have to get used to it."

Penelope's heart flew off a cliff at the sound of the announcer clearing his throat. She'd known this day was coming for months. She'd prepared for it. She'd attended dress fittings and meetings and listened to Beck rant, and rave about becoming General for the last thirteen years. And yet, the time had come for her to ascend the steps to the dais and show her face. Every screen throughout the Realm would display it. Everyone would see it, even the Dark King and his wretched son.

"I present to you Heir to Princess Penelope VanCamp, heir to the Idonian Throne, and Lord Cedric Chamberlain, nephew to the Elven King and King," the announcer finished as Penelope felt the color draining from her face.

As if Cedric could read her mind, Penelope felt him take her hand. She was startled by his touch but calmed by it all the same. His fingers intertwined with hers, and he took the lead. The next thing Penelope knew, she was climbing the steps as gracefully as her body allowed her. The Realm came alive, clapping and cheering in places as far as the Regal Mountains to hear.

Although the sight of thousands of people made Penelope's stomach flip and flop, her heart was warmed by how welcoming they were. Her fear and nerves disappeared as she and Cedric took their places beside Vincent and Mika. The only person left to wait for was the guest of honor: Prince Beck Chamberlain.

13

Beck stepped onto the dais clad in shining armor; pride radiated off him like a waterfall. For as long as Cedric could remember, this was all that Beck had ever wanted. He'd practically flown out of his mother's womb, reaching for the General's golden badge. Cedric had never understood why more men would rather reach for swords instead of books, but all that mattered in the end was happiness. If someone could get what they wanted out of life during such dark, depressing times...well...all the power to them.

When he glanced sidelong at Penelope, whose firm grip was still wrapped tightly around his fingers, Cedric fought against a smile. *So, this is the Idonian Heir, shaking like a leaf,* he mused as the prior General Helevyre began to give a speech. He hardly heard a word of it, too lost in how beautiful Penleope's hazel eyes appeared in the bright afternoon light.

"In the past, kings would choose the perfect person to present the General's badge to its new owner. I was lucky enough to be given my badge by Graham VanCamp over a hundred years ago. He was the best warrior of his time and the only VanCamp to become a Dragon Rider. Though those days are unfortunately behind us, to me, this badge was always a reminder of the dragons that used to flood the Idonian skies. It was also a reminder of him." Cedric finally tuned into the speech, now intrigued by the General's mention of legendary Dragon Rider Graham VanCamp. "There will never be another man quite like Graham, but there are warriors throughout this Realm he would have considered worthy of this honor."

Beck seemed to be vibrating with anticipation to learn who would be presenting him with the badge. Cedric smirked at the sight of him like a child on Giving Day morning. He may still seem youthful at twenty-one but wouldn't dare face him in battle. He had heard the rumors. During Beck's four years defending the Elven border, he and Aveo had earned the names *'Beck the Brutal'* and *'Calloway the Cruel.'* They were twin swords, shredding hoards of Pandora, leaving nothing but carnage in their wake. He shivered at the mere thought of them.

Aveo stood before the crowd, clad in his light gray uniform and shining golden armor, his cape fluttering at his back. Cedric's chest tightened as he realized how much he looked like his eldest brother, Halvar. They had the same long, honey-colored hair and bronze eyes. Looking at him, it felt like he was looking at the face of one of his dearest friends brought back to life.

"Over the last thirteen years since the calamity that shook our Realm to the core, many formidable warriors have shown bewildering promise. Much like Prince Beck, they spend each day fighting to defend our Realm from the Darkness that threatens to swallow it whole. There is one, in particular, that holds a special place in all of our hearts. One who laid his life on the line the night Solaris fell to ensure that High King Gideon and High Queen Meera's heirs survived."

Penelope went rigid beside Cedric, her hazel eyes shimmering with tears threatening to spill over, her heart thumping so ferociously that Cedric could hear it clear as day. He squeezed her hand as if to remind her that she was here, not back in time, suffering through the trauma of that dreadful night all over again.

While Penelope fought to calm herself, Cedric watched as a man he'd seen in the papers approached the dais, clad in Draconian Armor. He knew of him, and yet, he'd never had the pleasure of meeting him.

"Humphrey Adams," General Helevyre introduced. "He, alongside Lucinda Cross and Marcus Bonaventure, completed what many would have considered impossible. Many of Idona's strongest warriors would not attempt what they accomplished together. Because of them, Prince Vincent VanCamp lives and breathes."

The Realm Sorceress, Lucinda, sniffed as Humphrey took his place before Beck and clasped his hand. Beck took it quickly, and the two of them hung on to each other in a way that made it appear that they were about to arm wrestle. Cedric wasn't a man of war, but he knew this symbolized unity and camaraderie between the two Immortal armies. His lips twitched, nearly smiling at the sight.

"I'm honored to give this to you," Humphrey told Beck, releasing his arm. "The Realms need men like you to aid the Messenger whenever they surface. I look forward to fighting alongside you when that day comes."

Beck's eyes grew misty as Humphrey pinned the badge to his armor. It was clear that although they had just met, he looked upon his fellow Immortal with the utmost respect.

This generation of Immortals, Cedric thought, his heart soaring, *will change Si Realtra for the better.*

The ceremony came to an end, and the participants and noble guests all flooded toward the Elven ballroom for a celebration. Cedric wasn't particularly in the mood for a party, but he found himself there anyway. He located his nameplate on a table and couldn't help but grin at seeing the one beside it.

"So, how does it feel being back in the limelight?" Beck mocked, handing his cousin a tall glass of ale.

Cedric stared down at it, having never really cared for the drink. He preferred whiskey and made a mental note to locate some later. "Like shit," he replied, leaning against the table as he searched for a certain someone he knew was somewhere within this room.

"If you're looking for Vincent, he was sent to his suite," Beck grunted. "I practically begged my parents not to, but they said he's still too young for parties of this caliber."

"That's a shame," Cedric agreed as he searched the room for Penelope, who he found with her Guardian, both of whom were talking with Lucinda. "Tell me, what do you know of Marcus Bonaventure?"

Beck recoiled, lips parting with surprise. "Why?"

"I find it odd how vague everyone becomes when he's mentioned," Cedric said, narrowing his eyes in Beck's direction. "No one will willingly admit what happened to him that night or whether not he truly died. I find it suspicious."

"Oh," Beck said quickly as his eyes fell upon the princess. "Well, I'm afraid I don't know anything." A lie. "What I *do* know is that he was gravely injured the night Solaris fell. Lucinda and Humphrey tried to save him, but whether they succeeded is a mystery."

Cedric gave his cousin a long, skeptical look. Still, he understood Beck's position and wouldn't press him. However, that didn't mean he couldn't share his theories.

"He's the tracker they always talk about. The one King Loren placed in charge of finding the Missing VanCamp."

Beck remained still, his expression stony, revealing nothing. "There are plenty of trackers searching for her from every jurisdiction."

Cedric gave in and took a long sip of the ale that he hated so much before he said, "Sure, but there's only one the papers talk about. Whoever it is, they only have five years left before that deadline. The one pertaining to the Sectra."

Beck flinched, his golden eyes flashing with surprise. "How did you know that?"

"Common sense, really," Cedric said, shrugging. "The Idonian Council would have already placed it around either Penelope or Vincent's neck; it wasn't meant for them, which leads me to believe that it's meant for the Missing VanCamp instead. It's why they're still looking for her, isn't it? If it weren't, they'd have given up by now." He took another sip, grimacing at the taste. "Whether the tracker is Marcus Bonaventure or not, I hope they find her soon. This problem with the Rebels seems to be getting out of hand."

A muscle feathered in Beck's jaw. "What do you know about the Rebels?" he asked, whispering so softly his words were hardly a brush of air.

"Not much," Cedric replied. "Their presence has agitated the Pandora so much that Malachai feels threatened. So he's creating more powerful weapons, like Amorian fire." He lowered his voice enough that only Beck could hear it despite all the Elven ears surrounding them. "If we don't get a handle on this situation soon, the two parties will tear this Realm apart, and they will take us all down with them."

Beck was silent for a time. He drank his ale down to the dregs before he said, "Cedric, I thought you were a scholar, not a politician."

"I'm many things," Cedric replied, lips spreading into a

devious smirk. "I'm not great with a sword, but I can throw a dagger with perfect aim. I've dabbled with sorcery here and there out of pure boredom. I'm not great with people. I don't like them; they certainly aren't fond of me. But one thing I'm great at is *listening*, learning, and adapting. If there's something I can do to help, I would. For her."

Beck's eyes followed to where Cedric's finger pointed to Penelope, who was laughing musically at something her Guardian had said. "Penelope?"

"Yes," Cedric answered, facing the new General entirely. "Because putting the VanCamps back on the Idonian throne means life or death for Si Realtra," he explained and tipped back the remainder of his glass. "And honestly, I'm not incredibly fond of thieves, especially the type that steal thrones."

14

Valentina pulled in a nervous breath, filling her lungs as the rest of the Idonian Council flowed into the Round Table Room. Cedric was the last one to enter, his gaze falling upon her. She offered him an encouraging smile, which he returned despite the apparent fear reflecting in his silver eyes.

"You were invited here today to tell us everything that you know about the Rebels, amongst a few other things," Valentina announced as everyone lowered into their seats.

Esmeralda lifted a brow down the table at the mention of *'other things.'*

Cedric nodded, the lump in his throat bobbing. "I'm afraid I don't know much, just rumors."

Valentina rested her palms upon the round table, leaning forward to peer at him. *The eyes are the window to the soul; her* mind echoed Amelia's words, causing an old, familiar ache to torment her heart. "Are you one of them?" Gasps sounded throughout the room. Thaddeus and Esmeralda's features twisted into matching scowls, their eyes narrowing into deadly slits.

The Elf shook his head, seemingly unbothered. "Of course not."

Valentina's brow furrowed. "What do you know about Malachai and his family? I want to know everything. Every strength and every weakness." Her visions never told her nearly enough. She wished that instead of seeing the actions of others, she could see within their minds. Learn their deepest desires and be privy to their plans.

Dreamwalking was an ability pertaining to a species that was now extinct—Arebus Archers — the original Immortals. The last of the Archers perished during an incident involving Lucinda at the end of the Five Realm War. Valentina's lips dipped into a frown at the thought of their leader, a complicated man that none had trusted yet had once saved her life.

"I thought we were going to discuss the Rebels," Lucinda said from her usual place on the other side of Richard, crossing her arms. "You don't think we know enough about Malachai and the Pandora? We've been dealing with them for decades. Not to mention, it's not like he and Xavier were strangers before all this started."

Valentina sucked on her teeth and shook her head. "There is still plenty that we don't know. I can feel it. We only know what we've experienced and what my visions have told us. Cedric, on the other hand, has heard from the Idonian people. He's been out there." She dramatically waved a hand at the floor-to-ceiling windows around the room. "And I specifically recall how close Cedric and Malachai once were," she added, staring at Cedric expectantly.

Cedric's jaw clenched. "*All* the heirs were close. Now, most of them are dead, and Malachai's to blame." Pure, unadulterated rage flashed in the Elf's eyes. "The man you're asking about and the man I knew are two entirely different people. As far as I'm concerned, Malachai died the moment he became the beast that he is today." Each one of his words dripped with venom.

Down the table, Cleo shifted uncomfortably in her seat. Aries reached out and took hold of her hand, a gesture of comfort. Valentina's heart sank with dread at the sight. Many of Idona's heirs, the next generation of rulers and leaders, had died during the Ballroom Battle. Cleo's only child, Elveana, was among those lost.

Valentina nodded, grinding her teeth. "I received a vision of his first transition. One second, there was only him, and the next, there was an army at his back." She shivered at the memory. "We still have no idea how the Dark Army gains so many numbers so quickly. Every time we eliminate one Pandora, twenty more take its place. Do you know anything about that?"

Cedric exhaled slowly and shook his head. "Not nearly enough. What I *do* know is mostly common knowledge. The species started with Malachai. Those that came next were volunteers. When their ranks weren't increasing enough, they invaded Southern Idonian villages and cities, turning people by force. Places that fought back were leveled. As for how they've managed to keep those numbers for so long, that's what the Red Winters are for."

"I thought the Red Winters were a gruesome way for Xavier and his army to celebrate the anniversary of their victory in Solaris," Cleo whispered in horror.

Thaddeus scoffed. "*I* thought they were designed to instill fear and force those to bow and accept Xavier's reign that have yet to do so."

Cedric shook his head again. "I'm sure you're both right, but just as many people wind up missing as others do dead. Every year, five thousand Mortals vanish, sometimes more. The Idonian people don't fear the Red Winters because their lives are at risk, but because those they love could be taken from them and forced to fight for a cause they don't believe in."

"And now, the Rebels are fighting back," Aries concluded.

Shrugging, Cedric reached for the glass of water before him and took a sip. "As I said, I don't know much about them or their goals. But I know they've managed to get under Malachai's skin."

"I'm sure they won't be a problem that much longer, then," Loren huffed, lips curved into a frown.

"What about Xavier?" Valentina pressed, changing the subject. "He's no longer a Mortal. I'm not entirely sure that he was one to start with. We knew very little about him. He kept his private life to himself and rarely spoke about any family besides Malachai. He never mentioned if he was married, who Malachai's mother was, or if he had any more children."

Thaddeus grunted with displeasure. "What would make you think that my nephew knows more about Xavier than we do? He hardly knew him."

"That might be true, but he knew Malachai," Valentina countered.

Cedric cleared his throat, drawing their attention back to himself. "I don't know *what* Xavier is, only that he isn't a Pandora. No one knows what sort of power he possesses or where it came from. As for his family, I know he was married to Malachai's mother, but she died unexpectedly during childbirth with his younger sister the year before I met him. I also met another boy when the other heirs and I paid Malachai a visit at his family home. He was around four then, and I never caught his name. Princess Soroya is alive and well, parading around Solaris without care. She's a powerful Witch, which leads me to suspect that Malachai's mother was as well. However, I've heard nothing about the other boy. It's like he never existed." He took in a deep, audible breath. "I do know that Xavier married again. A Witch named Kiara Phantom. He adopted the son she already had, a Warlock named Savron, and together, they had a set of twin girls: Jax and Trixa. I'd say they're around fourteen now."

Each Idonian Council member recoiled with surprise. "How do you know all this?" Esmeralda rasped.

"You learn dirty things in dirty places," Cedric replied as his features darkened. "People talk, and I listen. But, unfortunately, Savron's gained a lot of attention these last few years. He's now a Pandora Hybrid, and many fear him just as much as Malachai."

Someone let loose a long whistle, and Valentina didn't bother to look and see who it was. Instead, her gaze was fixated on Cedric, her thoughts whirling. "What about the Rebels? Do you have any idea what their goals are?"

"There are whispers," Cedric started softly. His gaze dropped to the table as though he was afraid to look anyone in the eye. "It is said that they believe the Immortal Kingdoms have failed the people by withholding the Amulet when a Sectra Holder could save so many lives every Red Winter, but also by leaving the Mortals of this realm to fight on their own. I suppose the premise of the organization is that if you're not going to stand up and fight, they will. In short, they're sick of waiting for the Messenger like everyone else."

Tension thick enough to choke on filled the room. Valentina clutched the velvet fabric of her skirts beneath the table, awaiting the inevitable — the same dreaded conversation she'd endured at every Idonian Council meeting since Solaris fell.

"They would not think that we're failing them if we could appoint an interim Sectra Holder," Thaddeus said slowly, a muscle quivering in his clenched jaw. "Someone who could use it to protect the people while we wait for the Missing VanCamp to be found."

Someone like Princess Mika, Valentina silently seethed, pressing her lips together as she met Loren's gaze. He gave her a reassuring nod and reached for her hand, squeezing it gently beneath the table. "I've received visions that lead me to believe that Xavier's reign will soon end. The Messenger will surface within the next five years. The Missing VanCamp is not dead." Her words caused a few council members to gasp while the others gaped at her in surprise. "And the Rebels will become a massive thorn in our sides. They want the Sectra, and they won't stop until they get it, which means we need to find that VanCamp and put it around her neck before they get the chance."

With narrowed eyes, Valentina watched the faces of her fellow council members, waiting for a reaction. Her fists began to curl so tightly that her knuckles were growing white from blood loss as she fought against memories of their lack of faith in her.

"And if we can't find her in time?" Cleo croaked.

Valentina sucked in a nervous breath, her stomach churning. "Then we give it to someone else."

PART II

FOUR SWORDS

15

Nearly a month had passed since Beck's ceremony, and every day, Penelope found herself amidst lessons all over again. Each morning, Cedric appeared at their front door and would sit down with Vincent in the study to tell him stories about the other Realms and how they worked. Although Penelope had finished her lessons last year, she couldn't keep herself from joining the two of them in awe of everything the Elf had to say.

Abernathy was always nearby, studying spellbooks or writing correspondence to his friends in the Regal Mountains. He occasionally participated in the lessons, eager to share an opinion on whatever topic Cedric was teaching. Today, that topic sent chills racing down Penelope's spine.

"Were the Arebus Archers Si Realtra's original Immortals?" Vincent asked, narrowing his eyes skeptically. "All the books I've read about the history of Immortals, here, in the castle library, state otherwise."

Abernathy scoffed at that. "Well, that's because *Elves* can't accept that they came *second* at anything."

"You're not wrong," Cedric chuckled at the Sorcerer. "But yes, the Arebus Archers were created first as the Great

Sovereign's Guardians. The Elves were created almost immediately after as her companions. Fae came afterward, then Witches, Mortals, and so on."

Vincent's brow wrinkled with confusion. "Guardians against what? I thought there was only the Sovereign in the beginning."

Penelope turned away from the conversation and fixed her attention on the windows, noting the storm brewing in the angry gray clouds coating the sky.

"That's a lesson for another day," Cedric replied quickly. He explained how unique the Arebus Archers were compared to the other Immortals. They had an impeccable aim and could not miss a shot within a three-mile radius. As if that weren't dangerous enough, they could possess one of five rare mental abilities: Telekinesis, empathy — better known as emotional manipulation — hallucinosis, teleportation, and dream-walking. Every adult member of the species carried an obsidian bow engraved with markings pertaining to their clans or personal, unique natures. Their uniforms were also so dark they might as well have been made of shadows. "They were Si Realtra's apex predators. One alone could take out an entire village, but an army of them...well, I'm sure you can imagine why they were feared. Unfortunately, an incident toward the end of the Five Realm War brought upon their extinction."

Abernathy's laughter filled the room. "An incident?" he repeated. "Lucinda opened the Underworld underneath their feet."

A bright, captivating strike of lightning lit up the sky outside. Thunder cracked a moment later, rattling the castle as Penelope rose from her seat. "I'll be in the observatory," she told Abernathy before leaving. Her walk to the library was short and accompanied by a pair of silent guards. Once she arrived, she went up to the third floor, where she climbed a ladder to reach a familiar title waiting on the top. Afterward, she went further up to where the observatory awaited her.

The glass, dome-shaped ceiling offered a perfect view of the evolving thunderstorm as Penelope settled onto one of the couches. She stared at the skies, watching as streaks of lightning ripped through the sea of gray clouds. She opened her book, a dreamy sigh sailing past her lips.

Flipping through the pages, Penelope again lost herself in Alexi Grimm's heroic tale. A sea of emotions ran rampant throughout her as she skimmed each line. She experienced everything from joy to anger to sadness as she inched closer and closer to the epilogue — Blair Grimm's wedding to Nevin Vancamp. It was *supposed* to be a happy ending, but Penelope knew what had happened after their heartfelt vows were spoken. Blair died of illness, and Nevin became so distraught that he abdicated the High Throne to his younger brother, Ashwyn, and begged the newly appointed Realm Sorceress, Lucinda, to help him make his ascension into the afterlife.

Hours had passed without the princess realizing it, and night had fallen by the time she was snapped from her reverie by a deafening clap of thunder. Penelope blinked, shocked by the night sky that hovered above her. Most of the clouds had disappeared, revealing thousands of stars that twinkled like diamonds against a black sky, sending her into a trance so beautiful that she hadn't heard anyone approach.

"You're in my spot," a familiar voice called, startling her.

"I'm not moving," she declared, her eyes falling on Cedric, leaning against one of the glass walls, peering down into the kingdom below.

"I didn't ask you to." His smirk was audible in his tone. "Your Guardian fell asleep."

Penelope's eyebrows flattened as she imagined Abernathy's eyes drifting shut as he curled up on the couch in front of their family room screen with some action film likely playing upon it just as he'd done every night since she'd met him. The Sorcerer might often suffer from inexplicable exhaustion, but she still trusted him with her life. She had to.

"Sounds like him." Penelope sighed, shutting her book.

"What were you reading?" Cedric's strange, silver gaze dropped to the title. "Ah, *Age of Alexi*. I used to love that book too, but I'd hardly call it more interesting than the Arebus Archers."

Penelope set the book aside and rolled her eyes. "I finished my lessons last year. I know enough."

"But *my* lessons are far more riveting than whatever you were taught," Cedric challenged as he turned to face her. His usual silk tunic was unbuttoned, revealing the plain white t-shirt he wore beneath. "I can tell you anything you want to know. I've visited every court scattered throughout Si Realtra and traveled through every Realm. All I know could prove to be beneficial for a future High Queen."

Penelope swallowed hard and hoped he hadn't heard her with his incredible hearing. "I doubt I'll make it that far, Cedric. This war is just getting worse. Now, we have not only the Pandora to deal with but the Rebels as well. Thaddeus tries to hide the gory details from me, but I'm not daft. I can read a paper," she grumbled and stood, walking to join him in front of the glass wall.

The Kingdom below provided a breathtaking view for the pair. Bright lights sparkled endlessly below them, glistening in the dampness provided by the frequent rainfall. Elves took to the streets despite the angry midsummer weather. Nightlife in the Kingdom of Elves manifested before their eyes, but that didn't cause Penelope's mind to wander too far from her thoughts. Her shoulders curved inward as she gazed at it, placing a single palm against the glass. She longed to escape into the Kingdom and lose herself in its chaos for a time — to forget who she was and what she may never evolve to be.

Penelope's cheeks warmed as Cedric took her hand in his, intertwining their fingers.

"You're wrong."

Penelope spared him a sidelong glance but found her eyes trapped once she became lost in his. "Xavier is undefeatable. The Messenger might not come in my lifetime. I may die before that rancid bastard is slaughtered. This is what my life will consist of. The constant need for a Guardian, always looking over my shoulder and always wondering when someone might come to aim at the target my bloodline has planted upon my back." She sucked in a deep, calming breath before she let it loose in a single huff. "If only I could be Immortal. Then I wouldn't age. I wouldn't be as easy to kill. I'd live long enough to see Solaris restored to its former glory."

Penelope knew that she would be the only one of her siblings to die of old age — if she were lucky enough to make it that far. Vincent's pending condition was no secret. In a few years, he would transition into an Immortal. The potion their mother had used to help them survive the harsh labor a twin delivery can bring upon a mother, and the babies within her womb came with side effects. Usually, those given this potion were eliminated due to the risk that they'd turn into Hybrids. The Idonian people frowned upon such beings; Immortals and Mortals considered them abominations. Penelope's great-grandfather had banned them, insisting that any Hybrids discovered be executed. While Vincent would survive because the Idonian Council had excluded him from that fate, Penelope still worried for Ash. If she was alive somewhere, she might not survive much longer.

"Why do you think I'm here, Penelope?" Cedric asked, pulling the princess from her depressing thoughts.

"Well, your estate *was* rendered uninhabitable via Amorian Fire, courtesy of the Prince of Darkness." Penelope chuckled at the sight of his responding scowl.

"That's not the only reason. I could have gone anywhere. I'm welcome anywhere, even the Regal Mountains, where the outcasts thrive, the Witches, the Giants, the Trolls. All those untrusting species are unifying on one mountain range. So I'm welcome even *there*. Yet I'm here, in the same Kingdom I couldn't get out of fast enough twenty years ago." Cedric clenched his jaw, returning his attention to the view before them. "I want to help you and Vincent, and Ash, one day, if I get the chance. Nothing means more to me than returning the VanCamps to where they belong on the High Throne. Whether it's tutoring Vincent or standing here to reassure you, there's nothing I wouldn't do to help prepare you all."

Penelope's lips parted with surprise. "Why?"

"Because I believe it may be my life's purpose," he whispered. "What? Was I to waste my abilities hiding in some old estate, watching as a war raged around me? Absolutely not. I may not be a decorated soldier or a Galaxy-renowned warrior, but I'm still a damn Chamberlain."

Lost for words, Penelope stared at him, her hand still wrapped around his. Moonlight streamed through the glass walls, and she couldn't help but be mesmerized by how it danced upon his sharp features.

"You'll ascend to that throne one day. I don't care what price I must pay to get you there; I'll pay it." Cedric met her gaze once more, his iridescent silver eyes bearing into her like harsh blades. "I've seen enough suffering, Penelope. Enough death. I'll pick up a sword myself if that's what it takes to end all this."

Penelope's stomach flipped, and her heart skipped a beat. "Where do we begin?"

Cedric slowly shook his head. "I'm not quite sure. But there's one thing I know: don't trust anyone," he whispered.

"What exactly do you mean?" she asked, matching his soft tone.

Cedric stared down at her, pursing his lips. "Last month, I attended an Idonian Council meeting. Mostly, they asked me questions about…well…everything: Malachai, Xavier, the Dark Army, and the Rebels. So, of course, I told them everything I knew, which wasn't much. Still, there are things I should have told you about it long before now."

"Things like what?" Penelope pressed, nerves fluttering in her gut.

"I can't be sure..." he trailed.

"Spit it out."

"Well, I couldn't shake the feeling that all the members were at odds somehow," he replied slowly. "Especially the Elves. It almost seems like they're playing a game of their own."

Penelope's heart dropped. Her mind swam with ideas of what the Elves might want to gain from this Dark War. She thought of the history of the Elves, the constant battles and hatred between them and the Draconians. In the past Civil Wars, they had started, their goal was to take the main throne for themselves.

"Throughout history, Elves have always considered themselves the most powerful Immortals in Si Realtra. They tried to claim that they were the original Immortal species at one point. Still, the true original Immortals, the Arebus Archers, were quick to put them in their place," Cedric explained as if he could read the princess's thoughts, a grave expression upon his face. "They've craved that throne since the order was established throughout our Galaxy. While they've been complacent for the last few centuries, I fear that the peace will eventually end."

"What makes you think that?" Penelope blinked back tears, bothered immensely by the thought of Esmeralda and Thaddeus betraying her in such a way.

"Cedric's gaze fell to the floor, a muscle feathered in his jaw. "The matter of the next Sectra holder came up since it's clear that that's what the Rebels are after. We discussed the urgent need to give it to someone in the next few years before they attempt to take it themselves." His voice trembled. "Your mother's will states that it was to go to your sister Ash, but she hasn't been found. If she isn't found by the time she turns eighteen, the Amulet will likely go to Mika."

Penelope gasped, her blood turning to ice in her veins. "The Sectra holder to the main throne holds the Galaxy," she whispered wide-eyed. "Mika could take my throne for herself."

"Exactly." Cedric nodded slowly.

An emotion Penelope rarely felt began to overwhelm her: rage. Her cheeks flared red, her fist curling around Cedric's fingers. "I see," she hissed through clenched teeth.

"But there's one more thing," Cedric mentioned. "Valentina is positive that the Missing VanCamp is still alive."

Every hair along Penelope's neck rose up in response, her pulse thrumming like the beat of a drum in her ears. She fought the urge to double over. Of course, Ash's death had never been confirmed. Her tiny, newborn body had never been located. But the idea of ever seeing her sister again had been far from Penelope's mind. She'd lost hope ages ago. "We need to find her then," she breathed. "We need to find the Missing VanCamp before it's too late and we're *all* forced to bow down to the Elves. Me included."

Cedric grinned. "Where should we start?"

16

Abernathy sat in silence as Penelope paced before him. He'd never been one to understand the inner workings of a woman's mind, and yet, she was an open book. In the month he'd spent so far as her Guardian, he'd begun to notice how easy she was to figure out. Her pacing told him something was incredibly wrong since she only did such a thing whenever she was in distress with a constantly running mind.

"Are you going to tell me what's bothering you, or do I get to play that famous guessing game again?" Matt asked, leaning back on her bed, bracing himself with his hands.

Penelope stopped pacing and whirled around to face him. Her hazel eyes were bright with rage, her back as straight as a rod. "Who do you answer to?" She hissed the question, taking a step toward him so quickly that he flinched.

Abernathy scrambled to find an answer, alarm bells screaming in his mind. "Well, you, I suppose."

"You *suppose*?"

He cleared his throat, wondering what had gotten into the princess. "I report to Lucinda."

"Not the Elves? You *do* live in their Kingdom now," Penelope said, her face inches away from his own.

The Sorcerer shifted uncomfortably beneath her, a blush burning his cheeks. "I don't answer to the Elves. I might live in this castle, but I live with you. I'm here to guard *you*. So, I don't give a shit what they say," he replied. "Why?"

Penelope groaned, backing away from him to grab a letter off her nearby vanity. She returned to hand it to him, a deep frown etched upon her face. "Read this."

Abernathy took the letter from her and skimmed the delicate script. "They're giving you an eighteenth-year ceremony? That's wonderful!"

"No. Not wonderful." Penelope snatched the letter back, crumpling it within her hand. "They're using a Mortal tradition to ensure I marry an Elf so that they can weasel their way onto my throne. That's just in case the Missing VanCamp *does* turn up, and she becomes the Sectra holder as my mother intended for her to be. They're covering *all* their bases now."

"What are you rambling about?" The Sorcerer glowered.

Penelope huffed, blowing a strand of chestnut-colored hair away from her face as she placed her hands on her hips. "It's come to my attention that the Elves aren't as pleasant as they appear. Think about it. I've never been allowed to leave the Kingdom, though Mika gets to travel about the Elven jurisdiction and visit Dracus at least once a year. Beck is hardly ever inside the golden walls now that he's the General. Vincent is lucky enough to leave the castle at all. They're keeping us under lock and key, brainwashing us to think that they have our best interests at heart while they only think of themselves."

It was no secret that the Idonian Throne hadn't always trusted the Elves. For centuries, possibly a millennium, they strived to take the High Throne for themselves. They saw

Mortals unfit to rule Si Realtra and viewed themselves as the superior race. When another powerful Immortal species came into existence, such as the Draconians, Esmeralda's parents sought their destruction. The Scarlet Era ensued, and Idona suffered one of the most gruesome Civil Wars in history.

"I can't say I'm surprised. I thought Esmeralda was different, though," Abernathy admitted, running his hands through his silky hair. "Let me guess, they want to give the Sectra to Mika or Beck?"

Penelope nodded quickly as her face flushed. "And now that she's pregnant *again*, she'll likely use that baby against me one day too."

"And this eighteenth-year ceremony is just a ploy to betroth you to an Elf?" He shook his head in disbelief.

"It has to be." Penelope groaned, falling onto the bed beside him, her eyes fixed on the ceiling. "And that's not even our biggest problem. We need to find the Missing VanCamp before it's too late. Marrying an Elf is one thing. At least I'll still have my throne one day. But not if they give the Amulet to Mika."

Abernathy's evolving anger flared. "The VanCamps were the best royal family Si Realtra had. Mortal or not. They are the only ones who can keep the peace throughout our Galaxy." He pushed to his feet, fighting against the urge to pace. "I never thought I'd consider this, but Penelope..."

The princess sat up to look at him, leaning back on her hands. "Yes?"

He approached her, placing his hands on his shoulders and staring into her eyes. "I might know of a way to derail their long-term plan. If what I think works, then your reign will never end even if they marry you off to an Elf."

"How?" Her eyes narrowed slightly.

Abernathy pressed his lips together. "There are two ways.

It depends on who's more willing to undermine the Elves, Lucinda or Loren," he revealed, and Penelope stifled a gasp. "Tell me, who else knows about this?"

"Cedric," she admitted. "He told me everything last week, and now that I've received that letter from Esmeralda, it seems he'd been right in thinking his aunt and uncle were up to something."

Abernathy stared at her, his mouth agape as his hands dropped from her shoulders. "Let me get this straight," he started. "An *Elf* told you that the other Elves are conspiring against you?" He could hardly believe it. "He's their *nephew*."

"I know," she replied. "Which means he knows them better than anyone else. Think about it, Abernathy. He left this Kingdom, abandoning them without a second thought. So, he's clearly not their biggest fan."

The sound of the front door bursting open startled them, and Penelope rose from her bed, her eyes growing wide with fear.

"Cedric!" a familiar voice roared, and Abernathy rushed to see what the fuss was about. Had the Elves listened in on their conversation? His stomach churned at the thought.

Penelope followed Abernathy down the stairs, keeping close behind him. His wand fell from his sleeve, landing perfectly in his grip as he rounded the corner into the foyer. He'd fight his way out of this castle and kingdom if he had to.

What he found wasn't a threat. Instead, it was Elven Commander Aveo Calloway, standing in Penelope's foyer with a letter in his hand, trembling with what could only be rage.

"Where is he?" the Commander demanded.

"He's tutoring Vincent in the library," Penelope replied dryly, her eyes narrowing. Her hatred for Aveo wasn't exactly unknown, and it certainly didn't go unnoticed. "Why?"

"It's classified," Aveo spat, turning to leave the suite.

Abernathy seethed, following Aveo without a second thought, his wand still in his hand. The Elf was at *least* two feet taller than he was, with long, honey-colored hair and eyes that reminded him of liquid bronze. Power seeped through his pores and the impenetrable fabric of his dark gray uniform, causing the Sorcerer's stomach to knot with unease.

It's no wonder Penelope despises you. He fought the urge to snatch the silver cape from the Commander's back and wrap it around his neck. Instead, Abernathy's fists clenched at his sides. He was all too aware of Penelope behind him, her mind likely running with ideas about what the Sorcerer might do, and he didn't want to do anything that caused her any trouble. He tried his best to remain dangerously calm as he continued his pursuit.

"Why are you following me?" Aveo asked as he continued down the marble halls of the castle, headed toward the library.

"You seem threatened," Abernathy replied honestly. "I'm Penelope's Guardian. If there's a threat, I need to know about it."

Aveo glanced over his shoulder, his gaze lingering on Penelope long enough to infuriate the Sorcerer.

"Don't look at her; look at me and tell me what the fuck is going on," Abernathy snapped, venom dripping from his tone.

"Someone left us a present less than a mile from the golden walls. The charred corpse of one of my subordinates. They were kind enough to leave a note." His admittance was chilling, and Abernathy glanced toward Penelope just in time to watch her complexion take a green hue. "Beck went to track them, and it's my job to use this note to figure out who did it. The Rebels, or Malachai. That's why I need Lord Cedric."

"He didn't go alone, did he?" Penelope asked, her voice trembling.

"Of course not," Aveo grunted. "He took a platoon with him and called for Draconian assistance."

"Draconian assistance?" Penelope squeaked. Abernathy slowed, brows shooting upward with surprise. When did the Elves go running to the Draconians for help?

"Supposedly, the Electric Immortal was carrying out his investigation on the Rebels nearby. He confirmed that Malachai was in the Elven jurisdiction as recently as yesterday, thanks to a few witnesses who saw him in the Lakelands. Craven's on his way to help Beck as we speak," Aveo explained as they approached the library, the doors to the magnificent multi-leveled room in view. "If that man is involved, I doubt the Rebels will be a problem much longer. But, if Malachai's at fault, then I'm not sure what this incident means for the future of our kingdom."

Cedric was in the middle of telling Vincent about the fourth Zerinian Civil War when a certain angry Commander burst into the library with Matt Abernathy and Princess Penelope in tow. His heart halted in his chest as he imagined why Aveo, of all people, was with them. Had Penelope taken what he had told her, decided it was untrue, and ratted him out to the Elven Guard?

Cedric straightened in his seat and ran his hands over the smooth fabric of his silken, emerald tunic. "Can I help you?" he asked as kindly as he could manage.

Aveo slammed a letter onto the table so hard that it trembled the chandeliers above. "Read it," he ordered. Cedric scowled and reached for the letter, examining the wax seal bearing a familiar mountain symbol. His brow furrowed, having seen it somewhere before. He opened the letter, only to find four simple words. "Our silence has ended," he read aloud. "What's the meaning of this?"

Aveo growled so viciously that it sounded more like an animal than a man, gripping the top of a chair with so much force that the wood splintered. Vincent stared at him with wide, fearful eyes, but he didn't acknowledge the prince. "We found the body of one of my subordinates outside the walls, burned to a crisp with this note pinned to his chest."

Vincent trembled in his seat, his complexion turning ghastly.

"It was clearly the Rebels," Abernathy insisted. "If it were Malachai, there would have been a lot more blood involved. But, the last I checked, he doesn't fight with fire unless you count that incident at the Grimm Estate."

Cedric's eyebrows flattened. "This wasn't Malachai. First, this isn't his kingdom or family's symbol. Second, he doesn't leave notes. His actions are always enough of a statement."

The Commander's shoulders relaxed, the tension in the room easing just enough for Vincent to stop trembling like a leaf. "Well, at least we know that the Rebels are at fault. We have their wax seal." He pointed to the letter. "What does that symbol mean to you?"

Staring down at the seal, Cedric ran his hand over the three mountain peaks etched in the wax. "I've seen it before. In a book," he said, deep in thought, waiting for his memory to reveal the required information. Finally, he closed his eyes, his patience wearing thin. "A book about legends."

"What book?" Aveo gestured sarcastically to the thousands of books displayed on the three floors' worth of shelves around them.

"It was published a hundred years ago," Cedric explained, his eyes still shut. "I could read it again and then give you all the information that I found, but it might take some time." He gestured to the books as well. "I'm going to have to find it first."

Aveo's expression hardened. "Time is of the essence. Beck is going to need this information before the Draconians join him. So, I suggest you start looking."

Cedric pulled in a nervous breath, filling his lungs while Aveo stormed out of the library. "What an angry Elf." He blew out a long whistle before rising from his seat, his eyes falling on Abernathy and Penelope. "As long as you're here, you might as well help. I believe that all books about legends are on the third floor. Unless they did some rearranging while I was away."

"I can help, too," Vincent offered, jumping to his feet.

Cedric looked down at him as a smile spread across his face. "Good. Help me retrieve every book of legends you can find," he directed, and Vincent bolted from the table and up to the third floor.

Penelope and Abernathy sat quietly on the other side of the table, flipping through the pages of book after book. Dessa had been kind enough to deliver their dinner to them, and Cedric was glad to take a break from the searching to nourish himself. He'd grown increasingly frustrated by the second, wondering why his memory hadn't revealed the truth about the mountain symbol.

Oddly enough, a riddle began to replay in the Elf's mind as he scanned the pages of a book he knew he'd read before. "Deep in the mountains where no one goes sits a village that no one knows," he recited, causing those around him to cease reading and look up at him. "Down a path of twists and turns, in a location the naked eye can't discern. Be careful not to be led astray for one wrong turn, and you won't live to see another day."

Abernathy cringed in his seat. "That's… dark."

Penelope nodded in agreement. "What's that about?" she asked, her eyes alight with curiosity.

Cedric rubbed his temples, fighting against a coming headache. "The mountains. The village," he murmured before finally coming to the realization he'd been begging for. "The Hidden Village!"

Vincent gasped. "Here!" He pointed to a page in the book he'd been searching through. "These mountains are the ones from that symbol!"

Cedric reached for the book, skimming it over. "Indeed, they are," he agreed, his features twisting with confusion. "Are the Rebels trying to say that that's where they hail from?"

"I doubt it." Penelope surprised him by saying, "It's probably just a ploy to lead us astray. They'd have to be idiots to give their location away so easily," she explained, sipping her tea.

The princess seemed unlike herself, which amused Cedric. Her long hair had been tied into a messy bun, and her sweater dripped off her bare shoulders. She yawned as she pushed her reading glasses back into position. "The odds are that they're in Central Idona," Penelope continued as she reclined in her chair. "That's where the Immortal silence is the strongest. The people who live there have developed a hatred for Immortals. They hardly see them and believe they could do more to defeat the Pandora. As a result, they're more disconnected than those who live closer to the Kingdoms."

Astounded by her way of thinking, Cedric fought not to stare at her in awe. "We should station more men in Central Idona then," he stated as he slipped his communications device from his pocket and sent Aveo a quick message about the matter.

"I bet the people in Mayfire know a thing or two about them," Penelope mentioned. "Maybe we should go there and investigate."

"We?" Vincent scoffed at her. "We won't be allowed anywhere outside the walls until the Rebels and the Pandora are both gone for good. I don't understand why we don't just pin them against each other. That way, they'd destroy one another."

Cedric's brows shot upward at the sound of Vincent's suggestion. "That would be a dream," he agreed. "But he's right. And so are you, Penelope. Mayfire would certainly know a thing or two about the Rebels. It may technically be in the Elven jurisdiction, but it's close enough to Ardon Lake to be considered Central Idona."

Abernathy sighed in his seat, drawing their attention. "They also might know a thing or two about the Missing VanCamp," he mentioned softly. "A wealth of information is likely available there."

Cedric's eyes widened at the sound of his words. He stared at the Sorcerer for a while before his gaze fell on Penelope again. "You told him," he accused.

"He's my Guardian," Penelope reminded him sweetly. "And he's going to help us. Besides, he's had quite a few wonderful ideas so far," Penelope added with a bright smile. "Like undermining the Elves."

Vincent dropped the book he was holding and gawked at his sister. "Excuse me?"

Cedric had nearly forgotten that Vincent had been seated at the table. He sucked in a breath and exhaled slowly, doubting the prince was ready to know the truth. "Shit," he groaned.

"He's going to find out eventually," Abernathy said. "Might as well tell him before they off him or something."

Vincent gasped. "*Off* me?"

"You're different," Cedric reminded him. "You could turn into a Hybrid in a few years, and they could kill you for it. They would, too, because it means getting a VanCamp out of the way. But they can't. The Idonian Council signed an agreement to ensure that doesn't happen to you." He felt terrible, watching Vincent's face twist as he processed all he'd learned. His eyes were growing misty, and Cedric couldn't help feeling horrible for causing it. "Listen, Vincent. This Realm and this Galaxy are filled with people praying for the VanCamps to take back their throne. At the same time, the Elves have always prayed for the opportunity to take that throne for themselves. So if we don't find your twin before your eighteenth birthday, the Idonian Amulet will go to Mika, and they'll use that to their advantage. That damn Sectra is the biggest loophole in Si Realtra. A straight shot to the High Throne, where Mika will sit, not Penelope."

The princess nodded sadly in agreement. "And to make matters worse, they're giving me an eighteenth-year ceremony. They will use one of our family's *Mortal* traditions as an excuse to marry me to an Elf. That way, even if Ash *does* turn up and accepts the Sectra, an Elf still winds up as High King of Si Realtra. Since I'm Mortal, I'll age and eventually die, and that Elf will remarry another Elf. And the Elves will hold the Galaxy in their hands anyway." She shivered as she finished her rant. "Unless Abernathy and I can find a way around that."

The Guardian gave her a wink, and she smiled in return.

Cedric's lips parted with surprise, having not considered the possibility that his aunt and uncle would try something so devious. "You've got to be kidding me."

"Not one bit," Penelope said sadly, shrinking in her seat.

Abernathy nodded. "I read the letter Esmeralda sent to her myself."

Vincent growled, and everyone around the table looked at him, brows raised. "That's it!" He shot to his feet, his fists slamming down onto the table. "We need to find Ash."

"If she's still alive," Abernathy added.

"She is," Cedric said, "Valentina's sure of it. That

Prophetess is the only thing standing between my aunt and uncle hanging that amulet around Mika's neck."

Tears began to well in Vincent's eyes, and Cedric figured that the news that the baby he'd shared his mother's womb with was still alive had struck a nerve. He could only imagine what Vincent had gone through, likely yearning for his other half for thirteen years. He could see much of his younger self in Vincent and had grown to know him well enough that all the emotions the young prince had buried were surfacing.

"She's also sure of something else." Cedric thought he might as well mention it. Clearly, the people around the table were the only ones he could trust now. "The Messenger will surface within the next five years."

18

Another Red Winter had begun, and Valentina's mind was aching from the surplus of visions she'd received. Ever since the Pandora had come into existence, the snow that blanketed Idona every year had become their playground. They were stronger in the cold and took the opportunity to strike fear into Idonian villages and cities. The entire ordeal was part of Xavier's plot to break the Idonians so that they would finally bend to his will.

Most recently, The village of Greystone had suffered a vicious attack. Valentina had seen the attack coming, but due to its location across the Realm, the Draconians couldn't get there in time to aid them. The Elves hadn't made it there in time, either, despite their proximity. While Valentina had tried to reach out to them, she found it was too late. By the time the Elves and Draconians arrived, the village was in ruins, and the few remaining survivors were found trembling with their coming transitions into Pandora. Blade, who'd led the mission to aid them, had had no choice but to end their lives.

"Another village wiped off the map." Chills slithered down Valentina's spine as she walked toward the Training

Center, hoping to find relief. In the past, she would have been on the front lines. But, she was too valuable for Loren to send out, as was he. If she died, who would aid the Messenger when they arrived?

The Training Center had been closed for the evening, but since Valentina was a Draconian Council member, she knew the code to unlock it. She pressed her palm against the identification pad, watching red lights flicker green. After she typed in the code, she heard the latch unclick and made her way inside.

As Valentina walked down the hall, she saw that a light was on in one of the arenas. Curious, she approached it and glanced through the glass walls, watching as a man trained aggressively.

Holographic Pandora leaped at him from every direction. He moved so quickly that it was breathtaking. Sweat dripped off him, dribbling onto his bare chest as he fought angrily against their sharp fangs and claws. Valentina couldn't help but be enamored by the power he'd obtained in recent years.

Muscles flexed and rippled as he raised his sword above his head, bringing it down so hard onto the holograph that it shattered, sending pixels flying in every direction. He fell to his knees, sucking in deep breaths, and wiped his brow.

Valentina thought she should leave him alone, but something told her he could use the company. So, she made her way into the arena, and her presence didn't go unnoticed. He looked over his shoulder at her, his eyes wet with tears.

"You look like you need a drink," she mentioned softly.

He shook his head, trembling with the rage that his memories brought on. "It's been fourteen years," he reminded her, though he didn't need to. She knew very well what day it was. "Fourteen years since the Ballroom Battle. Fourteen years since I failed."

"You didn't fail," Valentina declared, her tone so stern that it startled him. "So, help me; if I hear you talking like that again, I'll have you committed."

Frowning, the man rose to his feet and turned to face her. Sweat glistened over his scarred torso, the marks nothing more than a devastating reminder of that night. "I might have gotten those twins out of the Kingdom before it fell, but I still can't find one of them," he snapped. "I can't bring myself to face Penelope or Vincent because, so far, I've let them down. I've combed through every inch of this Realm, and she's nowhere to be seen. So, how can you say that she's alive?"

"I've seen her," Valentina reminded him. "I've seen her face."

Vivid green eyes began to tear again, and he quickly looked away as if to keep her from seeing. "We only have four years left," he said, the words wavering. "Do you think she knows who she is? That she might come to us herself?"

"I don't know everything," Valentina replied solemnly. "I saw her with Vincent in a library."

He met her gaze, a ghost of a smile on his lips. "You've always given me hope," he told her softly. "You're the only person here who shares the same faith that I do. Everyone else seems to have lost theirs."

Valentina nodded. "I'll never lose mine," she claimed, holding her hand out to him. He took it, allowing her to lead him out of the arena. "There are a few things you should know, Marcus," she explained as they went downstairs into Benjamin's office, where she knew he always kept a good stock of blood in his fridge.

"What?" he asked as he made his way toward the large glass table that centered the room, hopping onto it so he could sit.

Pouring two glasses of blood, Valentina handed the first to Marcus and kept the second for herself, taking a long sip before she said anything more. "Something is going on in the Kingdom of Elves. I'm not sure what, but there's a storm coming. One that might not be so obvious compared to others," she explained warily, the thought of it all causing her gut to twist with unease.

"Should we be worried about Penelope and Vincent?" Marcus's eyes narrowed.

Valentina remained silent momentarily, careful about what words she might say next. If she revealed that she thought the Elves might be conspiring and using Penelope to do it, Marcus would march into that Kingdom and use Whitefire to burn the entire damn thing to the ground.

"I've seen that they'll throw her an eighteenth-year ceremony in a few months when Spring begins," Valentina admitted to him. "They want to betroth her to one of their commanders. But, of course, we can't allow that to happen."

"What can we do to sway them?"

"Nothing," Valentina replied blankly. "Loren, on the other hand, might have a say."

When he smirked, Valentina knew he'd picked up on what she was trying to say. "It's time the Draconians get involved in what happens with the VanCamps," Marcus declared. "In the meantime, I'm going to continue to try and find the remainder of the royal family."

"Perhaps Lord Cedric Chamberlain might be able to help you," Valentina mentioned thoughtfully as she sipped her blood. "I've met him. He's brilliant, and he isn't close to his family. He's only in the Kingdom of Elves to tutor Vincent indefinitely. Something tells me that he's on our side." She was sure of it.

Marcus pursed his lips, his brow wrinkling with thought before he eventually said, "Send me his contact information."

For a moment, Valentina stared at Marcus. He seemed so different compared to how he'd been when she'd first met him at the choosing ceremony for Meera's Guardian. He'd evolved. When he'd arrived in Dracus, he'd been knocking on death's door, and although he'd been consumed with finding Ash VanCamp ever since, she could see how much he'd truly changed — for the better.

A long silence passed between them, all while Valentina gazed upon him. A blush began to dust Marcus's cheeks, and her heart skipped. "Are you going to send it?" he questioned nervously.

Valentina snapped out of her reverie, her cheeks burning hot from her own cherry-shaded blush. "Of course," she replied, shaking her head as if trying to get his image out of her mind.

Another silence fell as she retrieved her Communications Chip from her pocket and forwarded the contact. Once she finished, Valentina debated on what she should do next. Part of her wanted to close the space between them, craving his touch. But the other part wanted to do precisely what she had come to the Training Center for fight.

Valentina's lips spread into a smirk as her fingers ran over her soft velvet cloak. "Do me a favor?" she asked in her most sultry tone.

Marcus's brow raised, his eyes widening slightly as her fingers grazed the silver ties of her cloak. Valentina heard him gulp and swallowed her urge to laugh.

"Sure," he replied, clearing his throat nervously.

"Fight me," Valentina directed. Her smile dissipated as she pulled the strings to her cloak, letting it fall from her form and reveal the red-and-black Draconian uniform she wore beneath. She sucked in a deep breath as her mind drifted back to the last time she'd worn it. Dracus had suffered an attack at the end of the Five Realm War when Amelia and King Lionel Mason lost their lives.

Shivering against the memories, Valentina focused on

Marcus. He stared at her, his mouth agape. "You want to fight... *me?*"

Valentina shrugged. "Why not? Do you not believe that I could take you on?" Her words were laced with venom, and she watched as Marcus's surprise faded into a look of pure determination. He leaped from the table so quickly that she was stunned; his fist reached out to wrap around her golden locks. She ducked, avoiding his strike. Her palms pressed against the cold marble floors as she kicked outward, catching the back of his legs with her foot. A giggle escaped her as he staggered backward into Benjamin's desk, causing piles of paperwork to scatter into the air around them.

Marcus collected himself, grunting frustratedly. "You're fast," he admitted, the corners of his mouth lifting into a devilish smirk. The next thing Valentina knew, he'd used Immortal speed to push off the desk. She only saw a blur flipping over the glass table that centered the room, landing on the other side.

Growling, Valentina prepared herself for his inevitable strike. He was too far away now for her speedy tricks to blindside him. She quickly thought of a backup plan, her mind drifting back to days when she and Loren would train in the nearby arenas. They'd both been hand-to-hand combat specialists, although she'd been more likely to use her feet than he had.

"You're not a long-distance fighter," Marcus pointed out. "And now, this large glass table separates the two of us. There's absolutely no way you could get around or across it without me dodging your attack. And then, I could issue a counterattack, and you would lose."

Valentina's blood began to boil at the sound of his words, her sweaty fists now clenching at her sides as she thought of what to do. She scanned the room around her. Every surface was clean, with screens lining the walls and a few empty desks beneath them. There was nothing for her to use against him other than the table in front of her. The Prophetess began to realize that if she wanted to win this fight, she would need to do the unthinkable.

Snarling, Valentina used all her Immortal strength to lift the table before her. She'd expected the glass to shatter, but all it did was slip out of place, sliding right into Marcus's knees. They buckled instantly due to the force, giving the Prophetess enough time to leap across the room and wrap her fingers around his throat.

Snarling, Marcus reached for her hair, wrapping it around his fingers before he pulled hard, causing Valentina's head to jerk backward. She yelped, digging her nails into the flesh of his neck. The scent of his Immortal blood wafted through the air. Her mouth watered.

While she'd been distracted by the scent of blood, Marcus forced her off him and onto the floor. He hovered over her, a crooked smile spreading across his lips. "Got you."

"Nope," Valentina laughed as she sent her knee flying upward, catching him in a place considered every man's worst weakness. He cried out, releasing his grip on her hair as he curled onto the floor, completely stunned by her actions. "Do you forfeit?"

When Marcus forced a smile and rose to his feet, Valentina couldn't stop herself from rolling her eyes. "You're clever," he complimented. "I have to say, I've never fought anyone who thought to throw a massive table at me before kneeing me where the sun doesn't shine."

His words brought a smile to Valentina's lips as she placed her hands on her hips, chuckling lightly. "That's because you never fought me before," she replied proudly.

Marcus sighed, shaking his head in disbelief. "Wasn't Loren your battle companion?" he questioned, and Valentina nodded in response. "Well, I feel bad for him."

19

Convincing Esmeralda and Thaddeus to allow her to go to Mayfire wouldn't be easy. Penelope's plan to join Mika in the Fall had been butchered the second the Elves had issued a travel ban due to the Rebels' message and the body they'd gruesomely used to send it. Now, she wouldn't have a chance to go until the Spring, and her eighteenth-year ceremony was getting in the way.

"I don't really need one," Penelope told the King and Queen during their weekly family dinner. "There's just so much going on with the Rebels. We just started another Red Winter, and Greystone was destroyed. I would hate to plan such an extravagant party while such devastating things are happening throughout Idona."

Beck gave the princess a dubious look. He had finally returned home after his long search for the Rebel Headquarters, which had unfortunately been fruitless. "What princess doesn't want a party in her honor?"

"Me," Penelope replied dryly as she sipped her wine. It was a rare drink for her, but now that she was old enough, she supposed she could use the liquid courage.

"It's crucial that we betroth you just as your parents

would have. The entire Realm is looking forward to it," Esmeralda explained, her belly as swollen as ever. Penelope imagined the baby could come any day now, possibly any second. "Besides, aren't you thrilled? Rebuilding the VanCamp family must be your top priority."

Penelope's face blanched as she purposefully finished off her drink. She could feel all the Chamberlain's eyes upon her as she set held her glass out, a butler stepping forward to fill it. Her breath hitched as she watched Esmeralda run a hand over her stomach. *No, absolutely not!*

"Is something wrong?" Mika's high-pitched voice rang. "Every young girl always dreams of their wedding day and the family they'll start soon after. Even I have," she admitted as she cut her steak gingerly with her knife.

Cedric stared at Penelope from across the table beside his uncle, his gaze reflecting his sympathy for her. "She must be marrying a Mortal then," he mentioned, raising his glass of whiskey to his lips to hide his smirk.

"Not necessarily." Esmeralda's scowl toward her nephew didn't go unnoticed.

Penelope felt a wicked blush flow into her cheeks and hung her head slightly, hiding it with her hair.

"Well, since Hybrids are illegal, I naturally assumed," Cedric continued, causing Vincent to stiffen in his seat beside his sister.

"Not when a Mortal and an Elf or Fae have a child," Thaddeus revealed. "The child would only be a crossbreed, weaker than the usual Immortal. Hybrids are full-fledged Immortals."

Penelope fought the urge to gawk at him. *Oh, so* now *we're okay with interspecies children.* Her lips pursed as she bit back a response, focusing on her steak instead.

"What if Penelope prefers a Mortal?" Cedric pushed, and Penelope was beginning to hope that someone would swoop in and save her by changing the subject, "What about someone like Matt Abernathy?"

Mika nearly spit out her wine. "Her Guardian?"

"He's an *Immortal* Sorcerer," Beck chuckled.

"But he was a *Mortal* before he drank the Fountain of Youth potion. His genes are Mortal. Besides, maybe the child would become a splendid Sorcerer like him."

"But he's her Guardian," Mika repeated, her nose wrinkling with disgust.

Penelope's head was officially in her hands; her mind whirled as her stomach began to twist and turn. She swallowed hard, fighting against the bile creeping up her throat. It wasn't that there was anything wrong with Abernathy; the entire conversation had taken an incredibly embarrassing turn.

"We'll consider it," Thaddeus said, shocking the Princess.

"What about King Loren?" Mika earned a mean scowl from both her parents when she brought up the Draconian King. "You said that if a Mortal and an Immortal had a child, it would be a crossbreed, not a Hybrid. Therefore, why not? Dracus has no Queen. It would allow Penelope to rise to a throne before the Messenger arrives and reclaim the High Throne for her," she clarified, flashing her brilliantly white teeth.

Beck's brows shot upward with surprise. "She has a point. Why not make her a Queen sooner?"

Penelope felt herself growing queasier and focused intensely on cutting her steak. She hadn't realized she'd passed through the meat and was sawing the fine china instead; the sound of it shattering drew everyone's attention. She stared at the mess she'd made with a blank expression, blood pouring quickly from the wound, creating a puddle upon the white lace tablecloth.

Cedric rushed around the table, retrieving a cloth napkin

to wrap her hand. He shook his head in disbelief, a glare set upon his aunt and uncle. "See? You've stressed her out."

"I'll take her to the infirmary," Beck offered as he stood to join her. "Perhaps you two might want to rethink the timing of this ceremony. We could always wait a year," he reminded them as he led Penelope out of the room.

Thankfully, there were no stitches needed for Penelope's hand. The Healers rubbed a healing balm on it before bandaging it for her and then sent her on her way. She was relieved to leave the infirmary, stepping into the cold winter night. For the first time in ages, snow was falling within the Kingdom of Elves. All the Giving Day trees lined the streets were lit, sparkling at night. She smiled at the sight, having always loved this time of year even though outside the golden walls, another Red Winter ensued.

"I'll deliver you to your suite," Beck offered, stopping Penelope dead in her tracks. "What is it?" he asked, turning around to face her, concern flashing in his eyes.

Penelope shrugged, unsure of what to say. "I would rather not go home just yet," she admitted, her eyes falling on a pub across the street.

"Absolutely not," Beck growled. "If I take you into a pub, it'll be all over the papers in seconds. *Princess Penelope gets drunk with the Elven General.* I can just see the looks on my parent's faces now."

The princess scoffed at him, placing her hands on her hips. "You're the Elven General, Beck. They can't shun you for having a drink or two."

Beck was silent for a while, his brow wrinkled in thought. Penelope waited impatiently for a response, wondering when he'd finally let loose. From the moment he'd turned ten, she'd watched Beck train intensely to become the Elven General. At twenty-two, he'd achieved that goal, yet he was still following his parent's orders instead of making his own. "Fuck it!" he finally shouted, causing many passing by to glare in his direction. "Today's a sad day." He nudged her arm as he started toward the pub. "Might as well drink our sorrows away!"

When the pair entered the pub, they were surprised it was empty. The barkeep, a middle-aged Mortal man, stood behind the bar, appearing rather bored as he skimmed the day's paper. When he looked in their direction, his eyes grew wide, the sheet falling out of his hands.

"General!" His back straightened. "And Your Highness."

"Enough of the formalities," Beck ordered as he sat at the bar. Penelope slid onto a stool at his side. "We're here to drink. Two ales. Scratch that. *Three* ales, please," he insisted, and the barkeep lifted a curious brow before pouring the glasses. He set all three on the bar in front of Beck and then watched as the General slid one over to the princess before pushing one toward himself. "I meant the three of us," Beck stated proudly.

The barkeep blinked slowly, raising his glass to his lips. "This isn't a trick, right? I'm not going to be beheaded for this?"

Penelope winced.

"Of course not!" Beck insisted, having already finished half his glass.

A short while later, Beck and Penelope were happily slurring their words while the barkeep, named Timothy, told them brilliant stories of his past as a soldier in the Idonian Mortal Army. Beck offered him a position in his platoon, but the man declined because he was the only one who could operate his bar.

"I'll buy this bar," Beck insisted as he shot out of his seat, slamming a fist down onto the maple wood. "Right now."

Timothy stared at the General, his mouth agape, while Penelope giggled endlessly. "You're serious?" he slurred, smiling.

"As serious as a Pandora attack, my friend!" Beck raised his glass to him, and the ensuing cheers meant the deal had been done. Beck was now the owner of a pub on the Elven main street, and Penelope had a place to run to when things got a little too stressful in the castle.

When the door to the pub opened and two familiar men passed through, Penelope squealed out of excitement. "Abernathy!" she gasped as she ran to hug him.

The Sorcerer stiffened beneath the princess, clearly afraid he might wind up dead on the street if he hugged her back. As Penelope released him, she couldn't help but notice Beck staring at him with eyes comparable to daggers.

"Did you hear?" Penelope shoved the General from her mind and focused on the Sorcerer instead.

"I heard that it was almost one in the morning, and you still hadn't returned home," Abernathy replied, sporting a withering glare. "You scared us half to death. This is the last place we expected to find you!"

Penelope looked over to see Cedric standing beside the bar, holding a glass of whiskey. "I'd say worse things have happened," he said.

"But did you hear?" Penelope returned her attention to her Guardian, repeating her question.

"Hear what?" Abernathy grumbled as she swayed in front of him. He placed his hands on her shoulders to steady her, causing her cheeks to burn as she watched him fight against a laugh.

"That we're getting married!" Penelope announced, grinning from ear to ear.

The Sorcerer's hands fell off her shoulders. "Excuse me?" he croaked.

"Whoa, there," Cedric interjected. "No one's getting married," he assured the Sorcerer, who sighed with relief, reaching out to brace himself on a nearby table. "Well, I can't say that for sure. But you *are* on the list."

"So are you, though," Beck slurred from his seat at the bar, the ink still drying upon the check he'd just written for the barkeep. "Did you hear I bought this pub?"

Penelope gasped, clapping her hands excitedly. However, Cedric stared at his cousin with eyes the size of silver dinner plates.

"Hmmm." Penelope's gaze shifted between the two men. "I pick you," she announced, poking Cedric in the chest.

20

Abernathy had decided it was best to get Penelope home, leaving Beck to his own devices while Cedric assisted him with the drunken princess. He doubted the General would return to his suite anytime soon since he was knee-deep in a conversation with the barkeep about the renovations he was planning for the place. The Sorcerer's eyes rolled at the thought of it all. He'd seen drunk men tattoo themselves or mistakenly take the wrong women home only to wind up married with a newborn nine months later. But, he'd *never* seen someone buy the pub they got drunk at.

Penelope had fallen asleep in his arms, and he glanced down at her slumbering face, shaking his head in disbelief. "Looks like she might have a bit of a crush on you that we didn't know about," he teased Cedric, who walked silently beside him.

The Elf scowled in his direction. "Let's not talk about that. If what Beck said was true, it could be either of us that my aunt and uncle chose for her."

"Am I allowed to decline?" Abernathy bit his lip. "I'm not

sure that marriage is in the cards for me. I'd be a shit husband and father."

"You think I wouldn't be?" Cedric groused. "I don't even know what to say to a woman. When it comes to me, they usually don't speak. They just tear my clothes off."

Abernathy snorted. "Lucky man." The moment the words left his mouth, a dark-cloaked man appeared before them on the cobblestone. Abernathy froze, his arms tightening around Penelope, leaving him defenseless and without access to his wand.

While this could be just an average man, or Elf, making their way home after a late workshift of an evening spent at tavern, there was no mistaking the faint tickle of Magic that seeped into air.

"Cedric," Abrenathy whispered. "My wand. It's in my sleeve."

Glaring in the figure's direction, Cedric reached into Abernathy's sleeve, withdrawing the wand. "What should I do?" he asked, pointing the wand toward the threat. "Are you sure this isn't something we can work out with words? I happen to be quite the conversationalist with prompts."

The figure remained still, his head cocking slightly to the side. Power seeped off of him, tainting the atmosphere, the very air Abernathy breathed. "I'm sure," he replied through gritted teeth.

Nodding in understanding, Cedric cursed under his breath. "You wouldn't happen to have a knife I could use instead, would you?"

The Sorcerer growled in frustration before holding out his foot to the Elf. "In my boot."

Cedric retrieved the knife and tossed it into the air, allowing it to spin twice before snatching it by the hilt and sending it flying toward their opponent. Unfortunately, it landed right in the center of his chest, and the man cried out in pain, falling to his knees.

"Well then." Abernathy blew out a long whistle. "Looks like you're not completely useless."

"I have a few talents that I rarely get to use," Cedric told him with a prideful smirk. "Wait...what's he doing? He should be dead." Abernathy returned his attention to the figure and watched as he rose back to his feet, now holding something in their hand—a wand.

Whoever this person was, they were out for blood. Had Xavier hired a Sorcerer, had one of Lucinda's defected? There was no way of knowing. Still, there was something eerily familiar about the figures. It was so potent that Abernathy could smell it. Whoever this enemy was, they hadn't come to fuck around.

"Take her," Abernathy said urgently, thrusting the princess over to Cedric, who handed him back his wand. His eyes closed, and when he opened them, they had turned from his usual blue to a color comparable to a thunderstorm. "Get back," he ordered, sparks flying off the wand, a swirling cloud raging above the sky. The wind whipped around them so strongly that it nearly knocked Cedric off his feet.

"Storm's Eye!" he roared, holding his wand to the sky. Lighting began to strike around him, white-hot and crackling as it splintered the stone street. The ground became uneven. The entire kingdom seemed to be swallowed by blinding light, trembling with the force of Abernathy's spell as he roared.

Buildings shook, and stone fell around them as the portion of the street they'd been standing on rose up further while the opposite sank. The Sorcerer watched with fury in his eyes as the enemy tried to evade his strikes but failed miserably. Then, finally, he buckled down, covering his ears with his hands, releasing an agonized scream as the lightning coursed through his body.

The scent of burning flesh filtered through the air, strong enough to make Cedric gag. "Fucks Sake, Abernathy. Something smaller and less destructive would have likely done the trick."

"No, it wouldn't have," Abernathy said, voice low and dangerous.

The storm quieted, and the swirling clouds in the sky calmed as his gaze darted about their surroundings. How could no one have seen that? Why were no Elven guards rushing their way?

And that's when he noticed it. The man's body was gone.

Abernathy gripped his wand, preparing himself. Something strange shifted in the atmosphere. "That thumbprint," he hissed, staring up into the sky. "I've never sensed it before. Whoever this is, they haven't crossed my path."

"What do you mean?" Cedric asked, his eyes fixed on the place where the man's body had just been moments before.

"He's a Sorcerer. A powerful one," Abernathy explained, finally glancing in the Elf's direction. "Get her out of here while you still can. Get somewhere safe, and prepare for another earthquake."

"Another one?" Cedric scoffed.

"No one is going anywhere," an unfamiliar voice whispered in Abernathy's ear, causing him to jump backward, bothered by its proximity.

Unable to see anyone, the Sorcerer swallowed hard. "Go. *Now.*"

"I *said* that no one is going anywhere!" the voice roared. A strange mist swirled around Abernathy and Cedric, reeking of Black Magic. Abernathy's stomach rolled with nausea, his limbs turning leaden, darkness ebbed along the edges of his vision. He fell to his knees, watching as Cedric did the same, rolling out of his grip onto the cobblestone. She stirred, eyelashes fluttering as she began to wake.

No, the Sorcerer pleaded, watching as the man materialized a few feet in front of the Princess. "N-NO!" He managed, willing his arms to work as he forced himself over, only to be forced back down so hard that he felt his lip split against the ground. Blood filled his mouth, coating his tongue with the taste of iron.

As he watched helplessly as the man pulled Penelope into his arms, tossing her over his shoulder, Abernathy screamed at the realization of who he was. The mist, the invisibility, the ability to render your opponent useless. Hans of the Mist; a rogue Sorcerer who could turn his body to mist whenever pleased. He was so skilled that he could seep through cracks in floorboards and beneath golden walls.

And he was a Rebel.

Cedric's eyes drifted open to the white, tiled infirmary walls. The scent of cleaning products churned his stomach. His head throbbed, and he winced, reaching his hand up, feeling fresh stitches pull against his skin. Frowning, he tried to remember the events that brought him there. The last thing that he remembered was standing in the street, holding Penelope while Abernathy lit up the sky with a five-caliber spell.

As for what happened afterward, Cedric's memories were murky at best. He fought to recall them as he glanced at all the *get well soon* cards and bouquets of flowers scattered about the room. How long had he been here? Where was Abernathy and Penelope?

Screams ripped Cedric from his thoughts. "Abernathy?" No other man he knew would curse at Healers and Nurses so decoratively.

Rolling out of bed, Cedric winced as the wound at his temple gained its own pulse. He padded out of the room barefoot, wearing nothing but a loose pair of sweatpants as he approached the profanity Abernathy was spewing.

It didn't take long to find Abernathy's room down the

hall, and when Cedric entered, he found his uncle Thaddeus standing before the Sorcerer's bed, Aveo at his side. "You had one job," the King hissed.

"You're acting like I fucking invited the enemy to tea!" Abernathy spat. "I tried *everything* to stop them. It's not my fault he bloody transitions into the mist!"

"What's going on?" Cedric asked, announcing his presence; all their gazes fell upon him. "You're acting as if he's done something wrong when all he did was try to protect Penelope."

"*Try*," Aveo repeated the word, his tone laced with disgust. "Now, she's gone, and the Rebels have her. She could be dead already."

Cedric's heart fell into his gut. The idea of Penelope's death tore through him like an ax. "She's not dead," he insisted, refusing to believe anything otherwise.

"You're right," a voice called from the hallway. Cedric looked over his shoulder to see who it had come from. "She's too valuable," the man stated, pushing past the Elf and entering the room completely. He was clad in typical Draconian armor, a tracker's badge, and a Head Mentor's badge adorning the crimson stripe running diagonally across his muscled torso.

"Who are you?" Abernathy fumed, clearly not in a good mood.

Cedric noticed his uncle's wide eyes and quickly became curious. He stood impatiently waiting for the man to reply.

"Marcus Bonaventure. And I'm not sure I like your tone," the man announced, and Cedric recoiled so hard that he feared he might have popped a stitch.

This is Marcus Bonaventure. He used the nearby counter to brace himself. *Was this man Meera VanCamp's Guardian? The man who abandoned Penelope here fourteen years ago?* He shivered at the thought of it. *The one tasked with finding the Missing VanCamp?*

Thaddeus was struggling to find words. "You're... different than I remember."

Marcus looked in the King's direction. He no longer wore the silver cape he'd worn as Queen Meera's Guardian and instead wore one that was so black it could have been mistaken for a void. His bright Emerald eyes narrowed into slits, crinkling the four-inch scar running through his eyebrow down to his cheekbone.

"I am different," Marcus admitted. "I'm much angrier than I used to be."

"Good to know," Aveo mumbled, shifting with what was clearly unease. Cedric fought against a smirk at the sight. "Why are you here?"

Marcus crossed his arms, turning to face the Commander. "If I really *must* tell you, I came here looking for Cedric Chamberlain. Your Gatekeeper explained what happened last night. Now, I'm *really* glad I came, seeing as Penelope being *kidnapped* clearly wasn't necessary to inform King Loren about," he snapped, the words directed toward Thaddeus more than anyone else. "If you think I'm leaving you responsible for her search, you've gone insane. I suggest you back up and stay out of my way."

Cedric sucked in a breath, wondering how his uncle would react to the former Guardian's words. But, even though he had anticipated the worst, Thaddeus said nothing in return. "I'm Cedric Chamberlain," he finally said.

Marcus's head snapped in the Elf's direction, his gaze softening. "How convenient," he said. "I wanted to talk to you about helping me find the Missing VanCamp. I guess, now, you can help me find two."

Cedric sat awkwardly on his black leather couch, unsure what to do with his hands. He felt lost, knowing Penelope wasn't in the castle or the city beyond it. His heart broke at the thought of her, likely terrified, amongst the company of the gruesome Sorcerer who'd stolen her right out of his arms.

Marcus paced before him in, mumbling to himself, raking his hands through his chocolate locks. Cedric wondered how he felt about having left her in the Kingdom of Elves so many years, only to have the Elves fail to protect her as they had sworn to do.

"You wanted my help with finding the Missing VanCamp?" Cedric was the first to speak, breaking their silence. After a shower in his own suite and a fresh change of clothes, he felt better physically. Emotionally, however, he was spent.

Marcus nodded slowly, ceasing his endless pacing. "Valentina told me about your ability. I'm convinced you'd be a wonderful asset to me throughout my search. You probably know that we only have four years left, and what's at stake – the future of our Galaxy."

"I might be able to help you. But, to be honest, a few others and I were already looking into trying to locate her," Cedric said softly, his mind still stuck on Penelope.

"A few others?" Marcus's scarred brow arched as he stared the Elf down, expecting an answer.

Cedric clenched his jaw, having intended for the mission he and the others had taken upon themselves to remain a secret. He wasn't sure who he could trust; he thought long and hard about the words he said next. "Penelope, Abernathy, and Vincent," he revealed, well aware of how Marcus had dedicated the last fourteen years of his life searching endlessly for Ash VanCamp.

"Vincent?" Marcus gave him a disbelieving look as he reached for his thermos of blood. "Why involve a child?"

"He's barely a child anymore. He's fourteen and already showing signs of his coming transition," Cedric explained, bothered by the fact that Marcus thought so little of the young Prince he'd come to know so well. "The same will happen to the other twin, too. The only difference is Vincent won't suffer the fate that the Mortals of this Realm would hand to Ash."

Marcus's expression turned grave. "I was there, you know. When that potion was delivered to Meera. I disagreed with it. VanCamps were Mortals for a reason. That's what the Moons intended them to be. She might have ensured they survived childbirth, but she put their adult lives at risk." He paused, his grip around his thermos turning white-knuckled. "We have no idea what they're going to turn into or the details of the potion she used."

"I know what it was," Cedric told him. "The Everlasting Life potion. It makes them stronger and turns them into Immortals. The side effects are random transitions at the age a normal Immortal would transition for the first time. It's similar to the Fountain of Youth potion but different all the same. One simply turns you Immortal as you are; the other changes your entire genetic makeup."

Marcus seemed enthralled with everything the Elf said and lowered himself into a seat for the first time since he'd arrived at Cedric's suite. "Any clue on what they'll turn into?"

"It depends on their environment," Cedric replied. "Vincent has spent all of his life surrounded by Elves. So it's probable that he'll become one himself."

"But we have no idea where Ash is," Marcus reminded him. "She could be anywhere. Surrounded by all types of Immortals."

"She'll be a Hybrid." A chill snaked down Cedric's spine.

He wondered silently what a being like that might be capable of. "And in case you didn't know, Mortals aren't very fond of us. They're calling our wait for the Messenger the 'Immortal Silence.' They think we should be powerful enough to defeat Xavier and the Pandora ourselves."

"The people she's spent her whole life around would turn on her in seconds." Marcus groaned, cursing under his breath. "We need to find her."

Cedric nodded, agreeing with him. "Those transportation hatches that the babies were put in, are you certain you had all the exits correct?"

"I confirmed it with Aries."

"He's been around a long time. He'd know." Cedric sighed, unable to shake the feeling that something about that scenario was amiss. He sat, deep in thought about the matter, but despite his efforts to keep his mind on Ash, all he could think about was Penelope. "I hate to say this, but we have to put Ash on the back burner. We must get Penelope back, and I think I know where to start looking."

22

The scent of salt flooded Penelope's nostrils. The carriage that she was in moved quickly through the Lakelands. The most significant bodies of water in the main Realm provided a sight for sore eyes, and she wished she'd be able to enjoy it, but she was too busy to devise a plan to escape.

The mist man never left her side. Instead, he sat on the cushioned bench across from her, staring out the carriage window, mesmerized by the view. He seemed older, yet Immortal, much like what Penelope had seen of Richard Anster.

"What do you want with me?" she hissed for the thousandth time, hoping that he would answer her. "If you plan on killing me, the least you could do is tell me about it."

The dead of winter surrounded them, turning the landscape icy and desolate. The carriage wheels slipped occasionally, jerking her from one side of her bench to the other, sometimes sending her tumbling onto the floor. Every time *that* happened the mist man would have to help her back up. She despised him and his damp, macabre touch and wished that Esmeralda and Thaddeus had agreed to teach her to fight. Then, she might be able to battle her way out of this.

Penelope slipped off her seat again, and the mist man reached for her. She gathered up all her courage and bit his hand, watching as he faded into a mist that floated around her, hissing in her ear.

"Let me guess; you're in the carriage with me because you can't be near the snow?" Penelope teased, no longer caring about the snarls he might release. If he were allowed to hurt her, he would have by now. "Poor you." She smirked as he materialized, his hand colliding with her cheek, using enough force to thrust her head into the back of the carriage.

Penelope cried out, instinctively reaching her bound hands toward her head, but she couldn't reach. "Fuck you," she snapped, the warm sensation of blood creeping down her neck.

"VanCamp bitch," the mist man shot back. "I suggest that you start playing nice. You're only alive right now so that my superior can get the answers he needs."

Penelope's expression turned placid as she stared him down, unwilling to let him see even an ounce of pain or fear lurking in his gaze. "He wants to know where the Amulet is." Her conclusion was proven correct. She could tell by the way he lowered onto his seat, flicking an invisible speck of dust off his black sleeve, feigning indifference. "I regret to inform you that you're wasting your time. I don't know where it is."

"That's fine," he replied with a smirk. "Our leader has other plans for you. If you can survive them," he snickered as the words left his mouth.

Penelope's heart sank at the thought of what the Rebels might have in store for her. But, no matter what, she knew that she had no choice but to survive. Somewhere, deep within her, was the strength of her ancestors. Their blood ran through her veins, pumping through her heart. The Elves might not have raised the princess to be a brilliant warrior like her father before her and his father before him, but now, she had no choice.

"Oh, I will," Penelope assured him. "You won't."

Valentina pushed open the doors to Loren's office, the vision she'd just received still fresh within her mind. "They're going to take her somewhere underground," she claimed, watching as he dropped his quill. Ink splattered across the letter he'd been writing, "Which means their headquarters is *underground.*"

"Shit," Loren cursed down at the mess he'd made. "As in a basement? A dungeon? A crypt?" he rattled off, crumpling his ruined letter and tossing it into the wastebasket across the room.

"No." Valentina shook her head, not quite sure herself. "Like a tunnel that leads into one massive environment."

The King stared at her as he began to shrink in his chair. "You realize that we live in one *massive* realm and that that establishment could be *anywhere,* right?" He groaned, throwing his hands up in frustration.

"It's still a clue," Valentina snapped. "Have you any word from Marcus?"

"I received a message from him this morning. Cedric suggested that they head to Mayfire and that it's possible that the Justice Keeper there, Lord Ward, might know a thing or two about the Rebels. He requested reinforcements."

Valentina nodded as she sulked against the pale gray walls, as thoughts of Penelope ran through her mind. The Prophetess fought against the tears that threatened to pool in her eyes as she imagined how terrified the princess was. "More people helping means more people to cover ground.

Underground," she insisted with a satisfied smile, watching as the King glowered at her. "Who are you thinking about sending?"

Loren rolled his eyes. "Craven and Axel. Who else?"

Just as the words left his mouth, a knock on the door caused Valentina to jump. She frowned, reaching to answer it, but the door flew open before she could wrap her hand around the knob.

"You summoned me?" Axel grumbled as Craven appeared on the threshold behind him. "And this idiot?"

"I'd hardly call him an idiot," Loren said, yawning. Valentina knew that he'd spent all morning covering all of his bases, sending missives out to all the specialists they had out in the field, instructing them to abandon their current missions and begin tracking all Rebel activity. Neither he nor Valentina had slept since they'd heard of Penelope's kidnapping, and she knew Loren all too well. He wouldn't sleep until Penelope was safe. "But yes, you two must report to the Kingdom of Elves Immediately. There's no time to pack. You're going to assist with Penelope's retrieval."

The color quickly drained from Craven's face. "Retrieve Penelope? From where?"

"The Rebel Headquarters," Valentina told him. "It's underground," she added, smirking in the King's direction. His eyes narrowed, nose wrinkling in response.

The Electric Immortal stood in a silent rage before them, his unique violet eyes reflecting his fury. "How the *hell* did I not figure that out?" he hissed, and Valentina could see he was beginning to blame himself. After all, he'd spent weeks traveling the Realm with the Elven General, attempting to disclose the Rebel's location before they could strike. Now they had, and an heir to the Idonian throne could die because of it.

"I don't think we would have ever found out if I hadn't

had a vision of her," Valentina replied. "Don't blame yourself. Things happen for a reason. Now, we have the opportunity to defeat them."

"We've just begun another Red Winter," Axel reminded them all, his expression grim. "Who's to say the Pandora hasn't already sniffed her out, now that they've crawled out of their hole?"

"That's precisely why we need to move quickly," Loren informed him as he opened one of his desk drawers, pulling out a key. "Use the Portal Rooms," he ordered as he tossed it to the General before watching as he and Craven left his office, disappearing into the corridor beyond.

Valentina stayed a few minutes longer. Her heart raced from the constant anxiety she'd endured since the start of the Red Winter and for nearly twenty years before that. "Loren?"

The King looked up from his work; his expression hardened at first. But as he gazed at her face, Valentina watched it soften. "Yes?" he asked quietly.

"I have an idea."

His brows perked. "What sort of idea?"

"Penelope," Valentina said her name and the King's eyes widened slightly. She moved toward him, grinning. "The Elves don't have her best interest at heart. You received that invitation to her eighteenth-year ceremony in the Spring. You know what they're doing, or at least what they're trying to do. They're making a backup plan. They will marry her to an Elf, one who serves them wholeheartedly. And then, she'll grow old and die, leaving this Elf in complete control of Si Realtra. Perhaps this wouldn't be so much of a problem if they had good intentions." She sighed as she hopped onto his desk, crossing her legs.

"Why are you on my desk?" Loren scowled. "What exactly are you getting at?"

Valentina had never been fond of the fact that it took

Loren so long to figure out what she was trying to say. It was the same reason she'd never pursued him romantically. They might understand each other on the battlefield, but certainly not in the bedroom. They'd attempted that once…or twice. It didn't end well.

"We already know that they want to give the Idonian Sectra to Mika. Thankfully, that's in *our* hands, and we can weasel our way into giving it to Penelope or Vincent. Meera would have wanted *any* of her children to have that amulet if it couldn't be given to the one she chose. *But* that doesn't mean they won't fall back on their next plan, where they subtly take the throne over a span of eighty years, where they wait for Penelope to die at a ripe old age," Valentina ranted, her heart thundering.

The Prophetess watched Loren shift uncomfortably in his chair as she leaned closer. "You think I can prevent them from doing that? They raised her."

"Penelope is her own woman," Valentina retorted. "She has the right to choose what she wants or who she wants. Gideon got to choose, and so did Meera. They chose each other." Her heart began to warm as she thought of the two of them and how they'd appeared on their wedding day. "If they want her to marry an Elf, fine. But that doesn't mean the Elf has to outlive her."

23

"You should consider yourself lucky to be able to participate in this mission at all," Thaddeus snapped at Abernathy as he stared down at him from his golden throne. "Not only because you let Penelope slip right out your fingers, but because you don't know how to hold your tongue. I could have you beheaded for speaking to me like you did."

The Sorcerer shifted his weight, fighting the urge to roll his eyes. *Oh, where's Lucinda when you need her?* He sniffed. *This dude is on one* serious *power trip*.

"I'm her Guardian." Abernathy attempted to stifle his burning hatred for the King to keep his tone as respectful as possible. "What happened was because of the fact that the Rebels hired some freak of nature to do their dirty work. I know how to defeat him. Any water spell will do the trick."

Marcus released an annoyed sigh from the Sorcerer's right side. "If you're judging Guardians for failing, Thaddeus, you might as well stone me. At least Penelope is still alive," he told the King. "Now, we're wasting time."

"Agreed," Craven said. "Why are we bringing the scholar again?"

Cedric scoffed in the Draconian's direction. "My expertise will benefit you greatly. I suggest you not complain."

Craven rolled his eyes, only to be punched hard in the shoulder by his General. "Watch your attitude. I swear, sometimes I forget you're still a baby," Axel grunted.

"This all seems unnecessary. We should leave. We could use Abernathy's teleportation sphere to get to Mayfire," Beck suggested.

The Sorcerer glared. It was never a good idea to use Magic when hunting another Sorcerer — especially one as powerful as Hans of the Mist. "I wouldn't suggest using Magic until we're facing Hans. He'll sense us coming."

"Mayfire is a four-day walk from here. Two and a half at Immortal speed," Cedric said. "We'll tire ourselves if we use that ability the entire journey, and if we were to encounter the enemy, it would put us at a serious disadvantage. Besides, we know for a fact that Hans has Penelope. I'd rather him come to us, anyway."

"I hate to admit it, but I like how you think," Aveo said.

Abernathy couldn't disagree with this and held out his hand before the group. They all watched with curious eyes as the teleportation sphere appeared within it. "I've learned a few tricks throughout my three centuries," he bragged. "Let's do this."

When the sphere hit the ground, a portal to Mayfire appeared. The group all took turns bowing to the King before they passed through, though Abernathy's bow was half-hearted at best. He had a feeling that he and Thaddeus were at odds now, and he didn't care. The moment the Realm discovered what the Elves were up to, he doubted the King would live long.

Once through the portal, Abernathy took a deep breath of salty air. The Lakelands weren't far off, just a few miles south. His body trembled with relief, happy to be outside the golden walls for the first time in what felt like centuries. He smiled despite the circumstances, fighting the urge to fall onto the snowy ground and gaze up at the cloudy skies for a time.

"We'll head to Lord Ward," Marcus announced, taking charge. "He has to know *something* about the Rebels."

"Agreed." Beck's stomach growled, causing everyone to glance in his direction. "Although, I'll admit that I forgot to eat breakfast. Do you think there's a café on the way?"

Knowing the Elven General wouldn't be much use to them on an empty stomach, Abernathy and Cedric went with him to a nearby café while the others continued their trek toward Mayfire Manor. They entered the eatery, grabbing the attention of an older waitress bussing tables. She stared at the three of them with an open mouth for a moment before she found the proper words to greet them.

"Your Highness," the waitress said, taking a bow.

"Highnesses," Beck corrected, gesturing to his cousin beside him. "But there's no need for such formalities."

The waitress nodded quickly, turning her gaze on the mysterious dark-haired Elf beside the General. "What can I get for you?"

"If I recall, you have a mean meat pie." Abernathy's mouth was already watering at the thought of it.

"I'll prepare three." The waitress grinned, giving the Sorcerer a nod before returning to the kitchen.

The trio took a table in the corner, happy to sit for a while before they embarked on what could be the most stressful mission of their lives. Abernathy relaxed in his seat, fighting the urge to shut his eyes. Just as they began to drift for a moment, the sound of the door opening grabbed his attention.

A man walked in, appearing to be no older than eighteen. Yet, he had what Abernathy had always considered to be the 'warrior's walk' and one heck of a sword sheathed at his belt. Abernathy narrowed his eyes; he couldn't help but wonder who this young man was, unable to shake the idea that he was an important figure in the massive city of Mayfire.

"Bonny!" the man called flirtatiously as he made his way toward the counter separating the dining area from the kitchens. "When will you accept my proposal?"

"*Never,* you uncultured swine," the woman growled as she returned from the kitchen with a bag of goods, and a platter carrying three meat pies in her hands.

The man sighed, his shoulders slumping as she handed him the bag. "I don't know how I'll live with myself."

"Hop off it, Ward." Bonny rolled her eyes. "Hurry and get that back to your mother. Some things need to be kept cold, you know. And don't forget to tell her and Aislynn that I said hello."

Frowning, the man turned away from her, his eyes falling on the three men who sat in the corner. Abernathy bit back a laugh as he took in the look on his face.

"I apologize." The man smirked. "I didn't realize there was anyone here to witness my embarrassment. I suppose I'll go jump off a cliff now."

Knowing the ordeal hadn't been more than one big joke, Abernathy shook his head in disbelief. "You're funny," he declared.

"Meh." The man shrugged, clearly having thought nothing of it. "If you think so, sure. I don't think Bonny finds me very humorous, though."

"That sword," Beck said, his eyes glued to its hilt. Abernathy's breath hitched as he examined it himself, now able to get a better view. He needed to clench his just to keep it from hanging at the sight of the glass dragon's eye at the hilt's end and flames engraved in the silver. "Is that what I think it is?" The General asked.

The man's brow raised as he looked down at the sword sheathed at his hip. "Dragon's Breath," he confirmed. "It's a family heirloom. Now, it's mine. Pretty cool, huh? There's only a handful of enchanted swords within Idona. Four, I think."

Beck nodded. "Shadow Strike, Dragon's Breath, Whitefire, and the Soul Blade," he recited, his golden eyes wide and filled with wonder. "The location or owner of the Soul Blade is still unknown. Its last known owner was Alexi Grimm. No one knows what happened to it after he died on the battlefield during the Age of Monsters."

Clearly intrigued, the man walked toward the table and stole the fourth seat."Ward, I said those things need to be refrigerated!" Bonny snapped as she delivered the meat pies.

"Then put them back in the fridge, woman. I'm trying to have a conversation here," he told her as he returned the bag.

She scowled at him as she took the bag and stormed back into the kitchen.

"Last I heard, Shadow Strike was given to Craven Amsterdam after the Ballroom Battle." The man grinned. "But the others I have no idea about. From what I've gathered, they're missing too."

Beck shook his head, his lips curling into a knowing smile. "What if I told you Shadow Strike and Whitefire were in Mayfire right now?"

The man balked at the General. "You can't be serious!"

"Serious as a Pandora attack," Abernathy confirmed. "Whitefire has belonged to Marcus Bonaventure ever since he became the High Queen's Guardian. And both he and Craven are here in Mayfire with us to talk to Lord Ward."

Just as he said the name, a sudden realization caused his brow to wrinkle confusion. "Didn't that waitress just call *you* Ward?"

The man nodded quickly. "I'm not Lord Ward, though. That's my old man," he clarified. "I'm Alistair the Great. Or, at least, that's what I call myself."

Cedric seemed enthralled. "And you're the owner of Dragon's Breath? I figured your father would have kept it until the day he died."

Alistair shook his head. "I'm better with a sword than he is. Not to mention, I earned it last year when I managed to decapitate one of Malachai's right-hand men," he revealed, his smile widening. "You can tell the Pandora are important when they remain in their Mortal forms. I saw him overseeing the attack they were issuing on Mayfire. He was standing off in the hills. I snuck behind him, and off went his head."

"So...you're a reputable warrior," Beck said slowly, a hint of mischief shining in his golden eyes.

Abernathy wondered what was going through the General's mind, but he hadn't anticipated what he was about to say in the slightest.

"We could use your help," Beck said. "Three enchanted swords would be enough to obliterate the Rebels."

Alistair's brow perked, his smile turning crooked. "You guys are finally going after them? What took you so long? We would have done it, but there aren't enough men left in Mayfire. All the good ones are in the Elven Army." His smile faded quickly as the words left his mouth. "It makes every Red Winter harder than it has to be."

"What do you mean you would have done it yourself?" Cedric was now intrigued. "You'd have to know where their headquarters are."

"Exactly," Alistair agreed. "And I do."

"Excuse me, what?" Abernathy stared at him. "Why didn't you say anything?"

"I just figured it out, that's why," Alistair replied nonchalantly. "I watched a group of men enter a tunnel that I hadn't realized existed right on the other side of Ardon Lake. So, I followed them and realized there were a shit ton of tunnels underground, all leading to one place. Some type of intersection. I figured it must be their headquarters, and when I returned home to tell my father so that he could send a message to the Elves, he was away on business. He still hasn't come back. He's in Blackbay assisting with the aftermath of a Pandora attack. Man, I hate when Malachai visits the Lakelands," he scoffed, shaking his head.

"But the rest of our team is heading to Mayfire Manor to speak with him right now," Abernathy groaned.

"Well, sorry, I'm the only Ward here. Unless you want to talk to my mother and little sister," Alistair said. "If not, you'll have to make due with me."

Beck shot out of his seat, finishing the rest of his meat pie in one bite. "You're going to lead us to that tunnel right now."

24

"You want to take *him*?" Aveo stared at the Mortal warrior with a scowl unlike any other. "For what reason?"

Cedric glared at the Commander, his right eye twitching with aggravation. He fought to understand what had made him such an untrusting and angry person. *That's a noble privilege for you.* When the General didn't say anything, he figured he might as well help him out.

"Since Lord Ward isn't here, his son is our best option," Cedric said to Aveo, fighting the urge to grip his shoulders and shake some sense into the Commander. It had already taken them too long to track down the rest of their team in the complicated city of Mayfire, and Cedric preferred to carry on with the mission without any grief from his teammates. "He holds the enchanted sword, Dragon's Breath, *and* he knows where the Rebel headquarters are."

Alistair gave Cedric an appreciative nod. "I suppose I *could* just leave a mark on a map and *hope* I'm right," he drawled to Aveo.

Cedric snorted at the sight of Aveo's glower. He couldn't help but notice how different Alistair appeared compared to their team. His hair was nothing more than a golden mop upon his head, and his eyes the shade of the Minorian Sea. He wore a simple, fur-lined leather jacket and worn denim pants.

"I don't appreciate your sarcasm," Aveo spat.

"Can we just leave?" Craven growled. "Do you not realize what's at stake here, Aveo? Who the hell cares who assists? We could use all the help we can get. And I'm sure King Thaddeus wouldn't appreciate that you're dragging things on."

Cedric watched as Aveo turned toward the Draconian with a look of pure rage upon his face. He wondered what he might do or how a fight would play out between the two of them. Craven may be young compared to other Draconians since he had yet to turn fifty and wouldn't for four more years, but he'd heard the stories about the infamous Electric Immortal. And while Aveo descended from a long line of notorious Elven Warriors, he hadn't even reached twenty-five and possessed no special abilities. Unless you count his short temper, of course. Even so, despite his odds, Aveo's fingers twitched toward his sword.

In a flash, violet sparks began to swarm Craven's fingers, causing the Commander to take a large step backward. "*Don't*," the Draconian bared his stark-white teeth and the hint of a fang as he snarled. The act caused a chill to run down Cedric's spine and the color to drain from Aveo's face.

"Alright, I'm leaving," Marcus announced. "Alistair, lead the way."

The Mortal nodded, an excited grin upon his face as he pulled his fur-lined hood over his head and followed. "So, who are we looking for?"

"Princess Penelope VanCamp," Marcus said flatly, his eyes fixed on the hills surrounding Mayfire.

Alistair stopped dead in his tracks, and Abernathy absentmindedly ran into him. The pair slid momentarily on the snowy terrain before the Sorcerer released an annoyed huff. Cedric's eyes rolled as he watched Abernathy straighten his black cloak, pulling the hood over his head as he bypassed the stunned man.

"You're telling me that one of the two remaining VanCamps was kidnapped by the *Rebels*?" Alistair squeaked as he returned to walking.

"Indeed," Cedric confirmed with a frown.

"Well shit, then we'd better hurry," Alistair announced as he picked up speed, nearly a blur as he ran through the snow-covered hills.

Axel stared at where he'd just been standing. "How the hell can he run so *fast*?" he asked before darting off after him.

Cedric did the same, wanting to be included when they finally had a good lead. "Dragon's blood," he told the Draconian General as they ran side by side. "Just because dragons themselves are extinct doesn't mean that dragon's blood doesn't still run through the veins of those who would have been destined to be Dragon Riders. Mayfire is where most of the people with dragon's blood come from. It used to be a city filled with Riders. Dragons used to cover these hills we're running upon," he said, a dreamy sigh escaping him, recalling the only time he'd seen a dragon himself.

He'd been just five years old, and his parents had joined the Idonian Mortal Army in a battle against Erminian reinforcements alongside the Strip. Esmeralda had taken young Cedric to the balcony in her own quarters to watch the prestigiously beautiful Elven Sunset. She had thought it would make him feel better. However, they hadn't anticipated seeing a massive red dragon burst through the clouds, headed toward where the war was raging in Central Idona. There hadn't been a Rider atop it, but Cedric had always imagined that maybe his Rider summoned him.

Shortly after that night, Ryiah's Hailstorm army cut down the remaining Dragons to weaken Idonian forces. While they had undoubtedly been weakened, Zerin and Minora's aid to the Main Realm helped Idona win the war. Not without sacrifice, though. What the Hailstone army had truly done was bring a cherished species to an end, causing many Idonians to suffer.

"I remember," Axel told him. "I remember when they used to fly through the sky."

"It's devastating that they're gone." Cedric's lips dipped into a frown, his heart shuddering. "The Pandora wouldn't have stood a chance if they were still around."

"I agree," Axel said and smiled. "You must have been little more than a boy when they went extinct."

Cedric nodded as his memories still plagued his mind. The memory of the dragon had only brought back many of Esmeralda when she'd become more of a mother than his own had ever been. He couldn't stand the way things were now, especially since it was so easy to remember how things had been back then. She'd cared for him, holding his small frame in her arms as he cried to sleep when Thaddeus had returned without his parents. She'd allowed him to follow at her heels as she completed her daily duties as a Queen. She'd read to him every night, no matter the circumstances. There had even been one point where she'd used the Idonian Portal Rooms during the middle of a ball to return to the Kingdom of Elves so that he could read his favorite story.

Fighting against tears begging to spill from his silver eyes, Cedric pushed harder, traveling even faster. Esmeralda may have been a wonderful mother to him, but what she silently did to Penelope was wrong. He wouldn't stand for it. First, he would get Penelope back, and then he would end her conspiring for good.

The musty scent of earth flooded Penelope's senses; her lungs longed to fill with fresh air. First, they'd blindfolded her, and at one point, they'd even gagged her so that she'd stop harassing the Sorcerer. Now, they'd resorted to keeping her in a cage. Her back had become sore from lying on the cold, hard ground, and her head ached from when it had collided with the carriage.

Unsure if anyone could discover her location, Penelope knew she needed to find a way out. She was still uncertain of their plans, but she knew that if they wanted her to be traded for the Sectra, then she would never be free from the Rebels. An unending prayer sounded within her mind for the Idonian Council to sacrifice her instead. To not hand Si Realtra over to the Rebels. She hoped they wouldn't be so stupid as to consider her life over the Five Realms.

"I'm just one person," Penelope reminded herself. "One among billions."

Penelope was in the dark, with no idea about what was to happen next. With an Idonian Heir in their possession, the Rebels would use her to their advantage. But how? She wasn't sure she wanted to find out. If she wanted to live, there would be no waiting for someone to save her. Instead, Penelope would have to find a way out of this mess herself.

"I'm underground," she muttered, her fingers curled around the cast iron bars that contained her. *I heard the commotion of a city when we arrived, which means there were plenty of people down here. Hundreds of them, maybe even thousands.*

Shaking the bars, Penelope could feel that they were loose. Whoever had installed them had done it carelessly, which benefited her greatly. She shook them softly, careful not to draw any attention to herself; she could see screws beginning to slip from their holes.

"This is a good start," Penelope smirked.

"I'd stop that if I were you." A man appeared in front of the cell; his arms crossed over his chest as he stared down his nose at her. While shadows hid his face, Penelope recognized his voice and form, and she knew that this man had been someone she'd known in her past life. "Even if you were to leave this cell, you'd have to go through dozens of my finest warriors to escape. And even if you make it out of this intersection, you won't know which tunnel to travel down. You'll wind up in the Regal Mountains or the Forest of Fools. Either Witches, Pandora, or Queen Cleo's notorious traps will kill you."

I'm not afraid of dying. I just refuse to do it here; Penelope's mind whirled as her blood began to boil. "Who are you?" she hissed, clutching the bars harder.

"You knew me once," he confirmed her suspicions, lowering himself into a crouch so she could see his face. "My name is Kurt Walsh. I used to work closely with your father. I designed weapons for his army."

Penelope gasped, fighting the urge to rip the iron bars from the stone that surrounded them and whip them as hard as she could at his smug face. Red hair was accompanied by a long beard and piercing brown eyes shining brightly in the dim light the lantern he held offered.

"I know what you're thinking," he snickered.

"I'm positive that you don't," she retorted.

"You're wondering why all of your father's advisors have turned on him so easily," Walsh continued. "I could tell you why Xavier did and why I have if you'd like."

Penelope didn't care about their reasoning. All she knew was that one day, both Kurt Walsh and Xavier Trevayne would pay for what they'd done one day. Then, perhaps, her father's ghost would appear straight from the afterlife to choke them in their sleep.

"It's all because of how weak the VanCamps became the second they placed a fifteen-year-old Mortal man on the throne. That was the second their reign ended. Whether anyone intervened right then and there or over twenty years doesn't matter. The point is, the Rebels are unwilling to let weak VanCamps regain control of the Idonian throne," Walsh sneered, wrapping his fingers around the cell's bars above the Princess's. "I don't wish you to die, Penelope. Your ancestor's mistakes aren't your own. But I can't allow you to take back your throne."

Penelope didn't believe a word he said. He wouldn't have dragged her out from behind the safety of the Kingdom of Elves' golden walls if he hadn't wished death upon her. He wouldn't have blindfolded, gagged, or contained her in a cage.

"Xavier, on the other hand, has a similar goal. Although, he's gone about it gruesomely," Walsh continued, his expression revealing just how disturbed he was by the idea of the Dark King. "He wanted to be Immortal and as strong as those around him. I'm fine the way I am. I don't believe Mortals to be weak compared to the Immortals that walk these Realms. I'll prove it when I destroy the Pandora and wipe Xavier's dark reign from existence," Walsh said.

"And how do you expect to do that without the Messenger?" Penelope snapped, knowing very well that defeating the Dark King without the prophesized being was impossible. "It's impossible. You need the power of Moonlight, which only lies within one enchanted weapon, which is protected by a spell designed entirely to be broken by the Messenger's DNA."

Walsh tilted his head back, letting loose a manic laugh

that echoed throughout the dark tunnels. Penelope shrank backward, her heart plummeting into her gut."I have the Messenger," he announced. His eyes twinkled beneath his yellow lantern light. "Don't you understand, Penelope? *You're* the Messenger."

Valentina watched as Loren paced in his office, well aware of how much distress he was in. "Calm down," she insisted, knowing her words wouldn't likely do him any good. "The best men in our Tech and Communications departments are working on locating the Rebel Headquarters."

Loren scoffed in her direction, though his expression quickly softened as he ran his hands through his dark hair. "I'm sorry," he said a moment later, "That's not why I'm so bothered. It's what the Elves do to Penelope without her even realizing it. I need to stop them," he explained with a glare strong enough to send chills down Valentina's spine. "And here I thought that they had her best interest at heart."

Eyes narrowing accusingly, Valentina slowly rose from the seat she'd been settled within. "What exactly are you planning to do?" she asked, whispering as if someone might overhear.

"Pay them a surprise visit and put them in their place," Loren said, heading toward the closet on the other side of the room, where he kept a few emergency changes of clothes. "Remind them just how powerful I truly am."

Valentina's mouth fell agape; her palms began growing sweaty. "How?"

Loren reached for his finest silk robe and slid his arms into it, quickly buttoning up the torso. Black silk cascaded down his powerful form, perfected with red accents that pridefully portrayed the Draconian colors. Valentina knew he hated how the colors made him think of the Pandora these days, but he still chose to wear them proudly. Loren would not change the ways of Dracus because of one species that would eventually become an insignificant blip on the face of history.

Valentina gulped as he placed his matte-black, ruby-encrusted crown upon his head. She realized how much he reminded her of his father, the great Lion Mason. She wanted to smile but couldn't find the energy. "You look like King Lionel," she admitted softly.

"Well, he *was* my father," Loren pointed out matter-of-factly, "and he wouldn't stand for this idiocy. He'd have marched into that kingdom the moment he'd discovered what they were doing."

"What will you say to them?" Valentina asked. Her body trembled along with her voice; her heart racing at an unhealthy rate as she imagined what Loren would do, and how it would affect the two remaining kingdoms within the main Realm. "Just remember, we're already facing two wars. Between the Rebels and the Pandora, more of our men die everyday. Please, don't start a third."

Loren sucked in a deep, his fingers balling into fists at his sides. "I will not start a war. But if they do, I'll finish it."

Loren made his way to the Portal Rooms after informing the Draconian Council that he'd be away for a few days. It was time that he took matters into his own hands. His mind whirled as he unlocked the door to the prestigious room within the castle's east wing, and he couldn't help but wonder if he'd been a fool to believe that the Draconians and the Elves were finally at peace.

Seven portals sat around the room, bordered by elegant silver thresholds. Only one remained black, and the sight of it broke the King's heart. Solaris. He'd shut it down to prevent any of his men from attempting to pass through with the thought that they might be able to defeat Xavier themselves. Now, he swallowed hard at the sight of his reflection within it.

Loren looked more like a King today than he did the day of his coronation.

Shaking his head, Loren frowned, turning his attention to the portal leading to the Kingdom elves. Through it, he could see a hazy image of the Elven castle. He scowled at the sight, gathering all his courage before passing through, ready to end their conspiring once and for all.

Upon his arrival, he found a pair of guards complaining about their rotation schedule. "I don't remember the last time I was off duty," one complained to the other. "I haven't fucked my wife in what feels like a century."

The second guard snarled, "At least you have a wife. Mine left me for a Lord's second son. *Second*."

Laughter filled the hall outside the portal room, and Loren found himself leaning against the threshold, crossing his arms. "Well, if you didn't have such a tiny prick –"

Loren cleared his throat, causing both guards to turn around, their perplexions turning ashen as they dropped to their knees, hanging their heads. "Your Majesty," the first guard said. "What brings you to the Elves?"

"Business," Loren replied dryly. "Lead me to your King. Immediately, if you're not too busy talking about your blue balls and tiny pricks."

After being led through the complicated marble halls of the Elven castle, Loren arrived before a door within the royal corridor. He pushed any second thoughts away, and he raised his fist to the door, pounding as hard as he could three times.

"It's unusual for them to be in their suite this time of day. Ever since Princess Penelope was taken, King Thaddeus has spent most of his time in the Communications center, waiting for news," the guard explained, speaking for the first time since he'd left his angsty comrade by the Portal Room. "Speaking of King Thaddeus...you won't mention..."

Loren lifted a brow. "I have enough on my mind. I don't have the energy to work with guards that aren't wearing Draconian Colors. Or their inadequate dick sizes."

The guard's cheeks heated with shame as he bowed and bid the king goodbye, leaving Loren to knock on the door as hard as he could three times.

When the door to the royal suite opened, Loren was surprised to see Princess Mika Chamberlain staring back at him with a glare. Once she realized who she'd opened the door to, her features softened, transitioning into an expression of awe. "King Loren," she squeaked with bulging eyes.

"I need you to take me to your parents," Loren directed her, nostrils flaring. He'd had enough of this golden kingdom already, and he'd hardly been there ten minutes. "*Now.*"

Mika stifled a gasp; every one of her muscles grew visibly

rigid. "Now really isn't a good time," she told him, wincing as the words left her mouth.

A wretched scream sounded from within the suite, raising the hairs on the King's neck. His eyes fell on Mika, whose shoulders drooped with defeat as he pushed past her, letting himself in. What he found wasn't what he had expected in the slightest.

Loren fought the urge to turn around and run back to Dracus. "Sovereign's sake." His stomach churned as he turned the other way with his head in his hands.

"Loren, what the *fuck* are you doing here?" Thaddeus roared as he aided his wife in delivering her third child. Healers were all over the room, buzzing around like they were tending to the wounded after a battle.

"I came to ask you a few questions," Loren replied, his voice weak as he fought back the bile surging up his throat. He could slaughter thousands in one day, killing them in a thousand different ways. But his stomach couldn't reasonably handle the miracle of childbirth.

"Can they wait?" Esmeralda snarled as Loren turned around, butting his back to the grotesque scene.

"I suppose." Loren swallowed, sucking in a deep breath to ease his nausea.

"Great! Get *out!*" the Queen screeched.

Loren exhaled slowly as he moved to take a step, only to have all the events that had brought him to this moment flood his mind. "You know what? No. It can't wait," he announced, his eyes still fixed in the opposite direction where Mika was standing, her complexion growing green.

"Excuse me?" Thaddeus spat.

"One of the few remaining members of the VanCamp family has been captured by Rebels. Now isn't the time to wait. We must get her back immediately and touch base with those we've sent in the field to retrieve her. Because once she returns, she'll turn eighteen in the Spring." Loren tried not to ramble, ensuring the Elves could hear every hate-laced word he spoke. "And that's when she'll drink the Fountain of Youth potion."

"What?" Thaddeus roared, leading Mika to startle across the room. "That's absurd! The VanCamps are *Mortals*." His hiss dug deep into Loren's flesh, causing an itch he couldn't seem to scratch.

Loren bit his tongue hard, nearly drawing blood, attempting not to start the war Valentina had feared so greatly. "Not anymore," he said. "Vincent will turn into something far from Mortal in four years. His twin will do the same, even if we don't know where she is."

"What happened to those twins was a *mistake*," Esmeralda insisted, and Loren cringed as she grunted, and he didn't need to look to know that she was pushing. He pushed the image from his mind, shuddering at the mere idea of what the queen was enduring. "Why are you all of a sudden meddling in her life? It was decided all those years ago that Thaddeus and I would raise her. That includes deciding what's best for her."

Unsure of what to say, Loren fought to find the right words. He knew what he *wanted* to say and the trouble it would cause. *Fuck it*, he sighed, throwing his hands up as if he were admitting his defeat against the mental battle he'd been enduring. "Because I don't trust you."

The sound of a baby crying muffled Thaddeus's angry roars, and Loren was sure he hadn't been in such a difficult predicament throughout his Immortal life. Alarm bells range in his mind, telling him to bolt, but his feet remained planted where they were.

Across from him, Mika's gold-speckled eyes were wide with both fear and surprise. Loren could see the color draining from her face; her eyes focused on something behind him.

Loren reached backward, Instincts kicking in, his fist instantly curving around silk. He pulled as hard as he could, flipping the Elven King over his head and watching as he hit the ground hard enough to crack the marble tiles, a frightening stare reflecting on his face.

"Do *not* approach me from behind," Loren growled, standing over Thaddeus, fury flashing in his eyes. "You should know better."

"Please don't fight," Mika begged.

Thaddeus looked toward his daughter, grinding his teeth. Loren imagined he wanted to tear him apart so severely, but wouldn't out of respect for the circumstances. He rose to his feet, smoothing his tunic and straightening his spine.

While Loren was tall in his own right, Thaddeus loomed over him. His long brown hair hung down his torso, and the same gold-specked eyes of his daughter narrowed into slits. And even though he should, Loren didn't fear him.

"You can choose to marry her to whoever you want," Loren continued. "But she won't grow old beside the Immortal you choose."

Valentina's suspicions about the Elves' backup plan were all confirmed when Loren stared into Thaddeus's eyes. The way he attempted to hide how truly infuriated he was. The way he twitched slightly, fighting to keep all his rage beneath the surface.

Fearing that the Elven King might burst at the seams, Loren held out his right hand, summoning his ability. It wasn't seen or heard, but it was surely effective. Thaddeus began to drain slightly, and his knees grew weak to the point where he was forced to kneel before the Draconian King. He gasped for air, attempting to find the strength to speak as he stared up at Loren with the same angry eyes.

"What... are... you... doing?" Thaddeus managed to get out between gasps for air.

"Reminding you that I'm your equal. Not in power, clearly, but in title," Loren dropped his hand, watching as Thaddeus fell forward, fighting to gather his bearings. "My father, the great Lion Mason, was impeccable when releasing his roar of power on the battlefield. But what his opponents seemed to forget was that he could steal their roars as well."

26

It wasn't long after Penelope had been told she was the Messenger, a fact she disagreed with entirely, that Walsh had ordered his men to remove her from her cell. At first, Penelope imagined it was because he knew it wouldn't contain her much longer, but she was surprised when they began to bundle her up with a thick cloak, gloves, and a hat.

"Where are we going?" Penelope questioned as they bound her hands behind her back, ensuring they were hidden beneath her cloak.

Walsh sighed as he fastened his thick wool coat around himself. "Where do you think, Messenger?"

Penelope gulped, the realization hitting her like a bag of bricks. "I'm not the Messenger," she told him, panic beginning to grip her like a vice. "If you make me try to get that Scepter, the beast will kill me, and this will all be for nothing."

"You're wrong," Walsh assured her, placing his palm against one of her cheeks. She shivered beneath his cool touch, avoiding his gaze. "You are the Messenger, and once you retrieve the Sovereign's Scepter, we'll kill Xavier and take back the Idonian Kingdom together. And then, I'll rise to the throne. If you're lucky, I'll marry you, and you can still become the High Queen. But only if you behave."

When a pair of hands pushed her forward into the tunnel they were facing, Penelope wanted to scream so loudly that the earth collapsed, burying the Rebels' stronghold forever. But even when she opened her mouth, no sound came out. She was helpless, and she would die because of it.

The temperature was bitterly cold as the Rebels led Penelope from the center of the Realm toward the northwest, where the Forest of Fools was waiting. They'd been walking for hours, and she found that her frozen legs no longer wanted to move. She ceased walking for a few moments, sucking in deep breaths of frigid air, burning her lungs. The Realm around her appeared lonely, without a village or any signs of civilization. Hills covered in thick, icy snow were the only thing to be seen for miles.

A pair of hands arrived on Penelope's back, shoving her so hard that she fell onto the ice. With her hands tied behind her back, there'd been no chance of trying to brace her fall. The princess fell on her face as stars crowded her vision upon impact. The coppery taste of blood filled her mouth, coating her teeth and dribbling down her chin.

Hans stood over her, his arms crossed in front of his chest. Nothing but disgust for her reflected in his eyes, and although Penelope had concluded that no kind bones existed throughout his body, she couldn't understand why he despised her so much.

"Night will be falling soon. You'd better get a move on it," he snapped before walking off to rejoin the Rebels ahead. More of them passed Penelope by as she lay with her back in the snow, shivering endlessly. None of them offered to help her up, and she contemplated refusing to move.

It was only a matter of time before the Pandora came out to play, so Penelope sat up in the snow, wiggling her way to her feet. She nearly slipped but caught herself before she fell again, drops of crimson staining the snow below her, a solid stream of it running down the front of her cloak. Glaring toward the Rebels, Penelope could see that quite a few of them were watching, waiting for her. They were all large, burly men with broadswords and bows strapped on their backs. She figured she could escape their sharp blades but not outrun an arrow.

Groaning with frustration and defeat, she began walking forward to join them. She moved slowly on purpose, watching as their faces reflected their annoyance.

"Good of you to join us," one of them snapped as she arrived before them. "Another minute longer, and I would have left you for Malachai to find."

Penelope went rigid at the sound of the Pandora's name, her heart skipping a beat. She'd never seen him herself, but she'd seen his picture in the paper. For years, the news outlets had raved about him on the screens, showing pictures of when he'd been praised throughout the Realm. "The Idonian Kingdom's genius," Penelope muttered, cringing at the thought. While his father's betrayal had been shocking, Malachai's had been even more unexpected.

Shouts from the head of the party pulled Penelope from her thoughts. She focused, attempting to hear what they were yelling about. That's when she saw the sky turn black. At first, she thought a storm was coming, but then Penelope saw their red eyes. What she was looking at wasn't a sea of black clouds but a massive flock of Pandora headed right for them.

Unsure of what to do, the princess froze. Her gaze darted

around in search of a place to hide, but there was no sanctuary in this frozen wilderness. Her heart pounded, the sound crowding her ears as Walsh's distant orders echoed throughout the hills. *Run,* Penelope's conscience screamed, but there was no way of knowing where the closest village or city was. Even so, we weren't fast enough to outrun the Pandora, and separating from the Rebels would make her stand out, planting a target on her back.

"Horse," Penelope said, looking toward the head of the party, where what few they had were already running, having broken free of their handlers. "Fuck," she snarled, knees trembling as the Panora grew closer. She had no choice but to fight, but her hands were bound behind her back, and she wouldn't know what to do with them even if they weren't. "Curse the Elves for not teaching me a damn thing other than how to fucking curtsey," she hissed as the Rebels around her drew their weapons, loading their bows.

Arrows flew through the sky, impaling dozens of Pandora. Their corpses fell dead onto the snowy ground, while those that survived transitioned into a slew of different beasts. Penelope felt her blood run cold as the icy atmosphere surrounded her, her throat becoming too quick to swallow.

The Pandora barreled into the party of Rebels so ferociously that Penelope doubted anyone would survive, including herself. She fought back a scream as they began to make their way toward her, watching as Rebels moved to protect her.

A series of sharp teeth were just mere inches away from her throat when a man intercepted it, sending the ebony wolf sliding across the ice. The air rushed from Penelope's lungs as she fell onto her back in the snow. Her head bounced off the icy ground, opening the wound on the back of her skull sending her vision swimming. She coughed, trying desperately to breathe, but couldn't. This was it. This was how she would die. The Screams of Rebels being torn apart vibrating in her ears, the scent of blood coating the air.

Stuck on her back, Penelope found herself helpless as the future of a jet-black, ruby-eyed Lion stalked toward her. In a foolish attempt at escape, she attempted to push herself backward, the boots the Rebels had provided with her sliding against the slippery ground. Tears sprang to her eyes as the Lion moved to hover over her, its massive maw opening, revealing canines eager to sink into her flesh. Bracing herself, Penelope sucked in a final breath and shut her eyes, only to hear the sound of a blade cutting through flesh and bone.

Blood rained down upon the princess as if the clouds above had been filled with it. She opened her eyes just in time to watch the Lion collapse, an ax driven through its skull, sending brain matter spilling onto Penelope. Gagging, she scrambled to get away from the corpse, her eyes drifting upward to view the Rebel who had saved her. He had already moved on, leaving her to scramble back to her feet.

"Cut my bindings," she begged the nearest Rebel, only to be ignored. "You can't just let me stand here defenseless!"

The moment the words left her mouth, Penelope watched in horror as the Rebel was thrown off his feet and swarmed by Pandora, torn limb from limb, his agonizing scream piercing through the air.

The sight left Penelope frozen, every muscle of her body refusing to cooperate with her, the thoughts racing through her mind.

Don't just stand there, move!

Grab his sword; if you're quick, you can cut yourself free.

Lay down and play dead.

Do anything that isn't standing still!

Before Penelope's body had a chance to catch up to her

mind, a hard body barreled into her, stealing the air straight from her lungs. She landed hard against the ground, her left shoulder screaming in protest as a Pandora wolf hovered above her, sniffing and snarling, exposing fangs dripping with saliva. Drops fell onto her face as the beast surged toward her neck, teeth grazing flesh. Yet, before death could come, Hans appeared, a mesmerizing sword with a glowing purple blade in his grip. His fingers were wrapped around its skull-shaped hilt as he raised it above his head, forcing it down through the Pandora with such force that the beast split into two on top of her.

Penelope felt the tip of the sword pressing against her sternum. She stared up at Hans, hot, sticky blood coating nearly every inch of her. In his eyes, she saw nothing but hatred. She watched as he fought an internal battle, knowing that every part of him burned with the need to end her life.

"Kill me, then," Penelope urged, covered in blood that wasn't hers. "End my reign before it even begins. I dare you."

Hans's lips curved into a wicked smirk as he withdrew the sword, and Penelope watched as the strange blade absorbed a black mist that swam out of the Pandora's form. Recognition struck her like a lightning bolt as she stifled a gasp.

"The Soul Blade." Penelope glared.

"Finders keepers." Hans walked away, leaving the princess to shove the corpse off herself.

27

As promised, Alistair had led their team to where he'd discovered the tunnel, using his enchanted sword to light the way through their pitch-black, dusty surroundings. The weapon burned like an ember that could never be snuffed out, sending a heatwave toward the group as they followed behind. The sword enchanted Abernathy. For centuries, he'd heard stories of Dragon's Breath and its power, yet now, he could finally set his sights on it. Aiden Cavanagh, the legendary Dragon Rider and first High King of Si Realtra, had once wielded the sword.

Secretly, the Sorcerer wondered if Alistair would have become a Rider if the Dragons had not become extinct. He shivered at the thought, fearful of how powerful the man would be with that sword and a dragon. Those thoughts were what kept him occupied as they made their way through the deep, dark tunnels. Having been born in Erim two hundred years ago, Abernathy hadn't been incredibly familiar with Idonian history until he'd joined Lucinda's League of Sorcerers. However, he'd heard rumors about the tunnels created by the Monsters that plagued Idona three centuries ago.

The mere size of the tunnels alone was enough to prove that that rumor was true. They were easily thirty feet high, big enough to swallow a man whole. Every once in a while, Abernathy would glimpse what appeared to be claw marks embedded in the earthy walls, the sight of them sending shivers skittering down his back.

No one in their party was old enough to have witnessed the Age of Monsters, yet there they were, passing massive alcoves where the eggs possibly hatched, walking on the same ground they had. The mere thought of them made Abernathy clutch his wand as if he were heading straight into the past for a battle when, truly, he was heading into a fight in the present.

The group had been traveling at Immortal speed all day and night, and the Sorcerer knew that they had to be nearing the center of Idona. Abernathy wondered how much longer he could go on and how he would survive a battle with the enemy as exhaustion began to set in. He tried his best not to think of it and thought of rescuing Penelope instead, hoping that would keep him going.

"We're nearly there," Alistair announced. "Get your swords and wands, I suppose, ready."

Abernathy's wand hadn't left his hand since they entered the tunnels. He gripped it harder, preparing the best water spells in his mind, knowing he'd likely have to face Hans again. Only this time, the Sorcerer wouldn't get away.

When Marcus unsheathed Whitefire, the others were easily blinded by it. Aveo cursed loudly as he shielded his eyes, having been traveling right behind him, but the Draconian didn't pay him any mind. Instead, his eyes were fixed on the exit to the tunnel.

"Ready yourselves," Beck and Axel ordered in unison, surprising one another. Abernathy snorted, realizing how much alike the two Generals were. Even though they were from two entirely different species, and Axel was at least a hundred and fifty years Beck's senior.

Craven smirked, his grip tightening around the silver hilt of Shadow Strike; its poisonous black blade began flickering with his electricity. Abernathy sucked in a nervous breath, already aware of how mighty the enchanted sword was. Paired with the Draconian's unique electric abilities, it was no wonder Craven had been the only one to survive the Ballroom Battle.

Alistair was the first to enter the large intersection, his sword ready, gleaming in his grip. When he lowered his weapon, the other's stared at his back in confusion.

"What is it?" Abernathy snapped as he pushed forward, curious to see what it was they'd be facing. What he saw, however, was not an enemy but a massive underground city. A slope led down into was lined with houses and shops, a massive castle carved out right in the center of it all. More tunnel entrances – hundreds, even – were positioned along the same level at which Abernathy and his party stood, wrapping all the way around the dome they'd found themselves in.

The Monsters wouldn't have cared enough about where they hatched to build such a thing, and the Rebels didn't have nearly enough men, nor had they had enough time to construct such a thing. Which meant…

"Something else built this," Abernathy said, chills sweeping throughout him as he approached what looked to be a city square situated before the city beyond. A large stage took up the space where someone important would speak.

Alistair, who clearly operated without an ounce of fear, climbed the stage steps, Dragon's breath swinging in his grip. "There's boot marks," he announced, turning his skeptical gaze toward the city. "Someone was here recently."

"At least three hundred men," Aveo said, surveying the

space in front of the stage, kneeling to inspect more bootprints.

"Weird because it doesn't look like anyone's home," Beck said, squinting toward all of the houses lining the streets. "I don't hear a single soul."

Craven's nose wrinkled. "I don't smell one, either."

"Spread out," Cedric directed, and everyone turned to look at him in a way that said *who the fuck put you in charge.* "Just see what you can find. There has to be some sign of someone or at least a clue as to where they went."

Axel nodded in agreement. "Cedric's right. Move in pairs. Report back here in an hour."

An hour later, Abernathy and Craven returned to the square empty-handed. They'd found no signs of Penelope in any of the houses they'd explored. They'd hardly found anything at all. It seemed to them that no one lived there or hadn't in a very long time.

Aveo and Beck came back next, both shaking their heads.

"Nothing?" Craven asked.

"It's like this place is frozen in time," Beck said, looking over his shoulder, visibly shivering. "Gives me the damn creeps."

"I found a can of peaches in one of the pantries," Alistair said as he approached Axel, holding the can up as if it were some sort of trophy. "That's about it, though."

Soon after, Marcus and Cedric made their way to where the others waited. Abernathy watched them, noting their grave expressions. "What is it?" he asked as they arrived.

"I caught Penelope's scent in the castle dungeons," Marcus explained, sniffing, his gaze drifting up toward the tunnels. "This way."

Abernathy followed without question, making his way up the incline leading toward the upper level with everyone else. Marcus led the way, stopping before each tunnel entrance, his pace growing quicker and quicker.

"You can't smell her?" Abernathy asked Axel.

The General shook his head. "Not a whiff. There were too many people here, masquing her scent. But tracking is Marcus's ability. He can separate scents like no other. It's best to follow his lead."

"Here," Marcus declared, stopping abruptly turning to face another daunting, black tunnel. "She went this way."

Noting the direction, Abernathy's blood turned into ice crawling through his veins. He took off into the darkness without a word, his feet slamming against the earth, kicking up dirt. He could hear the shouts of the others, ordering him to slow down, but he didn't dare. He couldn't see where he was going, but he didn't care. He needed to get to Penelope before it was too late.

It didn't take long for the others to catch up, Craven at their lead. "Tell me this isn't headed where I think it is," he growled, summoning some electricity to offer them some light.

"Northwest," Abernathy ground out.

Craven's electricity flickered. "The Forest of Fools."

"Why would they take her there?" Aveo seethed from behind.

"They think she's the Messenger," Cedric blurted, panic tainting his tone. "Fuck, they're going to make her go after the scepter!"

28

It would take them another day to reach the Forest of Fools, and Cedric was beginning to think that they wouldn't make it in time. He now understood the Rebels' motives completely. They thought that a VanCamp would be the Messenger and had kidnapped Penelope to test that theory.

There wasn't a soul within Idona that didn't know what lurked within the Forest of Fools. At one point, it had been the Enchanted Forest, where all of the Realm's enchanted weapons had been created. But when the Dark War started, and the Pandora sprang into existence, Cleo had grown fearful that they would attempt to invade the Safe Haven. There were plenty of powerful artifacts and weapons within the Fae's notorious vault, and she was determined to keep them out of the hands of the enemy. Still, no one had expected her to turn the Enchanted Forest into what it is today.

The Forest of Fools was covered in deadly traps powered by ancient Fae Magic. No one went in there and survived unless they knew the secret path to the Fae's Safe Haven. A key was needed to unlock it, and that key was hidden in the vault. The Forest was where the Sovereign's Scepter was located. It sat deep in a cavern, entrapped by spelled soil that only someone with a specific genetic makeup could remove —the Messenger's.

Cedric supposed it wouldn't be impossible for a skilled being to maneuver their way through Cleo's traps, but those who tried weren't successful. Bodies were frequently found by the Fae that patrolled the area, and those people were always called fools, which was how the forest gained its new name: the Forest of Fools.

Cedric knew there wasn't a chance Penelope would successfully make it around those traps. She'd had no training other than to be a future Queen. He growled as he thought of how Thaddeus and Esmeralda should have taught her to hold her own in a battle. Perhaps if they had, she could have escaped the Rebels.

Even though Penelope might not be Idona's best warrior, Cedric knew she was brilliant. He wouldn't be surprised if she managed to slip away from them and hoped that she would. Escape was her only chance of survival now.

"Even if the Rebels manage to lead Penelope past the traps to the cavern where the Scepter is located, they'll encounter that beast," Marcus informed the group. "I've never seen it with my own eyes, but Cleo once told me that it was Xavier who put it there and that it's not a Pandora. It's some sort of lion-wolf hybrid, and it's vicious. Plenty of the best Fae warriors have tried to rid it from their forest, but none have succeeded. This means there's a huge chance that whenever the Messenger surfaces and attempts to make their move and retrieve the weapon, they won't be able to defeat the beast. He's thought ahead. Too far ahead if you ask me."

Cedric nodded, knowing all of this to be true. "Ever wonder if that beast is a person? Possibly a werewolf he experimented on?" he asked as the group pushed forward, leaving them in the rear.

"Malachai slaughtered them all when he destroyed Death Valley. All but one, Morghan Henning. His father was the Alpha, Archibald Henning. No one knows how he survived Malachai's attack or where he is now. He prefers solitude." Marcus rolled his eyes. "It's not like we could use his assistance or anything," he added sarcastically.

The party pushed forward until light began to spread at the end of the tunnel. Cedric knew they were getting close. It was only a matter of time before they faced the Rebels, and whether he was ready or not, Cedric would do *anything* to save Penelope. *Anything*.

"Can I ask you a question?" Marcus asked, his voice little more than a whisper.

"Sure." Cedric shrugged as he ran.

"Why are you on this mission?" Cedric slowed his pace, taken off guard by the question. "It's just... you're no soldier. You can use a bow and throw a dagger with extreme accuracy. But you've never joined the fight. So, why bother now?"

Unsure of what to say, Cedric fixed his gaze on the path before him. He wasn't sure what he'd been thinking when he insisted on attending the mission. But over time, he was beginning to understand precisely why. "I've grown used to Penelope's company. She and Vincent are the only people truly sound of mind inside the Kingdom of Elves," he admitted easily. "And what makes you think I haven't joined the fight?"

Marcus gave the Elf a suspicious look, chuckling as he shook his head. "You've been a recluse for decades now. I hadn't heard of you, and I certainly haven't seen your name in any papers. It's not like you spend your spare time out in the Realm, tearing through hordes of Pandora like Craven, Beck, and Aveo," he explained, eyeing Cedric curiously. "As far as Idona's concerned, until recently, you didn't exist. So, why start now?"

"There was once a time where there was rarely a paper *without* my name in it," Cedric explained, fixing his gaze ahead. "You would be too young to remember, but before the days of the Pandora, there was the Notorious Six. All the heirs throughout the Realm grew a fondness for each other. Elven, Fae, Draconian, Mortal...we didn't see each other as anything other than friends." His gaze shifted toward where Aveo ran beside Beck, the epitome of determination. "Lord Halvar Calloway," he started, his voice low. "Princess Sky Mason, Princess Eve of the Safe Haven, Lady Nilaena Orinac, Sir Yuri 'Red' Belmont, Malachai Trevayne, and myself."

Marcus stopped, his boots skidding in the snow as Cedric did the same, though less dramatically. "Malachai Trevayne."

It wasn't a question, and Cedric had expected such a reaction from the Draconian. "Yes," he confirmed as the other passed them by. "He was the brightest among us. A Healer so skilled that the Galactic Council wanted him to be the first to certify in every Realm. We followed, supporting him along the way. He made it all the way to Minora before he vanished. He left a note saying he was summoned back to Idona for family business. You can imagine what happened afterward."

Silence enveloped the pair, Marcus's features twisting with thought. "What happened next?" he asked, beginning to run again.

Following, Cedric said, "We assumed that he'd return and waited a bit, enjoying ourselves. Eventually, Halvar and Nilaena became worried and decided to head back to Idona to search for Malachai. Yuri and Eve followed shortly afterward, eager to get back to their families. Sky and I decided to head to Zerin and found ourselves with the Centaurs." He stopped for a moment, swallowing against the emotions that the memories brought upon him. "I received a letter from Halvar about the Pandora. He was sure Malachai was responsible. I refused to believe it, and I came back to prove that I was right." He steeled himself, focusing on the journey ahead. "I was wrong. The Galactic Gates shut, leaving Sky in Zerin alone. I've since spent my time trying to reach Malachai."

Able to feel Marcus's watchful Gaze upon him, Cedric forced himself to remain stoic. Unbothered. "Did you ever reach him?" Marcus asked.

"Once," Cedric admitted. Thankfully, no one else was paying attention. "In the Forest of Fools, where no one would bother us. I didn't expect him to show up. Either way, it was a waste of time."

"He didn't say anything?" Marcus pushed.

"It doesn't matter what he said. He's lost to us," Cedric told him, his tone far angrier than he'd intended it to be. "I felt helpless afterward like I needed to undo everything he did. But I'm just me. A scholar. All I can do is support Penelope and Vincent, perhaps help you find the Missing VanCamp." He looked toward Marcus, watching him nod, his expression solemn. "I'm here because I need to protect Penelope from the mess I made."

"This isn't your mess; it's Malachai's," Marcus assured him. "You're not responsible for it."

Cedric pursed his lips, shaking his head. "It's everyone's mess now. All we can do is attempt to make Idona right again. Starting with finding Penelope."

Nodding, Marcus started to run again, and Cedric followed, pushing all thoughts of Malachai and the Notorious Six from his mind. Those days were long behind them now. Today, they lead completely different lives, standing on opposite sides of a war.

"You love her," Marcus said after a while, thrusting Cedric

from his thoughts and back to reality. "I can see it in your face, through your actions. You remind me of myself when I look at a certain person."

Cedric opened his mouth to deny it, but the words never came. Instead, he said, "It doesn't matter how I feel. When we get her back, and we *will* get her back, she'll be betrothed to someone next Solstice. It could be anyone. Abernathy is even being considered."

Marcus shook his head at the thought. "They won't choose him. Not after what happened. I'll be surprised if they even let him continue to be her Guardian after this ordeal."

Cedric's heart sank at the thought. "Abernathy enjoys being her Guardian. It's not what he initially wanted, but those two are like peas in a pod. She's his best friend."

"I know, but you must look at the bigger picture. He's her Guardian, and she was taken right from his arms," Marcus reminded him.

"No," Cedric disagreed. "Abernathy fought hard against the enemy. You should have seen it. The skies lit up with lightning, and swirling clouds threatened to turn into tornadoes hung above him. You should have seen his eyes. It's not his fault that that enemy turned out to be Hans of the Mist. Besides, Penelope wasn't ripped from his arms. She was ripped from mine." His growl caused Marcus to flinch.

"I didn't know," Marcus admitted sadly. "But none of that matters now. What matters is getting Penelope back. And after that, we can find the other VanCamp."

Cedric nodded in agreement. "The fact that the underground city existed with no one knowing means there are probably plenty of other places in existence that no one knows of. When this is over, I will comb through the Realm myself. I will find every hidden place and search through every blade of grass. Trust me, plenty of things are at stake if we don't find her."

"I like the way you think," Marcus told him.

"I understand why the Rebels used the symbol that they did," Cedric said, loud enough for those around them to hear.

"What do you mean?" Aveo asked, his tone less jarring for a change.

Cedric waited for all the others to either slow down or catch up before he continued. "The mountains, the symbol pertaining to the legend of the Hidden Village within the Strips Swirl. People have combed through that area before, and its existence hasn't been proven. But that intersection we were in was right in the center of Idona, beneath the Strip's Swirl. That's why they used the symbol. They weren't in the Hidden Village, but right under it."

29

Walsh had been lovely enough to stop at an inn so that they could all lick their wounds. They'd made sure Penelope's face was concealed when they paid the innkeeper before guiding her upstairs, where she'd been given her room with a hot bath. She'd washed all the blood and grime off her flesh before changing into the fresh pair of jeans and a sweater that the Inn's staff had provided. She watched through the window as night fell beyond the Skyward Range toward the east. She swallowed the hard lump that had formed her throat, well aware of how close they were to the Forest of Fools.

"I need to get out of here before daylight tomorrow," she whispered, entirely aware of Walsh sitting in a chair just outside her room. "In a few hours, he'll be fast asleep, and I'll find a way to slip past him."

While it seemed like a great idea, Penelope knew the risks. Idona was in the midst of a Red Winter, which was still early in the Winter Solstice. The Pandora were at their worst. It was likely that she would reencounter them. She would escape Walsh only to wind up dead or in the hands of

Xavier, and she'd prefer death over the latter. A chill crept down her spine at the thought.

"Figures, the first time outside of the Golden Walls in fourteen years, and it's all because I was captured," Penelope groused, clutching the fabric of the blanket she'd draped around herself. She pulled her knees to her chest as the window seat grew uncomfortable beneath her.

A few hours had passed, and Penelope waited at her door for the sound of Walsh's snores. He may be the Rebel's leader, but he was still Mortal, and like all Mortals, they needed sleep. Besides, she doubted he was a skilled fighter. Otherwise, why would he send Hans to capture her and not do it himself?

Hans.

Penelope growled as she realized that even if she *did* manage to slip past Walsh, she'd never be able to make it past the Sorcerer who waited downstairs. That's when she turned her attention back to the window, examining the drop below. She cursed under her breath. *That's my only option, and I'm a shit climber.*

Darting around the room on quiet feet, Penelope gathered the sheets from her bed and the spares from the armoire. She tied them all together, creating a long rope, tying one end to the oak bedpost and dragging the other toward the window. Her fingers played with the lock, her shoulders slumping with relief as it clicked open, teasing her with freedom. She drew in a deep, rickety breath as she shifted the window open, cringing as it creaked. She stopped, listening for any sounds coming from outside in the hall, only to hear Waslsh's snores. Exhaling slowly, she turned toward the cool air flowing into the room, took hold of her makeshift rope, and threw it outside.

Nerves welling up within her like a river racing toward a waterfall, Penelope slipped her gloves and cloak on, careful not to make a sound as she stepped into her boots. She spared one more glance at the door before wrapping her hands around the rope and squirming out the window, trying her best not to look down at the ground below, praying that all her knots held. She bounced off the side of the inn until she came to another window. Hovering, she listened for any sign of life behind it, her mind racing with ideas on what to do.

There was a large chance that Rebels stood on the other side of that window, watching for more hordes of Pandora. Hans himself could be standing there, anticipating her escape. "Or, they could be sleeping," she said, looking down at where the rope dangled in front of the window. Surely, if they were awake, they'd have seen it.

The call of a Raven drew Penlope's attention, her head snapping in the direction from which it had come, just in time to watch it fly in front of the three Moons. Goosebumps pebbled along her flesh at the sight, blood turning to ice in her veins. Trembling, she looked down. There were easily six feet standing between Penelope and her escape. Her arms burned from holding herself upward, fingers cramping around the sheets. She didn't have a choice. She needed to let go.

"Sovereign's Sake," Penelope whispered, letting the rope loose, falling onto the ground below. Once she landed, she didn't waste any time checking for potential injuries. The princess took off, her boots slamming into the snow, sending it flying open in icy clouds. She'd never run so fast in all of her life, but she didn't stop. Not when her legs started to burn or when it felt like her chest had been set aflame. She kept going because her life depended on it.

After running nonstop for hours, Penelope slowed as the Forest of Fools appeared. It looked so beautiful beneath the early morning light. So inviting. How deceitful it truly was.

"I should have run the other way," Penelope growled as an image of an Idonian map appeared in her mind. "I could have gone to Mayfire. Maybe even back to the Kingdom of Elves. But I'm free, finally, so why go back there?" Her mind ran wild with ideas on who she might become or where she could go to escape the pressures of being the heir to a stolen throne.

"But what about Vincent?" Penelope asked herself, "And Cedric?" Cracks seared through her heart as she thought of his face. "And Abernathy?" She began to feel like the worst of people for even considering leaving them, never to return. All they would do was wonder if she was still alive. Or maybe they would devote their lives to finding her, wasting precious years.

Shouts pierced through the silence behind Penelope, startling her. She glanced over her shoulder to see a small army approaching with Hans at the lead.

"Shit," she growled, running straight into the Forest of Fools.

While Penelope ran toward her death, she didn't bother to look over her shoulder again. She might have seen a group of warriors led by an angry Sorcerer intercept that small army if she had. But, instead, lightning crackled through the sky, accompanied by one mighty heatwave as she flew past the tree line, immediately falling into something she wasn't sure had an end.

Abernathy saw a figure fly into the Forest of Fools out of the corner of his eye.

"No!" he shouted, temporarily driving his attention away from Rebels and back toward the tree line.

"What?" Axel asked, poised with his ax ready in his hand.

"Penelope just ran into the Forest of Fools," Abernathy replied, panic beginning to grip him like a vice as he turned toward the trees, debating whether he should abandon his team and run after her.

Marcus cursed beside him, fear racing through his eyes as his sword ignited in his grip, the blade swarming with white-hot flames. "I'll go," he offered, taking off toward the trees without another word.

When the Rebels saw Marcus make a move, three of them quickly followed. Hans and forty others remained for Abernathy and the others to take care of. He was ready. *More* than ready. "Alistair, heat wave. Now," he ordered and then watched as the man's sword began to burn like an everlasting ember, quickly scorching the battlefield. He swung the blade, a wicked grin playing on his lips.

The Rebels and the Sorcerer, their lead, hurried to evade the eight-foot slice of flame speeding toward them. A few weren't so lucky, their screams echoing through the atmosphere. Abernathy scowled, his eyes never leaving Hans. After a moment, he caught sight of the flicker of a shield just before the Sorcerer vanished into the mist.

"He's using some sort of barrier," Aveo said, having noticed as well. "Will your spells work now?"

Abernathy didn't respond. Instead, he sifted through the files of spells in his mind, searching for one that might prove useful. "I have an idea," he said, turning toward Craven, who lifted a prow in return. "Shock him. It'll break whatever hold he has on that shield."

"How?" The Draconian asked. "I can't see him."

"So, shock everything," Cedric suggested.

"Woah, woah," Beck said, holding up his hands. "See what we're standing on? It's snow. Know what it's made of? Water. He'll fry us all, and I just bought a bar."

"Well, whatever you're gunna do, you're gunna have to do

it fast," Alistair warned, his free hand resting on the ground while the other remained wrapped around Dragon's Breath. "Their friends are coming."

"Fuck me," Axel growled, his eyes darting west, nostrils flaring. "They reek of Pandora."

"Are you sure they *aren't* Pandora?" Cedric asked, fiddling with the dagger in his hand.

"Suns up, buttercup," Alistair chirped. "Pandora only plays at night."

Cedric scoffed. "Not anymore. You should have seen what they did to the Grimm Estate at fucking noon."

"Guys," Abernathy snapped. "I have a plan. Aveo and Beck, you distract the Rebels. Craven, you and I'll go after Hans. You hit him with your electricity, and I'll back you up with some lightning."

Craven gave the Sorcerer a sweet smile. "Hate to break it to you, bud, but I don't really need backup," he announced before taking off, a blur swarming with purple threads of electricity.

Wand ready in hand, Abernathy watched as the two elves barreled into the Rebels, shedding blood all over the snow, invoking screams. After a moment, they separated, running in two separate directions, confusing the Rebels. From where Abernathy stood, he could see them trembling, eyes darting from one direction to the other, lips moving with silent prayers.

"What are they do—" Alistair started to ask, only to have his question fall short when Aveo and Beck turned back around, heading straight forward the Rebels with enough force to trigger an earthquake. "Oh." The carnage that followed was enough to twist Abernathy's stomach into knots.

Meanwhile, Craven had ceased his running and was standing in a field to the right of the raging battle, taunting Hans. "Come here, Misty," he trilled, bolts of electricity slamming into the ground all around him. After a moment, Hans sent out a bolt of his own Magic, black as night.

Abernathy straightened at the sight of it, opening his mouth to shout a warning, his wand heating in his grip. Before he could say any words, Hans sent out another strike, this one barely missing the Draconian as he flanked to the side, violet eyes wide.

"Black Magic! Retreat!" Abernathy roared, surging forward to aid Craven, who was now dodging strike after strike, just merely missing them. Growling, Abernathy aimed his wand in the direction they were coming from, firing off the first spell that came to his mind.

"*Wind Burst!*" Abernathy hissed, watching as light streamed from his wand, invading the snow, curling it upward into a funnel that stretched towards the clouds, entrapping Hans in its wrath.

Craven stammered backward, electricity still thrumming in his palms, swarming his fingers. "He's fast," he said, jaw flexing with frustration. As if to take his annoyance out on anything else, he withdrew Shadow Strike and drove it into the earth, causing it to tremble so terribly that Abernathy nearly lost his balance.

Across the field, the Rebels' shadows began to reach outward, creeping toward the obsidian blade. Abernathy's attention drifted between the ordeal and where he held Hans with his snowy wind. It was only a matter of time now before the Sorcerer slipped, dropped his shield, and ceased to exist.

Aveo and Beck began to back away from their bloodshed, clearly fearful that their own shadows would get swept up in Craven's blade. They ran, joining where Cedric stood with the others nearby, just in time for the shadows to crystallize and jump upward, impaling those they originally belonged to.

"You just killed them with their own shadows," Abernathy said, stating the obvious.

Craven nodded, rolling his shoulders as he arose to his full height. "Just a little party trick."

"We're about to have some more company," Axel announced as he and the others ran up to join them. "Think you can continue to hold him?" he asked Abernathy, nodding toward the funnel.

"I haven't broken a sweat yet," Abernathy said, adjusting his grip on his wand. "He's not going anywhere until I let him, and that's if he doesn't get caught up in that snow. He can't hold his Magic against my own forever."

The second Rebel Army made up of at least sixty more men, emerged from the top of a hill, a dark line against the snowy horizon. Abernathy's breath hitched at the sight, his stomach bottoming.

"Hang back," Alistair ordered, stalking forward, swinging Dragon's Breath.

"Now just hang on a second, kid," Axel said, making to intervene, but the would-be-Dragon Rider paid him no mind. Instead, he continued spinning his sword so fast that it became a blur, and all Abernathy could do was watch with a slack jaw as a storm of pure flame erupted from the sword, forming a wall that raced toward the enemy.

The Rebels' front lines were diminished in seconds, only ashes remaining where men once stood.

Beck cheered theatrically, and Abernathy wondered if he might jump up and down with excitement like a kid on Giving Day morning. "Sovereign's Sake, Ward!" he said, unsheathing his own sword, ready to finish the rest off.

"Well done," Axel obliged, twirling his ax. "Now, let's finish this."

Abernathy stayed put while the others ran into battle, Cedric included. The Elf wore no armor and carried no sword, but nothing short of an armory of daggers was hidden under his cloak. He whipped each one, hardly needing to look at his targets before the blades embedded in their skulls. Meanwhile, Beck and Aveo tore into the enemy just as they had before, Axel at their sides now, carving through flesh and bone with his ax. Alistair ran in after them, proving his own yet again, his swordsmanship skills nearly an exact mirror of the Elven General and Commander fighting at his side. Craven's method of fighting was comically lazy compared to the others, seeing as all he did was graze his opponents, stopping their hearts with his shocking touch.

This was the sort of battle that went down in history. Abernathy couldn't help but grin as he watched it unfold, shaking his head in disbelief at what just five Immortals and a Dragon-blooded Mortal could do.

It was all too easy for Abernathy to get lost in his surroundings, which proved to be a near-fatal mistake; he was watching Axel whip his ax through the air, its blade crunching through bone and flesh, and the next the funnel he was controlling imploded.

Hans emerged, sending snow and wind flying in every direction, the force of it blowing Abernathy's hair back. "Impossible," he insisted, lowering his wand and taking a step back, putting more distance between them to give him a chance to calculate his next move.

"Once upon a time, that little spell of yours might have done me in," Hans laughed, his previous pale eyes now nothing but black orbs that stood out in stark contrast to his complexion, so pale that it was nearly translucent. "But as you know, the longer a Sorcerer lives, the more power he obtains. I've lived a long time, *Matt Abernathy*." He said his name as if it had been rotting in his mouth for ages as horns began to sprout from his skull, black, curvy, and gleaming.

"Impossible," Abernathy repeated, swallowing the lump crowding his throat. "There hasn't been a Dark Sorcerer for centuries."

Hans nodded, holding out his arms, jet-black threads of power seeping from his hands. "Yet here I stand," he cooed, beginning to walk forward, a wicked grin playing at his lips. "Now, you're at a loss. There isn't a spell in that pretty little mind of yours that'll take me down. No weapon on this battlefield that'll harm me." He reached toward his hip, withdrawing his own sword. Abernathy's blood ran cold at the sight of it, his heart thrashing against his chest, the sound crowding his ears. "Enchanted or otherwise."

"The Soul Sword," Abernathy acknowledged, spinning his wand as if it wasn't useless right now. The only weapons capable of killing a Dark Sorcerer were blood blades, which were incredibly rare...and the very sword in Hans's hand.

"Finders keepers," Hans mused. "Now, I get the pleasure of adding *your* soul to my ever-growing collection. What a treat."

With that, Hans surged, and Abernathy prepared to die.

PART III

NECESSARY EVIL

30

Years had passed since Mika had had the nightmare that left her panting in her bed, soaking in sweat. Still, she knew this dream for exactly what it was—a premonition or perhaps a vision. She hadn't thought too much about what name to give it, for every time she received one, she knew she needed to act.

Immediately.

How exactly was Mika supposed to act? She wasn't sure. All she knew was that her brother was in trouble and that the enemy he faced now was something she'd thought only existed in storybooks.

"A Dark Sorcerer," Mika said, shaking her head in disbelief as she wrapped an emerald silk robe around herself before stepping in matching slippers. "I need to wake my parents," she decided, flying down the stairs and into her foyer. She reached for the doorknob and stalled. "No, I can't wake them. Not with the new baby," she groused, opening the door and exiting into the corridor, wrapping her arms around herself as she thought of what to do. She could wake Griffon, but he'd insist it was just a dream and send her back to bed. The same would occur if she disturbed any Elven Council member.

Mika frowned as her gaze fell on a door down the hall. "No, absolutely not," she insisted, turning away. King Loren would think she'd lost her mind, and for her to go to him after how he'd treated her father earlier…

"Beck's in trouble," Mika reminded herself, turning around and approaching King Loren's door. "General Craves and Lord Amsterdam are as well," she added, raising her fist to knock. "Surely, a king would do anything to protect his most valuable assets…right?"

After taking a moment to gather up all her courage, Mika knocked three times. As expected, there was no answer. Through the windows at the end of the hall, she could see that the sun had barely begun to rise. Her dream had occurred shortly after sunrise, which meant she was racing against time. Mere seconds mattered right now, leaving Mika no choice but to let herself into Loren's suite.

Shutting the door loudly, Mika hoped the King would wake on his own, but as she waited in the foyer for a few moments, she heard no stirring sound. "Of course, he sleeps like the dead," she spat as she made her way through the suite, up the stairs, and to the master bedroom. "Mind yourself," she whispered. "You're about to wake up the Draconian King, who you hardly know, over a nightmare."

Rolling her eyes, Mika knew that she had no choice and opened the bedroom door. Her gaze fell on Loren, slumbering in the middle of a massive bed, on his stomach, majestic face tilted toward the right. *Moons, he's handsome,* she thought as she approached, holding up a hand to nudge him, only to second guess herself.

Clearing her throat, Mika called, "King Loren."

The King didn't move a muscle.

Sighing, Mika reached to shake his shoulder. "King

Loren," she said again, louder this time. He remained as still as a statue, eyelids fluttering with dreams. "Wake up!" she snapped, patience wearing thin, but to no avail. Scowling, she figured there was only one way to get him out of bed. "The Pandora are attacking!" she shouted.

King Loren's eyes sprung open, and he threw himself out of bed, nearly knocking Mika over. She straightened herself, watching as he rubbed his tired eyes and approached the wall, fumbling for a switch that wasn't there.

"You're in the Kingdom of Elves," Mika reminded, fighting against a smile. "Not Dracus." The Draconian castle was made up mostly of obsidian glass walls, offering a view of the kingdom. King Lionel Mason, Loren's father, had constructed it that way with the intention of being able to see his enemies coming from all fronts.

Loren whirled around, his raven hair messy from sleep. "Where are they?" he growled.

"My apologies," Mika began, fiddling nervously with her fingers. "There are no Pandora."

Anger flashed in the king's eyes, causing Mika to take a nervous step back. "Have you lost your mind, Princess Mika?" he scorned. "What gave you the impression about me that you can let yourself into my suite and wake me with serious threats?"

Looking toward her feet, Mika hurried to find a way to explain herself. "I rarely have nightmares, but when I do, they're always true." She went on to explain to Loren about the dream she'd had before they'd found Vincent in the forest, along with a few other examples. Once she stopped, she waited for the King's reply, expecting to be made to feel like a fool.

"Alright," Loren said, the word drawing out longer than necessary as he reached to throw a shirt over his bare, beautiful torso. "What was this nightmare about?"

"A Dark Sorcerer," Mika blurted. "My brother...your General, Craven...I know for certain that they're facing one right now. Or they're going to be shortly after sunrise."

Loren paled as the words left Mika's lips. "A Dark Sorcerer?"

"Yes, at least I *think* that's what I saw," Mika replied, watching as Loren lifted a brow. "Black eyes, pale skin, horns, Black Magic," she added in a rush, throwing her hands up theatrically. "I've never seen anything even remotely like it."

Pulling in an audible breath, Loren looked toward the ceiling in a way that said *I can't believe that I'm about to do this.* "Alright," he said once, pushing past her. "Alright," he replied, headed for the stairs, Mika following on his heels. "If you're right, then we're going to need a blood blade. To get one, we're going to have to use the Portal Rooms."

"The Safe Haven's vault," Mika presumed as they left the front door. She watched as Loren turned right, walking with the purpose of a warrior headed into battle. "Mika gasped, watching as he turned the wrong way down the hall. "Aren't we going to wake up my parents?" she inquired, biting at her lip.

Loren paused, turning around to give her a look that only made the princess feel daft. "Can you blame me if I don't want to? Besides, they'll just hold things up."

Mika nodded, completely understanding what he meant, and watched as he continued walking. "Loren, wait!" she called after him, watching as he paused again and released an annoyed sigh. "The Portal Room is this way," she told him, pointing over her shoulder.

When Mika arrived in the Safe Haven, she couldn't help staring at everything in awe. Every building, including the sprawling castle, was made of shining alabaster marble. The cobblestone streets were lined with vegetation, providing earthy, floral scents. The temperature was so warm that she needed to fight the urge to shed her silk robe, even in the dead of winter.

Mika didn't have much time to take in the true beauty of the Safe Haven. She and Loren were both immediately detained by the Fae Guard, who'd seemed perplexed to see the King of Dracus and Princess Mika Chamberlain of the Elves arrive at their doorstep in the middle of the night.

"We need a blood blade. Now," Loren demanded. The second the words left his mouth, they were both immediately escorted to the infamous vault where Queen Cleo was already waiting. Mika stared up at the gleaming ivory doors, her heart beating wildly at the sight of them.

The Fae Queen stared at them, her mouth agape as they approached. "May I ask why you two… unlikely allies… are requesting a blood blade?" she asked sweetly.

"There's a Dark Sorcerer with the Rebels," Mika told her, watching as Cleo placed a palm against an identification pad that sat beside the vault. The sound of it unlocking nearly caused the princess's stomach to flutter with anticipation. Was she truly about to set her sights on most of Si Realtra's historical artifacts?

"You aren't going to question anything?" Loren gave her a long, skeptical look as they were both led inside.

"Stranger things have happened," Cleo replied with a shrug. She led them through the many halls the vault contained. Mika was enthralled with everything she saw. Rows upon rows holding Si Realrtra's history were splayed out before her, each item upon them offering a different story. She felt as if she were in a massive library, but instead of books, priceless artifacts and powerful weapons surrounded her.

Before long, they arrived in front of a series of daggers. Some were enchanted, the power radiating off of them sending shivers down Mika's spine. She reached out to touch one with a shining opal handle, running her finger over the blade's smooth, jade surface. "Silas, Minora's Realm Sorcerer, gifted that dagger to my daughter, Eve. It was a proclamation of his love for her. It originally belonged to the Mer," Cleo explained, running her finger along the blade as well, her expression solemn. "But, what you're looking for is over here." She pivoted, moving toward the end of the hall. "This set of three was surrendered to the vault by the Elders or Ryiah." She reached for the largest of the black-handled daggers with red crystal blade and handed it to Loren. "Be careful with it. Without Magic in its purest form, we can't exactly make more."

"Of course," Loren replied, weighing the dagger in his grip and moving it from one hand to the other. "Do you have anything that can get us to Prince Beck immediately? A teleportation sphere, perhaps?"

"Unfortunately, I have no teleportation spheres, but I might have something that can be of assistance," Cleo said as she guided them toward the back of the vault, where cobwebs had taken up residence among the various books and artifacts. "It's an ancient Amorian artifact. I'm unsure of its name since many Amorian records, including the sixth Realm, were destroyed. Next to nothing was recovered. But, it should be right around this bend," she said as they arrived in a hall filled with weapons and artifacts coated with a labyrinth pattern.

Mika could easily recall the Amorian symbol, as she'd

seen it before in plenty of books she'd been forced to study. It was a four-pointed star, filled with the same pattern she was staring at now. The sight was chilling, as was running her fingers along things that had once resided in Amoria. The sixth Realm may no longer exist, but part of it remained in the Safe Haven's vault.

"Wait a second," Cleo urged as she stared at a blank spot on one of the shelves. She continued to look, moving at impeccable speeds from one spot to another, sifting through scrolls and objects, sending spiders scrambling. Mika scurried backward, revolution getting the best of her. "It should be here. Where else could it be? *Where is it?*" she asked, her wings stretching outward, becoming taught with rage.

Mika and Loren shared a wary look, neither of them having seen the Fae Queen quite so angry.

"Aries!" Cleo shrieked, and her advisor quickly arrived at her side. "Where is the Amorian sphere?"

Aries stared at the empty place on the shelf, his expression revealing nothing. "It appears that it's... gone," he replied, his features contorting into a scowl unlike any other. "I'll review security footage."

"Well, that won't help," Cleo hissed. "King Loren and Princess Mika need to deliver this blood blade to Beck *now*."

"I could teleport them," Aries offered.

"No." Cleo held up a hand, driving the Fae silent. Aries' body went still. "I will transport them. I could be very useful if Beck is truly battling a Dark Sorcerer. You, on the other hand, would be at risk. His Dark Magic would call to your own." She shared a look with Loren, who nodded in agreement, his lips pressed into a thin line. "I'll remove his soul and, with it, any memory of Magic. You, on the other hand, will review security tapes until you discover what happened to that artifact!" she roared. The artifacts around them shook on their shelves, clinking into one another. Aries nodded quickly before vanishing.

Mika gulped, not anticipating that they would be arriving on the battlefield this evening. "My parents are going to kill me when they find out," she muttered as Cleo placed palms on her and Loren's shoulders before teleporting them to where Beck was standing. One second, she was standing in the vault, and the next, she was flying into her brother, knocking him to the cold, snowy ground. She hardly registered what had happened at first, horror rippling through her as she took in her surroundings. Bloodied, scored bodies and blood staining the snow red. Death was everywhere.

And death incarnate, standing in the form of a Dark Sorcerer.

Beck grumbled beneath the princess, staring at her with wide, shocked eyes. "Mika? What the *fuck* are you doing here?"

31

Now, instead of *one* princess's life at stake, there were two. Cedric groaned at seeing his cousin, Mika, struggling to her feet in the snow. She was wearing nothing more than a silk robe and a very thin nightgown beneath. He shrugged off his cloak and handed it to her, the frigid air an unpleasant sensation upon his flesh.

"We came to help!" Mika announced, and there was no missing the nerves rattling her tone as she draped his gray wool cloak around her shoulders. She attempted to hide it, but everyone could see in her eyes that she was afraid. *Very* afraid.

For the first time, Cedric noticed that Mika hadn't come alone. His eyes fell on King Loren, and his spirits suddenly lifted. And if that hadn't been good enough, she'd also managed to drag Queen Cleo out of the Safe Haven.

"We bought a blood blade," Cleo told Abernathy, who'd been working to uphold a shield against Hans' power for far too long. "I'll weaken him, and you go in with this. Then, together, we'll send him to the Underworld, where he belongs."

Abernathy smirked as he took the blood blade from the

queen and pounded his fist against the Fae Queen's fist. Cedric breathed a sigh of relief, knowing that there was *no* way they would lose this battle now.

"Seems you did an okay job so far," Loren told the group. His nose wrinkled as the scent of scorched flesh and char lingered. His eyes quickly fell on the Mortal man, who held a burning enchanted sword in his grip. "Who's this?"

"Alistair Ward," Alistair replied, grinning as he held out his hand, unaware that he was in the presence of a King and Queen. "I'm the only son of Lord Angus Ward of Mayfire and the holder of the enchanted sword Dragon's Breath," he added for clarification.

Loren's brow perked as he shook the man's hand. "Well, it's nice to meet you. I'm King Loren Mason."

Alistair swallowed loud enough for the others to hear, and chuckles sounded around him. "I'm sorry, I didn't know, or I would have kneeled."

"There's still time," Mika mentioned softly.

"Don't bother. We have more important things to worry about," Loren said as he turned his attention to the Dark Sorcerer before them. Hans had pushed back, eyeing the newcomers skeptically. "Why isn't he trying to strike us? You think he would, especially with Cleo and I on the battlefield."

"His fight isn't with you," Cedric told him. "This battle is between Sorcerers. He may have evolved into something beyond what Abernathy is now, but his focus is still on him."

Abernathy scowled, his spelled shield expanding to cover everyone. "It's an unspoken rule among Sorcerers. When partaking in a battle, if there's another Sorcerer among you, you must kill them first. Out of respect and acknowledgment of power."

"Well, it's unfortunate for him that *I'm* his opponent right now," Cleo said, levitating as her translucent wings fluttered, sparkling in the early morning light.

Cedric couldn't help noticing how majestic and innocent she appeared, but he knew that was just a facade. Cleo was deadly, and she was about to ensure everyone knew it.

With one outstretched palm and the other hanging casually at her side, Cleo's eyes narrowed. Golden-white dust spewed from her fingertips, traveling as fast as the speed of light toward the Sorcerer's heart. He dodged her dust at the last second and smiled.

"He's fast," Cedric told her, frowning.

Pursing her lips, Cleo's eyes narrowed with determination. "Indeed, he is," she agreed, turning her attention toward the bloody and bruised men around her. "Ward, you said your name was?"

Alistair nodded, straightening his spine. "Yes, Milady."

"Your Majesty," Mika murmured.

"How much fire can you produce with that sword of yours?" Cleo asked, her perfect dark brows pulling together curiously.

Alistair. "How much fire are you thinking?"

"Enough to draw his attention from the back while Craven here attacks from his front," the queen explained, her wings fluttering as she hovered, her magic thrumming around her, sending tremors through the air. "Let me know when you're ready." She raised a hand, fingers twitching.

Alistair shared a glance with Craven before nodding. "I'm ready."

The Mortal was gone in an instant, teleported into the field behind Hans. He wasted no time spinning his sword, invoking a burning inferno so hot that Cedric needed to step back despite how far from Alistair he truly was.

"Now, Craven," Cleo ordered, and the Draconian took off at Immortal speed, Shadow Strike gleaming in his grip. The sword snatched the enemy's shadow straight from the ground. His electricity intertwined with it, and the others watched as a deadly rain of shadowed electric daggers embedded themselves in Hans's back.

The Sorcerer was stunned, forced to his knees as the force of Craven's abilities ripped through him. Purple threads of electricity began to bounce between his horns, leading him to twitch, a cry of anger escaping him.

"He's down," Cedric said, stepping forward.

"No," Aveo said, unsheathing his twin broadswords. "He's not."

Hans's limbs jerked as if he was forcing them to cooperate. He pushed onto his feet, facing where Alistair stood, utterly helpless against his Magic. A black mist began to roll outward from beneath his sleeves, swarming upward, turning the sunrise from an array of warm, welcome colors to an eerie gray.

"Loren," Mika hissed, and Cedric's brows shot upward at her forgetfulness of his title. "You're ability. It could keep him down long enough for –"

"I know," the king interjected as Cleo lowered to place her feet on the ground, giving her wings a break. "I'll hold him; you swarm him," he said to Cleo. "Abernathy, when the moment's right, throw that dagger."

Abernathy nodded, though his gaze never left where Alistair stood before the Sorcerer, now joined by Craven. Despite their low chances of survival, neither of them gave a hint that they were afraid. They stood as Allies as if they'd known each other for decades instead of days.

"Aveo and I can go at him from the sides," Beck offered, cracking his neck. "He'll be too distracted by the lot of us coming at him; he won't be able to give you enough attention to harm you."

"I'll back you up," Axel offered to his King.

"I'll maintain the Shield and protect Mika," Abernathy

said, glancing toward Cleo. "Give Cedric the dagger. He won't miss."

Cedric's lips spread into a proud smile. "No, I won't."

As if sensing their next movie, Hans turned around, his horns growing upward, teeth sharpening into points.

The next few moments flew by in a flash of power hailing from every direction. Loren surged forward, Axel right behind him as he held out his right hand, causing Hans to freeze where he stood, knees buckling beneath him. Beck and Aveo flew in from the sides, driving their swords into the Sorcerer's ribs while Craven and Alistair retreated, unable to use their enchanted weapons without harming anyone else. Cleo flew toward Hans, hands surrounded with golden mist that shot out in rays toward his heart, causing his back to arch backward, his mouth open for a silent scream, teeth gleaming.

"Now, Cedric!" Cleo called as she pulled back, dragging something from within Hans.

Cedric stepped forward, pulling in a deep breath as he closed his eyes, sensing Hans' frantically beating heart. This throw wouldn't be easy, not with all the people crowding the field. If he were ever to make a shot, it *needed* to be this one.

"Cedric!" Loren snapped, writhing as he fought to hold the Sorcerer.

Dipping his head, Cedric relaxed his shoulders, whispered a prayer to wherever would listen, and set the blood blade free. He opened his eyes just in time to watch it bury itself in Hans's heart, a raspy scream sailing past his lips.

Aveo and Beck withdrew their swords, stepping back as Loren dropped his hand, wobbling with relief. Cleo continued to work, ensuring she drained every ounce of power from Hans's form while the blood blade worked.

"Fucking prick," Abernathy said as he dropped the shield,

flexing his fingers. "Never thought I'd like watching someone die so much."

"Chamberlain!" Hans roared as everyone left him for dead, the life leaching from his cold stare, fixed right on where Cedric stood. "I'll see you in the Underworld. That's a fucking Promise."

At that moment, Cedric felt everyone look in his direction, his cheeks heating with anger. He watched with silent rage as Hans' form cracked like fine china, deteriorating right before his eyes, fading to nothing.

Cedric growled, his silver eyes narrowed toward Hans' corpse. *You just ruined everything, you fool.*

32

When Penelope opened her eyes, a scream escaped her parted lips. She could feel that one of her arms was broken, twisted with bone peaking through her flesh. White spots flecked in her vision, the pain so intense that she couldn't help but cry.

Without realizing that she would attract every being within the surrounding area, Penelope continued to shriek. Anything could hear her. The Pandora, if they were near, and she was sure they were. The Rebels, who were looking for her. The Fae, who she hoped would come and save her. Or maybe even the beast, craving blood, unlike any other creature to walk the Realms.

Penelope didn't care who found her or whether she was rescued or killed. She just wanted the pain to end. "As long as it's not the Rebels," she hissed, finally able to control her screaming. "I'd prefer Malachai over them any day. I won't give them the satisfaction."

The sounds of swords clashing above drew her attention, and Penelope stared at the exit to whatever she'd fallen into. A hole? A large crack in the earth? She wasn't sure. All she knew was that she was battered and bruised all over.

"I will *not* be the damsel in distress," Penelope insisted as she forced herself to her feet. She wasn't sure if she could climb, especially with one arm, but she knew she had to try for her sanity. She despised the books she'd read where princesses had been lost to the enemy and needed to be saved by men in shining armor. She *refused* to be one of those women.

One hand gripped the earth, and Penelope was thankful to find it embedded with uneven rock. She used that to her advantage, planting her foot upon the raised surfaces and pushing herself upward. Each move that she made caused her pain to fester and intensify, but she knew she had to continue. She couldn't fail, not today.

Blood poured from her wounds, hot against her chilled flesh. She tried to stifle her sobs, allowing silent tears to roll down her flushed cheeks as she forced herself to keep moving.

Penelope used the rocks for leverage while her hand continued to grip the roots protruding from the earth. The scent of dirt and fresh forest air surrounded her as she inched closer and closer to the top. She silently begged for her body not to give in. If she fell again, she'd only break another bone and would never make it out on her own.

"I need to do this," she told herself, her eyes fixed on her escape. "I will not fail."

Knowing she must have fallen at least fifteen feet into the earth, Penelope wept with relief. Heat wrapped around her as her hand grasped the edge of the crack she'd fallen into. The scent of smoke filled her nostrils and seemed all too familiar. She needed to pull herself over the edge with a single hand. It would likely be the most challenging thing she'd done all her life, but she didn't care. Freedom was mere inches away, and she would give everything she had to pull herself up over this ledge.

Marcus hadn't expected his three opponents to be as skilled as they were, and it had taken him too long to get them out of the way. Had he lost his touch? Despite his newfound Immortal strength, he missed the days when he'd been a Black Knight and Meera's Guardian. His heart clenched at the thought of her. In a way, she'd been more of a mother to him than his own had been in the past, though he couldn't remember her face even if he tried.

He exhaled slowly, scanning his surroundings. He was afraid to move due to the endless traps Cleo had set up throughout the forest. He'd battled while standing in one place, which had proven to be a difficult task. The ordeal had exhausted him, and his arm throbbed endlessly from swinging Whitefire around.

Marcus released a frustrated grunt as he searched for signs of life. His heart dropped once he saw a crack in the earth before him, so long and wide that it boarded the entire width of the Forest of Fools. "No." He fought back tears, knowing Penelope might have fallen into it. They'd been too late.

Just when Marcus gave in to the idea that her sprint into the deadly forest had cost the Princess her life, he saw a hand reach out of the darkness, gripping the crack's edge.

Marcus rushed toward it, sliding onto his knees, sending plumes of dirt up into the air. He couldn't care about any more traps laying in wait, not when her hand was in reach. Just when she was about to lose his grip, he took her hand and pulled, every muscle in his arm growing taught beneath her weight.

Looking down, Marus met Penelope's gaze. Everything about her had changed and grown older, but her hazel eyes had remained the same. Tears sprung to his eyes as he pulled her over, relief washing over him like a waterfall.

Penelope landed on the ground with a thump, letting out a pained cry. She coughed, settling on the forest floor, her teary gaze fixed on the canopy of leaves above.

Chest rising and falling with slow, careful breaths, Penelope reached to cradle her broken arm. Blood pooled on the soil beneath her, and Marcus's senses became alive at the scent of it. He hadn't realized that he'd barely thought to drink blood throughout his journey, and a burning hunger appeared deep in his gut. He tried his best to push thoughts of his need away and crawled toward her, placing his hand on her shoulder.

"Hey." His voice was so soft that Marcus wondered if she'd heard him.

Penelope tore her gaze away from the canopy above. She looked at him, and at first, nothing registered. All she did was stare.

"Am I dead?" she rasped. "I must be."

"No." Marcus fought back a laugh. "You might have broken a bone or two, but you're very much alive. By some miracle, might I add!"

Another cry passed Penelope's plump, chapped lips when she tried to sit up. Tears ran down her cheeks, dripping off of her jaw. "I must be," she repeated; her eyes were like knives digging into his flesh. "Especially if you're sitting in front of me right now."

Her words might as well have been a knife tearing through Marcus's heart. He'd been a fool. He'd been so caught up in trying to find Ash that he'd forced thoughts of Penelope and Vincent from his mind. He'd walked away from a girl he'd held the day she was born and stood beside every day after for four years. Marcus, her parents, and Dessa were all Penelope knew for a long time. Gideon died,

Meera soon after, and Marcus became a Draconian, embarking on a journey to find her sibling. None of it was fair.

"I'm—"

"Don't bother," Penelope cut him off as her hand reached for his. "None of it matters now. To be honest, worse things have happened as of late. You never returning seems minuscule compared to it all," she said, a faint smile spreading across her lips. "Let's just get out of here."

Marcus nodded, swallowing the lump in his throat. "Can you walk?"

"Damn straight," Penelope informed him, allowing him to help her. "My legs are fine. It's my arm that's the problem. It's broken, likely in more than one place. Nothing a few soaks in the healing waters within the Kingdom of Elves won't fix."

Marcus gave her a long, questionable look. "Yeah, I don't think the healing springs are going to cut it on their own," he advised, taking notice of the bone protruding from her skin. "Let's get out of here. Perhaps your Guardian can perform a healing spell."

Whatever tension that remained within the princess evaporated at the mention of Abernathy. "I take it that you've met him."

"Oh, I've gotten to know him quite well over the last few days," Marcus said, holding Penelope up with an arm guiding her steps. "I've gotten to know quite a few interesting people. Quite the interesting team was put together to track you down."

Something like a grimace, or maybe a snort, escaped the princess. "Truthfully, I'm just happy to see you again," she admitted, her gaze fixed on the terrain as she carefully took steps. "You haven't changed a bit."

"That makes one of us," Marcus replied, smiling. "I hardly recognized you."

"It's the arm, isn't it?" Penelope joked, a hint of mischief shining in her eyes. "Last time we met, I was all in one piece. Technically, I am now. The pieces are just…crooked."

Marcus laughed for the first time in what felt like days, and for the first time in over thirteen years, he held Penelope close to him, and this time, he had no plans of letting go.

Together, Marcus Bonaventure and Penelope VanCamp walked through the tree line, only to find a sea of people waiting for them. Penelope gazed at the sight of them all, fighting back the tears as she spotted Cedric and Abernathy standing side by side.

The Elf was moved to see her as well, trying his best to hide his tears as he looked toward his cousin, Mika, who was standing beside him with a broad smile on her face.

"You're alive!" she squealed.

"Just barely," Penelope muttered.

Abernathy released one large sigh of relief that brought a smile to the faces of those around him. "Thank the *Moons*!" he shouted as he stared into the sky, illuminated by a bright, rising sun.

Marcus's brow furrowed at the sight of his King. He laughed as he approached him, taking in Loren's odd appearance. "Pajamas on a battlefield? This has to be a first."

Loren's eyes rolled as he crossed his arms before his chest. "I told Valentina I would take matters into my own hands, and I did. Whether I was wearing pajamas or not doesn't matter. Now, Cleo," he said, turning to face the Fae Queen, "let's take that blood blade and the Soul Sword back to your vault before another masochistic bastard gets his hands on it."

33

Two months had passed since Penelope had managed to escape the Rebels and had nearly died doing so. Her arm had healed nicely, and she finally had full use of it once again. Vincent had been glad to have her back in the Kingdom of Elves. He'd hardly left her side for weeks. Because of that fact, Penelope had spent even more time with Cedric, and now the thought of him did something to her that she didn't quite understand.

"Are you excited?" Abernathy stood at the threshold of her bedroom, wearing a black tuxedo adorned with a gleaming pin on his jacket.

Penelope's eyes widened at the sight of it, a smile blooming on her lips as she slipped into her heels. "The VanCamp family symbol," she pointed out, nearly tearing at the sight of the three Moons. The two on the sides were in the shapes of crescents, while the center one was complete.

"Why not?" Abernathy shrugged. "You're my favorite person, and this is the symbol of your family. Not your family's reign, but your *family*," he clarified. "And you're *my* family."

"I guess that makes you a VanCamp, too, huh?" Penelope inquired as she gazed at herself in the mirror. The royal seamstresses had done a fantastic job designing the perfect dress for the occasion— Sparkling sapphire blue, with diamonds encrusted around the dipping sweetheart neckline. The Idonian symbol of three intersecting triangles was embroidered on the bodice, while cap-sleeves hung loosely off her shoulders. A long train followed behind her with silver embellishments of Idonian knots scattered about the fabric, standing out brightly against the dark background.

Abernathy snorted, finding her question quite amusing. "No, I'm an Abernathy. Our symbol is nothing more than a spell book, so it's boring. I mean, I see those every day. The Moons have a much higher meaning."

"I suppose you're correct." Penelope sighed as he linked her arm with his, patting her hand lightly as if to calm her nerves.

"If I turn out to be your betrothed tonight, I'll gladly take your name," he said with a dashing smile. Blood burned in Penelope's cheeks, painting them scarlet."High Queen Penelope Abernathy of Si Realtra doesn't sound right."

Penelope cleared her throat nervously, her palms growing sweaty. "You've thought a lot about that."

"Of course I have," Abernathy said as if it didn't matter. "Even though I doubt they'll choose me after what happened."

"Did you *want* to be chosen?" Penelope pressed, tilting her head curiously.

Abernathy was quiet briefly as he spared her a glance or two. "No," he replied. "I'd much rather be your Guardian and your best friend."

Hundreds of people had come to witness Penelope's eighteenth-year ceremony. After Abernathy had escorted her to the ballroom where everything was taking place, her stomach threatened to expel what little she'd managed to eat that day. All the guests kneeled before her, and the sight made her wish to run away.

"Oh, how wonderful your mother's crown of roses would look upon your head," one woman said to her as she passed her by.

"The amulet would pair wonderfully with that sapphire dress of yours," Lord Angus Ward said with a smirk.

"That arm of yours looks great," Alistair mentioned as he peered at it. "You can't even tell a bone was sticking out of the flesh."

Marcus rolled his eyes at the Mortal's words. "Must you be so disgusting?"

"Oh, it's fine," Penelope assured them both. "Isn't it cool, though? The Healing Springs here in the Kingdom of Elves are phenomenal."

"Next time I manage to hurt myself, I'll try them," Alistair said.

"You both disgust me," Aveo insisted as he walked away.

Penelope and Alistair sneered at his back as he disappeared into the crowd. "I think we're pretty awesome," he told her, nudging her gently with his elbow. "Did you get my gift?"

"I did." Penelope beamed, recalling the small, glass, black dragon she'd found outside the door to her suite as she was leaving for the ceremony. "I'll put it on my mantle. Every time I light a fire, I'll think of you."

"As you should," Alistair replied playfully.

A short while later, Penelope was seated for dinner and

surrounded by most of the members of the Idonian Council. Nanny Dessa had remained behind to assist Esmeralda with watching after her two-month-old daughter, Princess Trinity. Penelope missed her greatly. She imagined how she would run to her later and tell her everything about what transpired there that evening.

"Are you nervous?" Mika asked quietly at Penelope's left side. "I mean, it could be anyone in this room. Even someone at this very table."

Penelope's stomach twisted as her gaze flitted from person to person. Her heart skipped a beat at the sight of King Loren, dressed like the very King he was this evening. She forced herself not to focus on him for long, and her eyes fell on Valentina, who was staring right back at her.

"I assure you, you'll be pleased with the match," the Prophetess said coolly, but her words did little to ease her bundle of nerves.

Penelope frowned as she reached for her knife to cut through her steak.

"Oh, no, you don't!" Beck growled, darting over to her. He reached over her shoulder, cutting her meat for her. "The last time we let you do this, I had to take you to the infirmary, and then, we had too many drinks. And *then*, low and behold, you were kidnapped. Therefore, you cutting your steak is officially a bad omen," he insisted as he finished, quickly returning to his seat.

Penelope's cheeks flamed once again as she shoved a piece in her mouth and reached for her wine to wash it down. "Don't even *try* to tell me that alcohol is a bad omen, too, or else I'll be in for a slew of bad luck for the rest of my life," she snarled in Beck's direction. The entire table erupted with laughter.

"I like her." Richard Anster said. "She's got fire."

"You call *that* fire?" Cleo scoffed. "You should have seen her when she climbed out of that crack in the earth."

"You didn't even see it," Beck reminded her, brow knitting with confusion.

Cleo took a sip of her champagne. "No, but Marcus told me everything."

"And that was your crack in the earth that she fell in," Cedric retorted, causing the Fae Queen to bristol before sulking into her chair, defeated.

Once dinner was through, it was time for the ceremony to continue. Chills slithered down Peneleope's spine, goosebumps pebbling along her flesh. She trembled with both anticipation and anxiety as she sipped her wine. Her eyes fell on the door to the ballroom, and she contemplated just how fast she could escape, but she knew that too many essential warriors sat in this room. The Rebels were one thing; Craven was an entirely different animal.

Thaddeus took to the dais that centered the ballroom, providing the perfect location for all the guests to view the ceremony easily. Penelope's opinion of her adoptive father had changed over the last year, but her heart melted in her chest as she watched him. He may have the same goals his ancestors once had: to see Elves claim the central throne of Si Realtra. Of course, he'd have to undermine Penelope to obtain that goal, but she could see in his eyes that he loved her and always would.

"It feels like an eternity ago that Penelope VanCamp was brought to us for protection against the Pandora as they attacked the Idonian Kingdom," Thaddeus began with a sad smile. "While we knew there was a chance that young Penelope would remain with us, at that time, we'd still hoped that she would be able to return to her home to live alongside her mother and siblings. I can speak for everyone in this room when I say the Ballroom Battle's failure caused complete and utter devastation throughout our Realm." His voice quivered as his eyes scanned the room, eventually falling on the very woman he was referring to.

Penelope found herself clutching her skirts, fighting against her own emotions. *Please don't make me cry, Thaddeus,* she silently pleaded, batting her thick eyelashes as she willed away her tears.

"It's with pride that I can say a light came out of that dark day. Penelope and Vincent have been the best blessings the Kingdom of Elves has ever received. We all love them, but the Chamberlains love her the most." Thaddeus held his hand out, clearly summoning the young princess.

Panic seized Penelope, freezing her in place. Her grip around her skirts began to tighten so furiously that she wondered if she'd tear the fabric, but a pair of hands fell upon her shoulders, easing her.

"It's fine," Beck assured Penelope as he helped her to stand, linking his arm with hers as they began their walk toward his father.

Penelope focused on the Elven King, watching as he smiled widely at the sight of her approaching. She wanted to smile back, cry, or possibly release the slew of emotions within her as she climbed the dais' steps. Thaddeus reached out, extending his hand. She took it, and the King gently intertwined his fingers with hers. Like the still water of a lake on a pleasant spring day, a certain calmness fell upon her.

"We're Elves," Thaddeus stated bluntly as he gestured to his tapered ears and the signature long, straight brown hair beneath his golden circlet. "We weren't exactly sure how to raise Mortal children. Our children start training from the moment they can walk. So, it's safe to say that we had much to learn when discovering what was best for the two VanCamps. We made it work after much trial and error," he chuckled, and many others within the ballroom began to laugh as well. "And while we're unfamiliar with eighteenth-year ceremonies here in our own Kingdom, Esmeralda and I thought it was essential to continue Gideon and Meera's traditions with their children.

"It's with great honor that Esmeralda and I were able to do this for Penelope. She deserves hope and love after so much heartache. There were plenty of nights when Esmeralda and I stayed up too late, trying to pick the absolute best man for Penelope. Not only someone who would stand beside her and love her unconditionally but someone she would love too." Thaddeus took a breath, retrieving a velvet ring box from his pocket.

Penelope's breath hitched at the sight of it, knowing it was only a matter of seconds before her betrothed would be announced. Faces ran through her mind at the speed of light. Every man, Elf, Mortal, and Draconian she'd ever had the pleasure of meeting. It, indeed, could be anyone.

"With much consideration and even some advice from the rest of our Idonian Council, a betrothed was chosen. There were so many choices, some of them even Kings, some of them Mortals," Thaddeus explained as everyone inched toward the edge of their seats. "Most would assume that we would naturally choose an Elf, and we did, but not for the reasons one might think. Because this person deserves a happy ending as much as Penelope." As the words left Thaddeus's mouth, Penelope felt her knees grow weak. She fought to keep standing, shock beginning to rip through her so viciously that she could barely think straight.

When Thaddeus paused, it nearly drove all the guests insane. They held their breaths, waiting impatiently for the next High King of Si Realtra to be announced. This occasion was monumental, and Thaddeus and Esmeralda's decision would affect Idona's future significantly.

"Cedric Chamberlain," Thaddeus announced with a grin. The entire room seemed to gasp in unison before hundreds of people jumped to their feet, screaming and applauding. Then, the Kingdom shook terribly, and the chandeliers hanging from the ceilings began to sway.

Penelope stared with her mouth agape. Her eyes fell on Cedric, who stood immobile in front of his seat. People patted him on the back, congratulating him as if he'd been victorious in battle. He seemed frozen in time, only moving slightly when Vincent leaped onto him, shaking his shoulder forcefully. He blinked quickly and smiled before Vincent pushed him toward the stage.

To Penelope, Cedric was moving slowly as he approached her. Her heart ceased to perform a single beat as she watched him. Silver robes fell off him, swaying gently along with his movements. The shade made his nearly waist-length black hair stand out and matched his eyes. He walked with such grace that it was breathtaking, and those around him stared at him in awe. It was clear what he was destined to be. He was a High King, and although it would take some time for him to get to that throne, people were already willing to bow before him.

Cedric climbed the stage, a shade of pink painted across his cheeks as his eyes met hers. Thaddeus opened the ring box, chuckling like a schoolgirl as he watched his nephew retrieve the diamond ring from its place. With shaking hands, Cedric slid the ring onto Penelope's ring finger and held her hand in both of his for a few moments.

Women wailed, fanning themselves. Cleo dabbed at her eyes with a tissue while Aries patted her shoulder. Vincent shouted excitedly as he clapped while Beck whistled beside him. Marcus, Craven, Alistair, and Axel raised whiskey shots into the air before toasting the couple and downing them in one gulp.

Abernathy offered the princess a thumbs up when her eyes fell upon him with a bright smile on his face. And for the first time, Penelope realized how blessed she'd been for not only meeting Cedric but Abernathy, as well. Without the two of them, she'd just be another lost soul. And now, thanks to them, she never would be.

34

Once Penelope's ceremony had ended, an immediate Idonian Council meeting was called. Although it would be a strange meeting with an unexpected subject, Valentina looked forward to it. She was the first to arrive in the Round Table Room, taking her seat as she waited patiently for the others to file in.

Richard arrived shortly after, glassy-eyed and stumbling. Valentina rolled her eyes at the sight of him but couldn't keep herself from chuckling as she watched him nearly miss the chair he'd been lowering himself into.

"You knew this was going to happen afterward. You didn't have to go and get drunk," she chastised as she sipped the blood she'd brought.

Marcus walked through the door with the rest of the Council, slightly buzzing himself. "Why am I here again?" he asked as his eyes met hers. He smiled quickly and waved.

Who knew such powerful Immortals could become so weak before a woman? Valentina bit back a laugh as everyone took their seats. "Where's Penelope?" she asked.

"Lucinda is retrieving her," Esmeralda announced. "We're so fortunate the Sorceress was able to attend. Things have been heating up in the Regal Mountains. The Pandora think it's their playground."

"Well, it *is* where they were bred and born," Valentina reminded her, pursing her lips.

Moments later, Lucinda walked through the door with an awestruck Penelope at her side. The Princess seemed so shy as she approached the round table with the most important figures within Idona sitting around it. Eventually, she'd be leading these meetings. The idea of it brought tears to Valentina's eyes. A hard lump formed in her throat as she longed for the day Gideon's daughter could take his place.

"Why am I here?" Penelope asked.

Loren stood, gesturing for her to take a seat. She watched him with wide, curious, hazel eyes that reminded Valentina of Meera. Oh, how she missed the fiery Queen Idona used to have.

"Tell me, how much do you know about your brother's... condition?" Loren inquired.

Penelope swallowed, and every pair of Immortal ears around the room heard it. "It's fine, Penelope," Lucinda assured her, placing a comforting hand on her shoulder. "Just tell Loren what you know."

"Well..." Penelope began nervously. "My mother used a potion during her labor with the twins. I'm also aware that using magic on infants is bound to cause side effects later in life. But the particular potion she used, the Everlasting Life potion, turns babies into Immortals."

"Possibly even Hybrids," Aries added.

Penelope's eyes widened further. "But Hybrids are forbidden. They're slaughtered. Are you trying to prepare me for the fact that you're going to *kill* Vincent?" She shot out of her seat, her unease quickly transitioning into a rage that startled the Council.

"No!" Loren scrambled to calm her. "We're trying to offer you the chance to become Immortal as well."

The princess fell back into her seat. Her face drained of all color as she processed what the Draconian King had just said. Silence lingered between them. Council members fidgeted as they awaited the Princess's response.

Valentina continued to sip her blood before speaking. "I know what you're thinking," she accused, earning a slight scowl from Penelope, "VanCamps have always been Mortal. That's what makes them special. They could inspire billions without Immortal strength. Even as they aged, the Realms watched High King after High King faded away. You don't want to change that. But you're wrong."

"I'm *wrong*?" Penelope sneered. Murmurs filled the air, dying out as she spoke once again. "How can you say that when you're completely aware that every fact you just stated is true?"

"Because the VanCamps may have been Mortal, but many of them had dragon's blood." Valentina's admittance caused yet another wave of shock to sail through the room. "It's not something many people knew. It all began when Theo VanCamp married a woman of Mayfire. Their son, Graham, was the only one to become a Rider, but that doesn't mean the blood disappeared. VanCamps have always been in a class of their own because of this. So, while it may have withered away as your family line continued, it could still be running faintly through your veins. By becoming Immortal, you would amplify that fact."

"Valentina is right," Cleo said before the princess could argue. "Not to mention, both of your siblings will be Immortal. Now, the VanCamps will fall into a different category. So we're allowing you to live alongside them and not force them to watch you grow old and die."

Penelope's shoulders drooped as she sulked in her seat.

Valentina knew that the idea was a complex one. She was wholly content with her Mortal blood. But, like the other Mortals scattered throughout the Realms, she'd made peace that she would eventually die of old age while those she'd surrounded herself with would live on.

"I can assure you that times have changed," Valentina told her softly, and for once, the princess looked at her with curious eyes instead of a gaze filled with hate. "This war is far from over. I never know everything, but something tells me we haven't even reached the tip of the iceberg. Now is the time for Immortals to be upon the main throne, and we would prefer for those Immortals to be VanCamps."

Penelope nodded slowly. "Alright," she agreed, though it was hesitant. "How will I become Immortal? Am I going to become a Draconian?" Her eyes fell on Loren, who shook his head slowly.

"You'll drink the Fountain of Youth potion," Lucinda informed her. "I've already prepared it for you. It's the same one Abernathy and I drank when we became Sorcerers. If you take it now, you'll still age for some time. Usually, you stop around twenty-five like most Immortals. At your prime."

"That sounds less painful," Penelope admitted. Laughter came from the Council.

Marcus stood awkwardly, having never taken a seat. Valentina could see on his face that he had a different opinion but wouldn't share it immediately. Perhaps, when they were alone later, she hoped he would.

A small bottle fell out of the hunter-green sleeve of Lucinda's dress, landing perfectly in place upon the round table. It seemed simple. A glass bottle, an ordinary cork, and a purple-tinted liquid swirling within.

Penelope visibly shivered at the sight of it, but without a second thought, she ripped it off the table and pulled the cork out. She raised the bottle to her pink lips and paused momentarily as her eyes drifted shut. Valentina wondered what was going through the princess's mind as she allowed the liquid to sail down her throat, changing her genetics forever.

Valentina's eyes fell on the Elves. They didn't seem happy, though they were smiling. Likely for Penelope's sake. Loren's plan had worked. He'd managed to undermine them without starting a third war, and Valentina was pleased that they'd avoided more bloodshed and a second Scarlett Era. Although she didn't know if the peace would remain in the future, at least it was still in effect.

"You'll be stronger now," Lucinda told the Princess excitedly. "You'll stand more of a chance if you re-encounter the Pandora or the Rebels."

"We still haven't extinguished them completely," Marcus reminded the Council. "Kurt Walsh is still alive. All we did was defeat Hans and a good portion of his men. There are likely plenty more."

Valentina smirked, knowing something the rest of the Council didn't. "They won't be a problem for much longer," she said, earning curious glances from those around her. "I've seen that they'll encounter Malachai, and while I wish the Prince of Darkness was dead, I have to admit, we might owe him one after he slaughters them all."

35

After Lucinda swooped Penelope away, Cedric had thought it best to return home to his suite for the evening. His mind was still whirling. Of course, when Beck had drunkenly told him he'd been on the list of eligible bachelors, he hadn't thought his aunt and uncle would choose him.

Cedric had surrounded himself with silence and solitude. He'd despised the constant buzz of Kingdom life and had escaped from it the first chance he got. The Grimm Estate had been a blessing in disguise, filled with enthralling history.

Returning to the Kingdom of Elves was painful, but he'd endured. After a few days, he realized that he enjoyed the company with Vincent, especially Penelope. The two were nothing like the Elves he'd grown up with.

He hadn't anticipated falling deeply in love with Penelope over time. Cedric wasn't sure when he'd realized it but figured it was likely once he had awoken in the infirmary, knowing she'd been captured. He smiled at the memory of her in his arms, how soft she felt, and the warmth that had spread through his entire body.

Ripping off his silver robes, Cedric threw them onto his bed and shed the tunic and plain white t-shirt he'd been wearing underneath. Warm spring air flew in from his open windows, ruffling his white curtains and hair.

As he undid the Elven braids in his obsidian hair, Cedric couldn't help but smile. As he stood in the center of his master bedroom, he realized that he no longer preferred solitude. He preferred Penelope, and he was going to marry her.

"Tomorrow, if Thaddeus will let me," Cedric said aloud. He wanted Penelope to be his forever. She wasn't Immortal like him. There would come a day when he'd have to say goodbye to her and attempt to resume his life without her.

He grimaced at the tragic thought as he turned on the shower and returned to his room to collect fresh clothes. He doubted that he'd be able to sleep later as he glanced at his bed, knowing his mind would be running a mile a minute.

As Cedric moved to return to his bathroom, a knock on his front door drew his attention. "It's the middle of the night," he grumbled, wondering who could be so inconsiderate.

Another knock sounded, and then another, as Cedric rushed to answer it. He pulled the door open and stopped dead in his tracks. His eyes widened as he stared at Penelope. She seemed different... Her hair was left undone, falling in chestnut curls that framed her flushed face. She was carrying her shoes in her hand, and her chest was rising and falling quickly as she took rapid breaths.

"I'm Immortal!" she exclaimed.

Cedric stared at her as he processed her words. "Wait, what?"

"The Idonian Council summoned me, and Loren allowed me to drink the Fountain of Youth potion. I bet you he knew what the Elves were up to. So now, we don't have to worry about me dying of old age. All we have to worry about is making sure we find my sister so that she can be given the Amulet," Penelope rambled as she let herself inside. "They won't win."

Shaking his head, Cedric shut the front door. He watched as Penelope's eyes drifted down him. A furious blush burned on her face. "I didn't know I would be getting visitors," he admitted, sporting crimson cheeks of his own.

"From this day forward, you and I are going to work endlessly to find Ash before it's too late," Penelope insisted, paying no mind to his shirtless torso. "Also, we're getting married!"

"I'm aware," Cedric said. His eyes fell on the ring on her finger, watching it sparkle in the light cast by the chandelier hanging above them.

Penelope beamed, and he could tell she was just as happy as he was about that fact. "So, how do you feel?" she asked. "You're going to be the next High King of Si Realtra. You know, whenever the Messenger comes."

"I don't care much about that," Cedric replied. "I don't know how good of a King I'll be. All I care about, if we're being honest, is that I'll marry you when that happens."

Penelope blinked. "I didn't know you thought of me that way."

"Oh, I do," Cedric admitted, "I got lucky tonight. If I'd had to watch you get betrothed to anyone else, it might have killed me."

Penelope closed the space between them and placed her hands against his cheeks, pulling him into a kiss. Cedric swore he hadn't felt such a sensation all his life and knew how easily he would become addicted. Her lips parted as her tongue beckoned him to explore her, dancing in time with his own. Penelope's body melted against his as he wrapped his arms around her, feeling the curves of her body.

Cedric felt his pulse quicken and his cock twitch, straining against his trousers, begging for release. Chuckling, she bit his lip, pulling a growl from deep within his throat. He was like a damn genie, and she was his master. She'd flicked a switch within him, releasing the animalistic part that he'd kept leashed. He deepened the kiss, pushing harder against her. Penelope moaned into his mouth, accepting him with eager greediness. He lifted her into his arms without breaking away.

One hand wrapped around her waist while the other reached for the back of her dress. His fingers quickly undid the soft laces of her bodice as he walked them toward his bedroom. Thin straps fell down her bare shoulders as Cedric set Penelope on his bed. His heart thundered, and his mouth grew dry as he watched her slip out of her gown. She was so beautiful. She was his forever.

Her fingers wrapped around one of his belt loops, pulling him closer so she could kiss him again.

"We're not married yet," he breathed.

The Princess huffed, blowing a stray strand of chestnut hair away from her face. "You've taken me into your bedroom, where you aided me in removing my dress," she reminded him. He knelt before his queen, shivering as she ran a finger down his bare torso. "Finish what you started."

She was a damned goddess.

"As you wish," Cedric replied, pulling off his trousers until he, too, was just as the Moons had made him. He crouched onto the bed, backing her up until she fell. He hovered over her, watching as she smiled up at him. Her legs spread to make room for him, and he looked down, drinking her in. He swallowed. Oh, Moons, was she gorgeous. He wondered how she could look at him as though he were the most fantastic thing to exist within Si Realtra. But he looked at her the same way, and because of that fact, this moment was the only thing he'd ever considered perfect.

His mouth reached down to claim hers in a hungry kiss. Her fingers dug into his back as she moaned with pleasure.

"Cedric," she whispered, "I need you." And it was those words that were his undoing. It was with those words that he sheathed himself in her and relished in their union.

The sun began to streak across the sky as Cedric crawled out from beneath his sheets. He glanced over at Penelope, who was slumbering peacefully beside him, surrounded by an array of black silk bedding. His breath caught in his throat as he forced himself to look away, or else he feared he might wake her up and ravage her again.

"She must be a Sorceress," Cedric whispered as he pulled a shirt over his shoulders. His hair was still damp from the shower they'd taken before finally slipping beneath the covers they'd messed up so badly beforehand. "I'm so in love with her that it can't be real."

As legend states, there is nothing quite like an Elven sunrise. Cedric couldn't help but disagree as he stepped out onto his balcony, the crisp morning air greeting his bare arms. Penelope, to him, was even more beautiful than the sunrise he stared out into, and deep down, he wondered how he'd gotten so lucky.

"Thank you, Malachai," Cedric muttered as he leaned against the balcony rails. "For burning down the Grimm Estate and giving me a reason to return here. I almost feel like I owe you something in return." He tapped his fingers on the railing, humming into the early morning silence. "But, I tried to give you a chance. I offered you a chance toward freedom. Cleared a path for you. I never thought I'd forgive myself for failing you all. The Moons feel differently, apparently. Perhaps I should focus on my own happy ending for once in my life."

Black feathers cut across his vision as Cedric watched the blackbird. It was flying north toward Saloris. His heart sank as he imagined the worst. "Pandora," he seethed. Though he couldn't spot its red eyes, the hair rising on his neck told him it was true. Cedric couldn't shake the feeling that dark times were coming to the Kingdom of Elves.

Six months had passed since Penelope's eighteenth-year ceremony, and despite the lack of Rebel and Pandora activity, Abernathy and the others were still at work. He, Cedric, Vincent, Beck, and Penelope offered to assist Marcus in the search for the Missing VanCamp.

Penelope and Vincent were under restrictions when it came to leaving the Kingdom of Elves, which meant Abernathy had no choice but to stay behind with them. They communicated with others in the field using the technology Dracus had provided. It was a massive secret that Thaddeus and Esmeralda couldn't find out about. That specific technology was prohibited outside of the Communications Center.

Penelope would have opted to use the Communications Center, but none of them wanted the other Elves to find out they were aiding Marcus. Moreover, they weren't sure if Thaddeus and Esmeralda could be trusted, even though they agreed to allow Penelope to become an Immortal. Their second plan to gain the central throne within Si Realtra had backfired.

Cedric and Marcus were both traveling throughout the

Regal Mountains to look into a mysterious village that was thought to be impossible to get into. Although he was jealous that Cedric got to leave the golden walls, Abernathy wasn't having such a horrible time keeping Vincent and Penelope occupied.

"I don't see the point of this," the princess grumbled as she sat across the table from him at a local café. "We're wasting time."

"No," Abernathy disagreed as he sipped his tea. "We're enjoying the fresh fall air, and we're bonding."

Penelope gave him a skeptical look, knowing he likely had an ulterior motive. "We've already bonded. You've been my Guardian for over a year. We live together," she said as she pushed her salad around her plate.

"Sorry I'm late," Mika chirped as she lowered into the third chair at their table. "My mother stopped me on my way out of the castle. You have mail," she announced as she handed her adoptive sister the letter.

Penelope stared down at it, her brow furrowed as she quickly became confused. "Three intersecting swords," she said, showing the seal to her Guardian.

"I have no idea. Maybe one of the noble houses toward the Strip?" Abernathy asked.

"No." Penelope shook her head. She tore open the letter and immediately focused on the delicate script scrawled across the fine paper. When her eyes widened with surprise as she let out an audible gasp, Abernathy stiffened.

"What is it?" Mika inquired sweetly.

"Xavier," was all Penelope said as she stood quickly, throwing the letter down onto the table as if it had been poisoned.

Abernathy snatched the letter to read it himself.

Dear Penelope,

I'm so sorry I missed your ceremony this past Spring. I heard you've grown up to be a fine young woman. A spitting image of your mother.

He cringed, knowing that the Pandora had managed to survey the princess.

I heard about your spat with the Rebels, and it seems that we have a common enemy. I thought I knew about everything happening within my Realm, but apparently, they've managed to go unnoticed by my Pandora. That's my mistake. I can assure you, it won't happen again. I just want you to know that you're always welcome home. These castle halls miss you terribly, and I would happily make you High Queen. You'd make the perfect bride. And, of course, your sister would love to see you.

Abernathy stared up at Penelope, trembling rapidly with fear and rage. His chest tightened, and his breaths came in shallow puffs as specs of black danced within his vision. He closed his eyes, drew a deep breath, tried to steady himself, and slowly exhaled. His eyes flicked open, taking in the tears that streamed down Penelope's cheeks. "No," was all he said as he shook his head. "If he had Ash, we would have known long ago. He'd have dangled it in front of our faces like bait. But, instead, he's trying to draw us in."

"We're a threat, and he knows it," Mika agreed with the Sorcerer. "There's no way this is true."

"There were no hatch exits within the Idonian Kingdom. Only the entrance," Abernathy added for good measure.

"That doesn't mean his Pandora weren't out in the Realm, surveying the exits. They could have snatched her up and brought her back to him!" She was panicking now, repeatedly taking deep breaths.

"We need to take that letter to the Idonian Council immediately," Mika demanded.

The moment that King Loren learned about the letter Xavier had sent Penelope, he lost all composure. His stomach churned as he and the other Draconian Council members gathered in Dracus's Communication Center. While the Idonian Council members would have all preferred to meet in person, there wasn't enough time. They needed to discuss the matter and what to do about it, choosing to do so via video call.

Thankfully, Benjamin had designed a room in the Communications Center for the rare occasions it was needed. Five giant screens were positioned on the walls, but only three would be used. Loren watched as they each worked to connect to the Safe Haven, the Regal Mountains, and the Kingdom of Elves.

Cleo and Aries appeared first. The Fae Queen seemed pale. Aries looked calm, but Loren knew better. Aries' type of calm was always the calm before a storm.

Lucinda connected next; her amber eyes were wide with worry. Loren saw she was in her haven, a place that only she knew the location of. He scanned her background, smirking at seeing spellbooks lining the walls. It was no wonder that she was the most potent Sorceress Si Realtra had.

"The Elves haven't connected yet? Figures." Lucinda scowled. "Why *would* they be on time for a meeting like this?" she asked sarcastically.

"What's taking them so long?" Valentina grumbled as she paced behind the King.

"They're always late," Aries mumbled through the screen,

rolling his burgundy eyes so far back into his head that it was a wonder how he hadn't glimpsed his spine.

When the Elves connected, Loren's breath caught in his throat. He'd been expecting to see Esmeralda, Thaddeus, and perhaps a few Elven Council members, but he hadn't expected to see Penelope or her Guardian.

"I want to know what happened," Loren said slowly, "From the beginning."

Thaddeus's eyes narrowed in the Draconian King's direction, and it was clear to Loren that they might still have a bit of bad blood. "Penelope, tell him," he ordered. Penelope jumped slightly in her seat.

"I was out having lunch with Abernathy. We'd invited Mika, and when she joined us, she brought a letter with a wax seal reflecting three intersecting swords. Neither Abernathy nor I had seen it before, but now, I think it may be Xavier's family symbol." Penelope shifted uncomfortably, her bright eyes reflecting her horror. "He said he has Ash and wants me to be his bride and become High Queen."

"Disgusting," Aries hissed.

"Do we honestly believe he has the Missing VanCamp?" Anastasia Volden, the Draconian Fire Clan leader, questioned. Loren glanced to his right, noticing how infuriated she appeared to be. Her gray eyes seemed darker. Fire-like rings surrounded her irises. "Because if he does, I'll go in there right now and take her back. If I have to, I'll burn the entire place to the ground."

Loren glared in her direction. "Let's not get hasty."

"He's lying," Benjamin insisted, crossing his arms. "If he had her, he would have dangled her in front of our faces years ago."

"But why now?" Esmeralda asked as she stiffened in her seat, gripping the arms of her chair so tightly that her knuckles were turning white.

When Penelope's Guardian cleared his throat, Loren began to grow nervous. The look on Abernathy's face said everything he needed to know. He was guilty of something.

"I know why," the Sorcerer revealed, his fists clenched. Loren could see that he was fighting an internal battle and imagined he was debating whether he should tell the truth or not. "They know we're looking for her."

"*We?*" Esmeralda gasped.

Loren watched as the color drained from Penelope's face. She stared at her Guardian. Even through the screens, he could see that she was trembling. His head fell into his hands as he stifled a groan, realizing that Penelope had figured out that the Elves had a secret agenda regarding the Idonian Amulet. He'd hoped she was in the dark and hadn't learned that those she thought loved her would easily push her aside to take Si Realtra's High Throne for themselves.

"We've been helping Marcus look for the Missing VanCamp," Abernathy admitted, rising from his chair. It was clear to Loren that the Sorcerer didn't care about Thaddeus or Esmeralda's opinion. "It was pretty obvious he wasn't getting anywhere alone."

Loren bit back his tongue as he watched Penelope nod, confirming all that her Guardian had said.

"We're running out of time," Penelope added, rising from her seat. "We've been helping Marcus by researching legends about hidden places within Idona since Ash isn't anywhere that can be found on a map." She stood tall; her shoulders pressed back, utter determination visible across her delicate features. "If you want to get angry at us for trying to assist with finding her, by all means, go ahead. But we're not sorry."

The Council fell silent as they watched Thaddeus stare at Penelope. Loren held his breath, waiting for the shouting that would inevitably occur.

"Who else is involved in this?" Thaddeus's voice was so low that it sent a chill straight down Loren's spine.

Both Abernathy and Penelope remained silent, their lips pursed. It was clear that neither one of them was going to give up the names of the others without a fight.

"Penelope," Loren began, drawing the princess's attention. He barely knew her and had no idea about what might be running through her mind. He'd only met her in person three times until this moment. But he was beginning to see her for who she was: a passionate woman who would do anything to protect those she cared about. "It's evident that Xavier has discovered what you and whoever you were working with were up to. We need to know their names to protect them."

The princess softened as her attention fell on Abernathy. He nodded slowly. "Vincent, Cedric, and Beck," she revealed.

"*Beck*?" Esmeralda snapped. Thaddeus was trembling with rage.

Loren drew in a deep breath and slowly exhaled. The video call had been a mistake. If they'd all met in person, then he might have been able to use his abilities to silence Thaddeus before he did anything he couldn't take back.

"I sent Marcus to Cedric. I thought he might be able to help more than any of us could," Valentina admitted from behind Loren. "But I didn't expect the rest of you to get involved."

"Where is Cedric now?" Cleo asked softly.

Penelope gulped. "With Marcus."

Esmeralda rose from her seat, disappointment reflecting as her gaze flitted from the Draconians to the Princess and her Guardian. "Marcus was tasked to search independently for the Missing VanCamp for a reason. That way, he wouldn't draw any attention to himself. Can you understand why now? There's no doubt in my mind that Cedric's presence drew the Pandora's attention. And it's not exactly an unknown fact that he's your betrothed." Her harsh words were directed toward Penelope. It was unnecessary Loren knew, for the Queen to say as much to Penelope. She wasn't daft. He knew that all too well."You've put your lives at risk," Esmeralda continued.

"Summon Cedric home," Thaddeus ordered. "We have no choice but to call off this search. Completely."

"You can't be serious," Abernathy growled. "What exactly are you trying to do? Use this entire ordeal as a way to make sure that she's *never* found?" He hissed the accusation. "We all know you want that Sectra to go to Mika."

Another painful silence ensued, causing the hair on Loren's neck to rise. Finally, he lifted his gaze from the floor, wincing at the sight of Thaddeus's deadly demeanor. The Elf was visibly fighting against the urge to end the Sorcerer's life.

"Get out," Thaddeus ordered.

"Excuse me?" Abernathy snapped.

"Get out," Thaddeus repeated. "Get out of this room and out of this Kingdom, or so help me; I'll kill you where you stand."

"You can't do that!" Lucinda snapped. "He's Penelope's Guardian."

"Not anymore," Thaddeus replied, turning his back on all the screens and the Sorcerer.

Loren watched as Abernathy stood beside Penelope, fuming. He imagined that he could kill the Elven King in a matter of seconds but severely hoped that he wouldn't.

"Fine," Abernathy said and turned to face the princess. Penelope stared at him with tears trailing silently from her eyes. "Next time you see me, I'll be with Ash VanCamp," he assured her before storming out of the room.

It's only a matter of time now, her musical voice echoed in Xavier's mind. He cringed at the sound of it. It made him so furiously sick that he could barely stand the sound. He snarled as he held his hands against his ears, doubling over in his chair as if to keep from hearing her.

"Shut up!" Xavier hissed out loud, fighting the urge to rip his hair out.

I'd rather not, she replied sweetly. *You'd never know what was coming to you if it weren't for me.*

"I don't *care*!" Xavier roared as he shoved his arm across his desk, pushing through framed pictures and paperwork. The items went flying. Glass shattered all over the hardwood floor. He wanted to scream as loud as his lungs would allow him, but he knew it was no use. It wouldn't silence her; nothing would.

She was quiet for a few moments but not for very long. *You lied to her. You don't have Ash. Why lie?* she inquired, her voice tainted by heartache. *I swear, I'll never understand you. Every decision you make is a poor one. You may sit on my throne, Xavier, but it's nothing more than an extravagant chair to you. This Realm doesn't bow down to you; they bow down to me.*

"For now," Xavier retorted with a raspy voice, reaching for a glass of water that was no longer there. He frowned, realizing he'd pushed it off.

She'll surface. The Messenger, she assured him. *And when she does, you'll have to return your borrowed throne. Doesn't that bother you?*

Xavier trembled with rage. He wanted it all to end. Her voice, her comments, her constant observations of everything he did daily. She was always in the back of his mind, waiting for the perfect time to strike.

"You have a lot to say for a dead woman," he replied as he rose from his seat, staring out the window to view the Kingdom he'd won. "You're just mad because I was too strong for your magic trick. If it had, you'd have been able to control me completely. Now, you're just a powerless voice."

I wouldn't say I'm powerless. Everyone thinks you're insane because of me, she sighed. *And I'll never leave you. Not for as long as you live. I'll be a ghost that haunts you for the rest of your days, and you deserve it after what you did. How could you turn against my husband, a man who trusted you so entirely—and wrap your children into it all, too? Shame on you. Not to mention the one you left behind.*

Xavier's breath halted, and he shoved his fist through the windowpane. His hand began bleeding from the shards, but he didn't care. The pain had always been a great relief for him. And now that he was Immortal, it felt even better.

"You know nothing," Xavier told her. "You know nothing of my true goals."

What are your goals for taking over Si Realtra? On behalf of your fallen Amorian ancestors? I know all about that, honey, she assured him.

"You don't even know the half of it," Xavier snapped.

If you say so, she sighed once again. *But I've been in your head for almost fifteen years now. I've learned a thing or two.*

"And that matters why?" Xavier scoffed. "It's not like you can run and tell the Elves or the Draconians. Even if they did know, they could do nothing to stop me. I'm too powerful. It's why they haven't bothered to approach me. They spend their time attempting to control the Pandora, which is pointless."

The Pandora won't last much longer. Idona is adapting to your misery, Xavier. Idonians are growing stronger. They're holding their own, she informed him proudly.

"Perhaps I need to remind them who we are then," Xavier suggested as he turned his back on the broken window.

Sure, destroy another village. But you couldn't do any better if you tried.

"Watch me, Meera!" he hissed.

A knock on the door caused the Dark King to startle, and he rushed back to his chair behind the desk. "Come in!" he called, hoping whoever it was hadn't heard the conversation he'd been having.

When Malachai walked in, Xavier rolled his eyes at the sight of him. His son had evolved to be powerful, almost *too* powerful. Sometimes, the Idonians feared him more than they feared the Dark King, and it bothered him. "What is it?" he snapped.

"Our scouts say the Idonian Council has called off the search for Ash VanCamp," Malachai informed him as he approached the desk. For once, a hood didn't shield his face. Xavier's lip curled in disgust at the sight. Malachai looked too much like his mother.

Remembering your wife, are you? How sweet, Meera sneered.

Xavier stiffened in his seat at the sound of her voice, trying his hardest to focus his attention on his son. "Good. It saves me time." He sighed, reclining in his chair. "Is that all you came to tell me?"

"Yep," Malachai replied as he turned around and headed toward the door without a second thought.

"Wait," Xavier growled. "I have a mission for you."

Malachai paused; he turned and arched a dark brow clearly. "What kind of mission?" he inquired as he glanced at his father from over his shoulder.

"The kind where you get to do some stalking," Xavier announced, flashing an all-too-knowing grin. "I want to know who's in charge of the Rebels, and I want them dead. They're getting too ballsy, kidnapping princesses and shit. It's the perfect job for the Prince of Darkness. And while you're looking around, why don't you retrieve the man I want."

Malachai's face twisted as he heard his father's suggestion. "You know he's still too young. He's only sixteen. He can't even use the bow yet," he reminded him, crossing his arms as he turned to face him. "Bringing him now would be pointless."

"If you say so." Xavier glared. "Anyway, I've heard the Rebels reside in Central Idona. So, that's where you should begin."

"Fine," Malachai replied and turned his back on his father. He headed toward the door to his study once again.

"You should remember to kneel before your King, boy," Xavier warned.

The Pandora paused, glancing over his shoulder once more. "No, thank you," he said before disappearing into the hall, slamming the door behind him.

Thankful to escape the Idonian Kingdom for a change, Malachai quickly abandoned his father's side. He craved the sensation of air beneath his wings but knew he should gather a few subordinates in case he ran into trouble. Sighing, the Pandora headed toward the Great Hall within the castle and picked the first three men he saw, one of them being the most loyal man he knew.

"We have a mission," Malachai announced, "We leave immediately."

Alrich had been in the middle of finishing his dinner when his Commander approached. The Pandora frowned and pushed his plate away before he rose from his seat. "Where are we going?"

"Central Idona," Malachai replied blankly.

"For what?" one of the other men inquired.

"To extinguish the Rebels."

"Just the four of us?" The third stared at his creator's back.

When Malachai ceased his walking for a moment, the three men cringed. "Don't forget who I am," he warned before leaving the Great Hall. He quickly transitioned into a hawk, spreading his jet-black wings out before taking flight. Alrich and the others did the same, ensuring they weren't far behind as they began their journey south.

It had been far too long since Malachai had escaped his father's borrowed Kingdom and filled his lungs with mountain air. He was nearly trembling with anticipation as he flew farther away.

Thank the Moons; he rejoiced internally as he dipped downward, setting his sights on the forest below. His gaze fell on a small clearing where a particular cavern still stood—one without a door. The view sent a shiver down his spine as he recalled his near encounter with Lucinda Cross. While he was sure that he could take her down, a part of him didn't entirely want to. She was too powerful, and killing someone like that would be such a waste.

Memories of Lucinda weren't the only memories brought up at the sight of the clearing. He thought of the VanCamp twins as well. Vincent had been raised happily and kindly within the Kingdom of Elves, while the other remained elsewhere. Everyone else was continuing to look for her. Until now, anyway.

There were quite a few reasons why Malachai was deemed different compared to any other Immortal within Idona, and all of Si Realtra. His complex nature was likely the largest, as he resided in a constant fight between good and evil. But another factor that made him different was that Malachai knew precisely where the Missing VanCamp was.

And he wasn't telling anyone.

38

A year had passed since the search for Ash VanCamp had been called off and Abernathy had left Penelope's side. If not for Cedric, she was sure she would have fallen into a hole of depression that even a VanCamp couldn't crawl out of. But just as she was beginning to make peace that she may never see her sister's face, another Red Winter started. And this time, tragedy had struck close to home.

Penelope stood in the Throne Room before a memorial she never thought she'd see. Tears dripped from her eyes, streaming down her cheeks. Not long ago, she'd approached Esmeralda, having yet to see the Realm and its devastating nature. She'd wanted to go to Mayfire. She'd wanted to see what was once known as the *Land of Dragons* in all its glory.

Smoke from the attack on Mayfire still sailed through the air, burning Penelope's lungs every time she stepped outside —a constant reminder of what would never be and the faces she would never see again.

While many of the faces portrayed in the pictures that the Elves had displayed around the Throne Room were unfamiliar to the Princess, there was one person she knew very well. She stood before Alistair's picture, holding back a sob as she held a single red rose close to her heart, the thorns pulled at the black fabric of her dress. A small glass figurine of a black dragon sat within her grasp, gripped so tightly that the sharp edges cut into her flesh.

Penelope stared endlessly at his picture while others stopped at every single one, planting roses before them to pay their respect. She wanted to ensure she never forgot his face or the wide smile he had always worn. His blue eyes had constantly reminded her of the sky, and his sandy hair had always made her think of the pictures she'd seen of Minora's breathtaking beaches. She could still hear his voice in her mind as he told her of the dragons his ancestors would ride.

"Malachai," Penelope hissed under her breath, setting the rose she'd held on top of the pile before Alistair's picture.

"It wasn't him," Cedric said from behind the Princess, though she couldn't bear to look over her shoulder to view him.

"He was still there," Penelope argued. "He still gave the order."

Cedric couldn't argue with her, and instead, took his place beside her. "Alistair wasn't executed with the rest of the Ward family," he told her softly.

"It doesn't matter," she whispered, though she knew Cedric's Elven ears would hear her. "No one ever knows why the Pandora do what they do. Xavier probably got sick of Mayfire not bowing down to him, so he sent his dogs after it. We'll never know why they didn't kill Alistair with his parents and sister. What matters now is getting our vengeance and aiding Mayfire in any way that we can."

"Getting our vengeance?" Cedric asked, raising his brow.

"I swear I'll make this right. One day. I'll do something even the Messenger can't do." Penelope turned to him, finally tearing her eyes away from Alistair's face. "I don't know what yet, but it'll be something big. I'm going to erase all of this hatred and change this Galaxy for the better," she announced as she straightened her back and wiped the tears from her eyes before turning on her heels and gracefully walking out of the Throne Room.

Cedric watched as she disappeared into the hall, finally able to breathe easily. He wondered if he'd ever been as proud of Penelope as he was in that moment, and deep down, he knew she was capable of everything she'd said.

He's figuring it out; Cedric sulked silently as his eyes fell on the picture of Alistair's father, Angus Ward. His stomach twisted into knots at the sight of it, and by the time he glanced toward the vision of Ward's six-year-old daughter, he had to hold his breath to keep himself from hurling and screaming in frustration. *This is all my fault.*

The Prince of Darkness stood before one of his Pandora bases, watching as his men worked to extinguish the red-hot flames threatening to swallow it. He frowned at the sight, having worked too hard to take it over from the Idonian Mortal Army in the first place. Yet, all that work had been for nothing because of the Rebels. Was this their retaliation for Mayfire? Was this *truly* all they could do? *Pathetic.*

He was lucky he'd been so close, or he might not have seen the smoke. But instead, Malachai had given into his eternal, burning, rage without a second thought and used it to his advantage. He slaughtered one Rebel after another, shedding their blood on the icy blanket of snow beneath his feet. He hadn't even bothered to transition. His bare hands had been enough to get the job done.

"So weak," Malachai muttered as he stared down at the only man he'd left alive. He appeared so pitiful as he trembled at the prince's feet, fearing for his life.

Malachai's long, black hair swayed in the chilled winter breeze, his eerie red eyes igniting the night around him. "Say your fucking name." His voice was hauntingly low. Tears sprang to the man's eyes before him.

"Ku-Kurt Wa-Walsh," the man stuttered.

With a glare sharper than knives, Malachai lowered himself so that he was at eye level with the Rebel. "Rumor has it that you're in charge of the Rebels," he hissed the accusation, contemplating what he might do to his soon-to-be victim. "You escaped us during our siege of Solaris. Why make a scene? Why bring attention to yourself?"

"You have it all wrong!" the man rasped, pushing himself backward in the snow to put more distance between the Prince of Darkness and himself. "I'm not the one who started this!"

"Then who is?" Malachai snarled as he rose to his full height, walking toward Walsh, who was trying hard to escape him. Watching a man with two broken legs trying to crawl his way to safety was nothing short of amusing.

"Cedric Chamberlain," Walsh said, his eyes darkened with anger as the name left his lips. "He's the one who started it all. He's the one calling the shots."

Malachai closed the distance between them, his hands quickly transitioned into sharp claws. He didn't waste much time sinking them into Walsh's throat, forcedly ripping his vocal cords out.

"What are you going to do about this?" Alrich asked as he

approached from behind, a worrisome expression upon his scarred face.

Silence ensued between them as Malachai entered a deep state of thought about the matter. Eventually, he released a sigh tainted with annoyance. "I suppose that I'll kill Cedric Chamberlain."

"He's betrothed to Penelope VanCamp," Alrich snapped. "If you do that, there's no way the Immortal Armies won't retaliate. They might not be able to defeat your father without Moonlight, but they could do some serious damage to his forces. And killing you means ending the Pandora."

Malachai turned to face his closest ally. He reached out, placing a hand on Alrich's shoulder in reassurance. "All will be well," he replied. "Besides, let them try. They won't get very far without the Messenger. And the way I see it, you can either slay your way to victory or lay down and die. Your choice."

39

The Elves had always thought they were so protected behind their golden walls. Hadn't they realized the Pandora could shapeshift into anything with a beating heart? Everything from snakes to hawks, to bears and lions. It was unfortunate that dragons were extinct, or else Malachai would have transitioned into one to melt the Kingdom into a puddle of gold at his feet.

Sometimes a stealthy entrance is best; he thought as he flew over the golden walls in the dead of night, his eyes set on the castle. A grin swept across his lips as he recalled all the information his devoted scouts had gathered for him. Thanks to them, the prince knew precisely where to find Lord Cedric Chamberlain.

Malachai had never really been fond of killing nobles, but there were always occasions when he didn't have much of a choice. This was one of those occasions.

After stopping at the armory, where he'd managed to slip past the guards, Malachai stood before the collected weapons and chose his favorite. "I've never used one of *these* before," he mused as he wrapped his fist around a lance. "This should do just fine."

He quickly headed back toward the castle, his eyes fell on a balcony that he knew belonged to his unfortunate target.

Grinning, he transitioned into a raven and landed atop it, where he proceeded to transition into a smaller animal. He shivered with disgust in the form of a centipede, having never been fond of the creatures. They had far too many legs. *How offensive, making me transition into such a tiny, helpless creature,* he hissed as he slipped beneath the doors leading into Cedric's suite.

Malachai paused, surveying the Elf who sat on the bed. It was almost as though Cedric had been expecting him.

"I know you're there," Cedric announced. "I can hear you."

Malachai transitioned into his Mortal form, a smug look on his face as he stuck the lance into the floor, leaning against it for a few moments. "That dagger you're holding won't harm me, you know," he warned.

"It's enchanted." Cedric narrowed his eyes in the prince's direction.

"So?" Malachai shrugged.

"Even you are susceptible to enchanted weapons," Cedric insisted as he rose, clad in a thin t-shirt and sleep pants. He seemed like the scholar Malachai had heard he was and not a warrior. "And I don't miss."

Until now, Malachai laughed internally as he watched the dagger leave Cedric's hand. He snatched the lance from the floor, moving quickly to the side as he watched the blade sail past him, shattering the glass balcony doors before slipping off the ledge and falling into the Kingdom below. "Well, damn." Malachai clicked his tongue. "That's why I always say not to get cocky. Now you've gone and thrown away your only form of defense."

When Cedric surprisingly smirked, Malachai knew he'd been wrong. He hadn't noticed the wand in his hand and cursed under his breath as the Elf whispered a spell he couldn't hear. Ice quickly spread throughout the room, though it was far from ordinary.

"Ryian ice," Malachai growled as he fought to evade the deadly spikes piercing the floor. One punctured his black cloak, just barely grazing his flesh.

The ice settled, covering the entire bedroom. Every surface was slippery and deadly. "That was a good trick, but I imagine it was the last one you had up your sleeve," he said as his grip tightened around the lance. He carefully crossed the room.

"I suppose." Cedric shrugged as he sat back on his bed, silently admitting his defeat. "What do you want with me? My mind? My abilities? Do you wish to use me as a trade for the Amulet?" he rambled. "Or, have you finally come to your senses? The Notorious Six have always appreciated you more than that scum you called a father. Even if you only left three of us alive."

Malachai shook his head, driving the lance into the ice, burying Cedric's words into the depths of his mind. "Nope. I've come to kill you," He revealed. "I told you to back off, but you created the Rebels anyway. You've been leading them all along, and now they're out of control. I cleaned up your mess, and now it's time to finish it.

Cedric grimaced as the words left Malachai's mouth. "It's not what you think," he said, finally beginning to show emotion. However, he didn't appear to be afraid or sad. He wasn't trembling as Walsh had been. Instead, he was infuriated, and Malachai could see something was amiss.

"Feel free to explain," Malachai replied, growing weary of the circumstances. Extinguishing the Rebels had been one long, grueling task, and Cedric was the last of them. Then, he'd be able to breathe for a time.

"I *did* start the rebellion. But not to win Si Realtra for me, but to aid the VanCamps. The Mortals were becoming increasingly frustrated by the Immortal Silence, and I feared they would all turn on Penelope. So, I designed an organization to help prevent that. But when I came back to the Kingdom of Elves, Walsh took matters into his own hands. It was clear they'd all had different goals from the start," Cedric growled, clutching his white duvet cover in his clenched fists. "I severed all my ties with them the second that Hans appeared in the Kingdom of Elves and took Penelope."

Malachai's brow raised, enthralled with the Elf's tale. "You're a man of honor," he told him. "I can appreciate that. But, in the end, Rebel or not, you're still my enemy," he reminded him slowly.

"I'm your father's enemy," Cedric snapped.

The Pandora's eyes widened slightly out of surprise. "What, am I not good enough for you?" he asked, arching a brow.

Cedric's eyes narrowed as he pushed to his feet. "We all know what happened, Malachai. We all know you were forced into it," he said softly. "You can stop this, you know. You don't have to continue."

When Malachai laughed at him, the Elf's nose wrinkled with disgust. "That's sweet. Really," he replied, attempting to will his chuckles away. "But not possible." His smile faded, transitioning into a sneer as he ripped the lance from its place on the floor. Rearing back, Malachai threw the lance straight toward his enemy. Cedric's eyes widened just before the lance pierced his chest and sliced into his heart. The impact sent him flying backward with such force into the headboard.

Blood dripped onto the white duvet as Cedric choked, his life quickly leaving his eyes. Malachai watched until it was over. His heart sank as he surveyed the gruesome job he'd done. *What a waste,* he sighed, his heart crumbling in his chest. His legs quaked, causing him to drop to his knees as he stared up at what he had done.

"Did you think I'd let you go through this ordeal alone?"

Cedric had once said after surprising Malachai in Erim during his journey to become the first Healer to certify in all five Realms. "*Friends are meant to stand by one another. You study and test, and I'll be right there with you.*"

"We can't take any risks," Malachai reminded himself, the emotions welling up within attempting to get the best of him. Footsteps approaching Cedric's suite echoed within his ears. He wasn't really in the mood for killing. He'd had enough of it this evening. Still, he left the bedroom to at least see who it was. The Elves needed to know of the traitor living behind their golden walls.

Malachai stood in the foyer and waited for the suite's front door to open. "No, let me go first," he heard a man say. "No. I need to do this," a woman replied.

The Pandora rolled his eyes, growing impatient. But when the door finally opened, he needed to hide his shock. How idiotic were the Elves to allow Princess Penelope, of all people, to approach him? His lips pursed as he fought the urge to make his way through the castle, breaking each of their necks.

When the princess saw him standing in the foyer with a torn black cloak and clenched fists, her eyes widened with horror. Sometimes, Malachai hated how people looked at him but knew entirely why they did. He was despicable.

"I wouldn't go any farther," he warned softly, nearly ashamed of himself. "You won't like what you see."

A General appeared behind the princess, Rage burning within his golden eyes. Malachai knew this Elf would kill him without a thought and that he didn't have much time, but he needed to attempt to tell them the truth before he made his grand escape. "I don't wish to end any more lives tonight," he announced. "But as long as I'm still here, there are a few things you should probably know."

"Like what?" Penelope snapped at him, entering the foyer further, attempting to restrain herself from attacking him.

"Like the fact that your dear betrothed was the very man pulling the Rebels' strings," Malachai hissed. The princess jumped. Her eyes widened as the caliber of his words sank home. He could see her knees weakening as the truth sent a wave of shock through her. He knew that feeling all too well. "I did you a favor, whether you like it or not. He admitted it."

Tears sprung to Penelope's eyes, and the sight of it made Malachai turn his gaze downward, no longer willing to look at her. He'd suffered similar pain before, and this ordeal brought back unpleasant memories.

"Also, don't stop looking for Ash VanCamp," Malachai directed as he turned to leave, determined to escape out of the shattered balcony doors before the General decided to end his life. He transitioned into a hawk, flying as fast as he could through the rest of the suite and into the Kingdom of Elves. He could hear Penelope's screams as he fought to escape, and his heart sank. He concluded that she must have just found her betrothed pinned to his headboard by a lance Malachai had explicitly chosen for him.

I told you that you wouldn't like what you saw, Malachai internally snapped, fighting back his pained tears.

40

Penelope had been sleeping peacefully in her bed, dreaming of her coming wedding. She'd spent the last year with Mika and Esmeralda planning every detail down to the silverware. She was ready.

Yet, when the Princess awoke in the middle of the night, it was Mika standing at the end of her bed. It was moments like these when Penelope missed Abernathy the most, seeing as there was no way the Elf would have been able to sneak into her private rooms in the middle of the night as long as he was around.

"What is it, Mika? It's the middle of the night," Penelope mumbled, rubbing the sleep from her eyes. She blinked, taking in her surroundings, and frowned. She sat upright and alert in her bed as she realized the terror reflecting upon Mika's face. "What is it?" she repeated as she rolled out from beneath her covers, ready to go wherever Mika sent her.

"I had a nightmare," Mika admitted, biting her lip.

Penelope frowned. "You woke *me* up because you had a nightmare? For goodness sake, Mika, you're twenty-four years old," she chastised.

"No, you don't understand," Mika snapped. "I had a *nightmare*."

Unsure of what she was getting at, Penelope released an annoyed grunt. "Alright, Mika, I'll play your game. What would you like me to do about it?" she inquired.

"We need to summon the guard to this castle. Right now." Mika insisted."We need to summon *everyone*."

Penelope's heart began to quicken in her chest. "Why?" her voice was so soft.

"Malachai."

The news of Cedric's death had shaken Idona to its very core. The future High King had been murdered by Malachai in the middle of the night four days ago, and most of Idona had shown up in the Kingdom of Elves to pay their respects. Valentina found it hard to focus during his memorial, which took place within the Throne Room. Esmeralda wept terribly, which only caused tears to leak from Valentina's eyes.

Penelope stood as silent as could be between her younger brother and Beck, her back as straight as a board and her head held high. While the princess seemed strong on the outside, Valentina wasn't fooled. She knew she was dying on the inside.

After Cedric's death, Xavier had addressed the Realm through the screens scattered across it. His face appeared before them for the first time since he'd begun his Dark reign, and it had been nothing more than chilling. During his address, he'd revealed why Cedric had become a target. He'd been the creator of the Rebels, and he died because of that. Not because the Elf would eventually take Xavier's place.

Valentina didn't believe a word of it, but almost everyone else did. Some people who'd gone on the mission to retrieve Penelope from the Rebels alongside Cedric had recalled how Hans of the Mist had known him. They hadn't thought much of it back then, but it was beginning to make sense.

When the service was over, Valentina planned to retreat to Dracus when Penelope and Vincent intercepted her and Loren. She stared at them, having never been approached by Gideon's children before. Although there were many occasions when the Prophetess had spoken to Penelope, it was rare that the princess looked upon her with the kind eyes she bore now.

"Yes?" Valentina inquired, the sounds of someone approaching from behind flooding her ears. She glanced over her shoulder to see that Marcus and Beck had joined them, and her stomach twisted into knots.

"Take me with you," Penelope requested calmly, although she was attempting to hide her genuine emotions.

Loren's brow rose in surprise. "You want to come to Dracus? Why? This is your home. Esmeralda and Thaddeus aren't a threat anymore," he whispered.

"That may be true," Penelope agreed with him, "but Malachai told Beck and me something before he disappeared. He said not to stop looking for Ash VanCamp."

The Draconian King's eyes narrowed. "So, it's confirmed that she isn't with Xavier." He frowned. "But why would he tell you to search for her?"

"Everyone within Idona fears Malachai," Beck explained from behind the King. "But at the same time, no one understands him. So it's best we not read too much into it. We must look for her, and we can't do that from here."

"Well, obviously, *you* can't come to Dracus, Beck. You're the Elven general," Valentina reminded him. "But Penelope, I've seen that you'll spend some time with us."

"What's going on?" Lucinda's voice startled the small group. She stared at them all, clad in black instead of her usual green. Her amber eyes were filled with unspoken accusations. "You all look like you're up to something shady, and I want in."

"Great." Penelope beamed. "We're going to find my sister. But, first, I need you to summon Abernathy to Dracus."

Lucinda's face fell as her eyes drifted toward the marble floors of the hall. "I can't do that," she replied sadly. "After Thaddeus cast him out, Abernathy never returned to the league. He disappeared."

"But we need him," Vincent insisted. "He's no longer Penelope's Guardian, which means he can go out into Idona and work with Marcus."

"It's just impossible," Lucinda informed him, finally meeting his gaze. "I'll keep looking for him. But for now, you'll all have to do without him."

Penelope sulked at her words, and Valentina understood why. After losing Cedric, she craved the friend she knew she had in the Sorcerer. "Thaddeus and Esmeralda won't like you coming to Dracus with us. They're going to betroth you to someone again," she reminded her, knowing it was too soon to bring such a thing up.

"I'm nearly nineteen," Penelope snapped. "They can get mad at me all they want, but I have every right to explore the Realm I'll eventually rule."

"Alright." Loren held up a hand, hoping to stop her from speaking before she grew too angry. "You may come back with me. We'll say you just need a break from the Kingdom of Elves after all that's happened," he assured her, watching as she breathed a sigh of relief. "And I'll reinstate the search for Ash. Privately. No one else can know about this other than the people standing here."

"Well, we're going to need Grant," Marcus added softly.

Loren huffed, giving the newly appointed Mentor a dirty look. "And Grant."

Thaddeus and Esmeralda had allowed Penelope to spend a year within Dracus, and she'd thoroughly enjoyed her time there. For the first time, she'd felt less like a princess and more like an average person. The Draconians had treated her with respect, and she'd spent nearly every day in the Communications Center with Grant as they helped aid Marcus out in the field.

Axel had taken up the position of temporary Mentor while Marcus was away, but since he'd returned, he took to his usual duties as the Draconian General. Penelope had barely been able to see Marcus for a few moments before being forced to return to the Kingdom of Elves. He'd been kind enough to prepare her dinner, and she'd been in awe at how wonderful a cook her mother's former Guardian truly was.

The moment Penelope passed through the portals, entering the Kingdom of Elves for the first time in twelve months, a hole in her heart appeared. She missed Grant, Marcus, and even Valentina. But mostly, she missed Loren. He'd been so different than Thaddeus in the best of ways. He cared for her, and it showed through how he looked in her direction or how he delivered her lunch daily while she worked with Grant.

The second Penelope stepped out of the Portal Room and into the hall, her heart seemed to break again. Thoughts of Cedric flooded her mind, bringing tears to her eyes as her hand rose to her chest. Losing him had been like losing a part of herself, and although it was clear that not everything

Cedric had said had been true, she was having a difficult time living without him.

The first thing Penelope had to do was report to Thaddeus and Esmeralda, and she'd taken her time doing it. She'd strolled toward the Royal Corridor, watching as the sun began to set through the windows that lined the grand halls.

She forced her gaze to remain on their door at the very end of the hall, knowing she was passing Cedric's former suite.

Cedric was a traitor; Penelope fought to remind herself as she let herself into her adoptive parents' suite. They'd been waiting for her, both seated in the Tea Room with none other than Mika and Aveo.

"Where's Beck?" Penelope asked, frowning at the sight of the Commander she'd never been fond of.

"He's training with Vincent," Mika announced happily, wrapping Penelope in a warm embrace.

Confused, Penelope pulled away and glared at Aveo. "I thought you were in charge of that." She tried her best not to snap.

"Not today," Aveo replied, a wide smile upon his usually scowling face. He'd peaked, no longer aging as an Immortal. Instead, his long golden hair, sun-kissed flesh, and brass-colored eyes seemed more radiant than when Penelope had seen him last. But no matter how hard the princess tried not to, she would always despise him.

"His presence was requested," Esmeralda announced with a mischievous smile. "We have a surprise for you."

Two-year-old Trinity sat happily on her father's lap, waving at Penelope as she popped a piece of cucumber into her mouth. Her face twisted a bit before she decided that she liked it and chose another piece to eat. Penelope chuckled at the sight, having always been fond of children.

"Would you focus?" Mika snapped.

Penelope frowned, giving Esmeralda the attention she so clearly craved. "What's the surprise?"

"Aveo will be your new betrothed. Isn't that wonderful?" Esmeralda fanned herself, dreaming of their wedding day.

Bile quickly crept up Penelope's throat. She swallowed hard, willing it away, though she wished she could bear the embarrassment of unleashing it all over their white carpet. Then, at least, she'd be excused. "I don't want to marry Aveo," she informed them, crossing her arms.

"You're the heir to the Idonian throne and a noble within this Realm. The fact that you're now twenty and haven't married is absurd," Thaddeus insisted. "We've allowed you the time to grieve Cedric, but the show must go on. Aveo is a Callaway. Their family is known throughout history for being the most respected, powerful Elves. He's an excellent match for you."

Penelope shook her head, disagreeing with her adoptive father entirely. "You chose Cedric because you knew we were fond of each other," she reminded him. "I despise Aveo, and that's a well-known fact."

"What's done is done," Esmeralda snapped. "You'll marry him at the beginning of Fall Solstice."

When Penelope turned her back on the royals, she knew she'd find a way out of it. She would choose a husband, knowing well what they were up to. The Callaway family had remained by the Elven throne's side since establishing order nearly two millennia ago, and it was no secret that Aveo was in Thaddeus's pocket.

Penelope wouldn't stand for it. She wouldn't be manipulated. She was an adult and no longer the responsibility of anyone but herself. She was mere years away from becoming the High Queen of Si Realtra. She could feel it in her bones.

"Don't go too far, dear. We have a wedding to plan!"

Esmeralda called after Penelope as she slammed the front door to their suite.

"The Sectra holder controls everything that happens within Idona. They can stop this," Penelope insisted as she marched toward her suite, her skirts swaying furiously along with her movements. "Where the hell are you, Ash?"

41

Throughout his life, Vincent had come across too many unanswered questions. He'd lived in fear, wondering how his mother's use of Magic during his birth would affect him. And if that weren't bad enough, he'd encountered many sleepless nights as he fought to figure out where the Missing VanCamp could be hiding.

Day after day, Vincent had gone about his everyday life while staring at a secret map in his room. One that Grant had created for him. He ran his finger along a hidden switch beneath his desk and watched as the invisible screen displayed the map. Red dots covered it almost completely. Every place Marcus had searched for Ash was marked, and he'd been everywhere.

Everywhere but one single place.

"It doesn't exist," Vincent insisted, throwing his pack over his shoulder. At least one of his questions had been answered, and even though his eighteenth birthday was still a few weeks off, he'd transitioned into an Elf just as Cedric had predicted.

Vincent knew Marcus and Cedric had used one of Dracus's drones to fly over the Strip's Swirl, revealing no village hidden within its center; he couldn't get the riddle out of his mind. "Deep within the mountains, where no one goes, sits a village that no one knows," he recited as he flipped the switch, causing the map to disappear again.

His eyes fell on a pile of folders and notes on his desk. Cedric had worked incredibly hard to try to find Ash. He'd been relieved when he managed to sneak into the Elf's suite before the royals had cleaned it out so that he could retrieve all of his records.

Something within Vincent told him that the answer to where the Missing VanCamp was located was written on the pages of Cedric's notes, but he'd never found anything that made any sense. His breath hitched slightly when he noticed an envelope he'd never seen before sticking out of the back of one of the folders.

Aries of the Black Winged Fae had signed the envelope, and it appeared that Cedric had never opened it. "He must have received it right before he... died." Vincent stared in wonder at it. And then, without a second thought, he tore the envelope out and grasped the paper hiding within, pulling it gently until he could see what was written.

"The hatch exits." Vincent's mouth flew open as his heart began to race. "There were supposed to be ten, but eleven were written here. These are their coordinates." His heart felt like it would fly out of his chest as he flicked the map back on, finding the coordinates to the eleventh hatch exit within seconds. "No way."

Vincent shut the map back off, clutching the paper as he barreled out of his suite. Once in the hall, he nearly ran into his older sister, who snarled at him in response. "What the hell, Vincent?" she snapped.

"Look." Vincent shoved the paper in her face. "I found an unopened envelope from the Fae in Cedric's files," he explained. "There are *eleven* exits, not ten."

"What?" Penelope shrieked. "Where are those coordinates?"

"The Hidden Village," Vincent told her, watching the color drain from her face. "It's real. Cedric and Marcus must have missed something. I'm going to Dracus right now to talk to Loren."

"You're not cleared for the field yet!" Penelope called after him. "Thaddeus and Esmeralda will have your head!" she warned.

"Thaddeus and Esmeralda can go fuck themselves!" Vincent snapped from over his shoulder. "I'm going to get the Missing VanCamp!"

Loren stared at the map in awe, knowing very well they'd once missed something. "I could assemble a team, and we could storm the village," he suggested, watching Benjamin and Grant shake their heads.

"We need to be subtle," Benjamin told him. "Send Vincent as a scout first. Then, let him survey, and if he spots her, we'll send the entire damn army if we have to."

Loren couldn't disagree with this. He turned to Vincent, who was nearly trembling with anticipation. Thaddeus and Esmeralda were furious with him for breaking into their Portal Room and escaping to Dracus without explanation. He'd avoided all their video conference requests and responded to none of the numerous scrolls they'd sent. They would be at his throat in seconds if they knew what he was about to allow Vincent to do.

"You look pretty good in a Draconian uniform for an Elf." Valentina patted the young Prince's shoulder. "Just make sure you're careful. The snow has begun to fall. We don't know if the Pandora know about this village," she reminded him slowly.

"Any idea why Marcus missed it yet?" Benjamin asked, chuckling as he handed Vincent the pack he'd prepared.

"I'm guessing there's an invisible barrier. A powerful Witch or Sorceress must have put it there at some point to keep it hidden," Vincent explained. "It's the only explanation."

Loren nodded, wondering if this barrier would become a problem. "Go and update us regularly. Just make sure Marcus doesn't see you leave. He'll have my head for letting you leave this Kingdom without backup."

Vincent nodded and turned to leave the Communications Center. "It'll take me a week to get there from here," he reminded the Draconian King. "Don't worry, I won't die on this mission. And the next time I see you, I'll have brought my sister home."

42

It had been nearly three weeks since Vincent had left, and Penelope hadn't heard from him. It was driving her mad, but he knew that the Elves had all of her forms of communication tapped. They watched for him and wouldn't stop until he was brought back behind the Golden Walls.

At one point, Thaddeus attempted to go to Dracus, but when he'd gone to the Portal Room, he'd found that King Loren had shut down all portals leading to and from the Draconian Kingdom. He'd been infuriated, screaming so loudly that the entire castle could hear him.

Dessa was in pieces without Vincent, but the truth was, she'd grown ill. She'd spent her last few days begging for him, and Penelope held her hand as her last breaths left her lungs. They'd buried her nearby to Cedric, and the two were now laughing musically in the afterlife. Penelope smiled at the thought, though her cheeks were still wet with tears as she sat before the screen above Vincent's desk.

Yesterday, the entire Realm had been shaken due to a dragon sighting. The minds of Idonians were whirling because one had managed to survive and had a Rider as well.

Penelope couldn't stop smiling at the idea that dragons would finally take to the skies of Idona once again.

Penelope was happy to focus on thoughts of dragons instead of thinking about today's date. She knew the two Kingdoms had reached their deadline. It was Vincent and Ash's eighteenth birthday, and the Sectra would go to Mika as soon as the ceremony could be planned. It wasn't that Penelope didn't trust her adoptive sister; it was just that she knew her loyalties lay with her parents.

When a call began to come through, Penelope was shocked. She'd been under the impression that the screen had only been a map, but clearly, she'd been wrong. So she answered it, knowing it was likely a call from Dracus.

"Penelope!" Grant grinned at the sight of her, clearly out of breath. "You're not going to believe this."

The Princess's brow raised, wondering what he might be referring to. "If it's about the dragon sighting, I already know. Beck is considering looking for the Rider," she informed him, knowing very well that a dragon would come in handy when fighting the Pandora. "It seems Red Winters might have finally gotten easier." She smiled back at him, reclining in her chair.

"That's not why I'm calling." Benjamin shoved Grant out of the way, and Penelope smirked at the sight of him. He also appeared to be out of breath, and the Princess couldn't help wondering what they'd been up to over in Dracus. "Are you sitting?"

She gestured to the chair she was comfortable within, arching a brow. "Obviously," she retorted with a snort. "Why?"

"Because the Dragon Rider, the Missing VanCamp, and the Messenger were all found," Benjamin announced.

Penelope felt as if her world had begun to spin around her as she slowly rose from her seat, her heart racing wildly within her chest. Was it true? Had Vincent indeed retrieved the Missing VanCamp? And for the Messenger and the Dragon Rider to show up in Dracus simultaneously? The entire thing was beyond bewildering. It was fate.

"I'm on my way," Penelope told him, smiling as she shut off the screen and ran to pack her things. "I hope you're ready, Xavier because your time is up. My throne was never stolen. It was simply borrowed, and the time has come for you to return it."

To be continued...

And now, here's a sneak peek into The Messenger, book two in The Five Realm Chronicles.

THE FIVE REALMS
THE MESSENGER
Volume 2

M.L DARLOW

PROLOGUE

Cedric Chamberlain was a chaser of legends. There was nothing he loved more than to solve their mysteries and indulge in their history. For years, before the War began, he'd travel throughout all of Si Realtra and learn everything there was to know about each of the Five Realms.

Now, Dark times had fallen upon Idona. And the High King had shut the Galactic Gates without warning. Since then, matters had only gotten worse, and Cedric could see the Realm he'd always called home falling apart.

The Mortals and Immortals throughout Idona were now at odds as everyone waited for the prophesied Messenger to surface. At first, Cedric hadn't believed that a single person would be enough to slay the Dark King and end the war. He couldn't fathom the Immortal Kingdom's reason for waiting, and not striking back. He didn't understand why it was that the different Kingdoms and communities through Idona couldn't band together and take the Idonian Kingdom back.

When Cedric had learned of a legend in Idona, it was only natural that he found it's truth. Perhaps if he approached the Sovereign's Scepter, he might be able to break the spell surrounding it. He did happen to have a vast knowledge of spells, and had evolved to be bit of a novice Sorcerer himself. And if he could break the spell, he'd be able to end the Immortal Silence, and unite the Realm. He'd be able to slay Xavier and return Idona to it's peaceful state.

All Cedric wanted was to keep his Realm from falling apart at the seams, therefore he braved the Forest of Fools. He'd skittered around it's plethora of deadly traps until he'd found the very cavern the legend spoke of. It had taken him four days worth of searching and avoiding death at the same time. But he'd finally made it.

The Elf had faced a whirlwind of emotions as he'd traveled through the complicated cavern. Yet, after traveling beneath water and through tunnels nearly too small for him to fit through, he encountered a beast placed there by the Dark King himself. Cedric's only saving grace had been his wand, and after using the Incepstasis spell to keep it from moving, he approached the scepter with a dagger in hand.

The blade bit at his palm as he dragged it agross. His deep red blood swam from the wound and he pressed it to the earth surrounding the Scepter and waited. Nothing occurred. The ground didn't tremble, as the legend said it would. The Scepter remained chained to the earth around it. Imprisoned.

Cedric had failed. He would not be able to break the spell and wield the weapon. He would not be able to slay the Dark

King and return Idona to its peaceful state. He would not be the one to end the Dark War.

Even though it was hopeless, Cedric wrapped his bloodied grip around the Scepter and offered a silent prayer to the Moons. If he could not break the spell himself and unify the citizens of Idona, he asked that they show him another way. He would not sit around and wait. And as he removed his hands from the ancient weapon and turned his back on the cavern, he began to devise a plan. He would find a way to keep the peace between the Immortals and Mortals by gathering as many people as he could find, and anyone that would listen to what he had to say. Together they would rebel against Xavier's Dark reign.

1

Eliza Snow never thought she'd see the day the Idonian Kingdom fell. But now, she could smell it burning. Ash and smoke sailed through the wind, surrounding her as she left the comfort of her cottage. As a Mortal, Eliza didn't share the impeccable vision of an Elf. But, she knew all that remained of the Kingdom was nothing more than a glowing red ember in the distance, smothering beneath a cold winter's night.

And though the night had begun like any other, Eliza couldn't shake the fear consuming her since the Red Winter began a fortnight ago. She couldn't rid herself of the feeling that this year, the Pandora's vicious nature would change the course of history. And now, with tears beginning to prick her icy blue eyes, Eliza needed to accept the fact that she'd been right.

News of the High Queen's death had traveled across the main Realm as quickly as wildfire ripped through dry brush in the fourth Realm, Zerin. By midnight, all of Idona had learned of what had occured in the Idonian Kingdom, and that a Dark King now sat on Si Realtra's High Throne.

Once Eliza had learned of the Queen's demise, she knew any chance of resting had escaped her. Now, she found herself out in the cold with her bow clutched tightly in her grip and her quiver fastned at her thigh. A chill crept down

Eliza's spine as the frigid air bit at her exposed face, as she watched her icy breath curl in tendrils before disappearing. She sucked in a deep breath and pushed forward, now leaving the village of Crane behind.

Throughout her youth, during a time where Idonians hadn't needed to fear what lurked in the shadows of night, Eliza would often find herself in the mountains that surrounded Crane. When her thoughts began to spin wildly in her mind, the views from the East Cliff, or a hunt never failed to calm her. Now, dark times had fallen upon Idona. Midnight hunts and breathtaking views were a thing of the past. Yet tonight, Eliza knew there would be no Pandora in sight.

Eliza's eyes fell on the forest trail leading up to the mountains that surrounded the Hidden village. So far, winter solstice had made quick work of covering the trail in sheets of icy snow, but she would still be able to find her way using the village symbol carved into the trees, marking the safest route for villagers.

For centuries, Crane had gone unnoticed. While it had been the inspiration for songs, riddles and legends, very few dared to seek it out. Nestled within the center of Idona's longest mountain range, The Strip, it was nearly impossible to get to. Idonians had long referred to the Strip's center as its swirl because of its peculiar shape. There are many stories about the Strip's intriguing center, little do the storytellers know of the people who reside there.

Eliza, herself, was only aware of two occasions where strangers crossed through its deadly borders. And while deadly they may be, those borders were no match for the Pandora. For the first time since Crane had been built in secret, the villagers lay awake at night, waiting for their turn to die.

Four years ago, when the Pandora first attacked the

hidden village, Eliza had lost her husband, Erick. She could still feel his warm blood seeping through her fingers, staining the snow around his lifeless body. Her breath hitched as she endured the painful memory. Tears that she had been fighting to hold back sprung from her eyes and rolled down her cheeks. Her hands instinctively reached to wipe them away before they froze in the winter air. Eliza's breath became ragged as she fought to calm herself. She pulled in a series of deep breaths, willing the memory away.

On this night, on the seventh day of the second week of Winter Solstice in the year one thousand and thirty one, the Idonian Kingdom has fallen to the proclaimed Dark King, Xavier.

The voice of Crane's Justice Keeper, Drake Waters, rang in Eliza's mind as she maneuvered through the complicated mountain terrain, the snow crunching beneath her boots. "May the High Queen rest in peace," she muttered to herself as her eyes fell on lights flickering off in the distance, casting a warm glow upon the freezing forest.

The McBride Estate.

Eliza's lips curled into a smile as she saw it, knowing her dearest friend lived within.

Right now, Claire was likely fast asleep, nearly full term with her third son. However, she could see that she wasn't the only one tormented by today's events.

Pat McBride kicked at chunks of ice as he made his way down the stone path leading away from the miraculous cabin-like mansion that he had built for himself. It was unlike any cabin Eliza had ever seen, forged from logs that had once belonged to the trees that covered the plot he'd built his home upon. The path led up to the large front porch where two rocking chairs swayed in the harsh winter winds. A candle flickered in each window throughout all three stories, which only made the magnificent estate seem even more inviting. And to think it had all been built by one man.

Eliza could recall when she'd first met Pat, the day he'd appeared in Crane. Like many, she'd feared him at first. Who was he? Where had he come from? But, soon enough, Drake had begun to trust the stranger, and Claire had fallen deeply in love with his dark chocolate locks and sparkling blue eyes, which meant Eliza had no choice but to put up with him after all.

After he'd finished building his cabin, Pat planted crops that he donated to the village, providing for tables that were often lacking. He became a living legend within Crane, the first man to successfully grow anything so deep into the mountains. People had often whispered that he'd put magic in the soil, and it was thought that he was a Sorcerer who'd gone rogue. But, despite all of the curiosity and rumors surrounding Pat McBride, it wasn't long before every villager depended upon him for fresh fruits and vegetables. He delivered a bounty every harvest season that would last the village through the Red Winter. Without him, Eliza was sure that many villagers would have starved since the Dark War began.

"You shouldn't be out here alone," Pat chastised once he caught sight of her, standing at the end of his pathway.

"Something tells me the Pandora are occupied this evening," Eliza replied, her face twisting into a scowl as he arrived before her. "And where do you think you're going? Claire could go into labor any minute," she groused, using the long end of her bow to poke him square in the chest.

"Turn that accusing stare of yours in a different direction, " Pat sneered as he pushed her bow aside and passed her, heading off into the forest.

Eliza huffed, a cloud of icy tendrils erupting into the air

before her. "I was going to go on a hunt," she explained as she turned to follow him.

"At three in the morning?" Pat snorted, looking over his shoulder to give her a long disbelieving look.

"If I wait until sunrise, I'll have to compete with everyone else. Besides, we all know now that Xavier took over the Idonian Kingdom, nothing will come out of it. Witherow will no longer be able to assist us. We'll have to survive off of your farm, and hunt for protein," Eliza began to rant, her pulse beginning to quicken, pounding in her ears. The future was uncertain, and the idea of what might happen now that the Idonian Kingdom was lost led her stomach to churn. "Starvation is not a part of my five year plan."

Pat nodded slowly as he ceased his walking, turning around to face her completely. Eliza's lips pulled down into a frown as she took in Pat's expression. He looked at her the way he always did, with a single lifted brow and a crooked smile that made her feel daft.

Eliza found herself fighting the urge to load her bow and mount him above her fireplace.

"You're lucky Claire loves you so much," he teased, his lips spreading out into the smirk that always caused the blood to boil in her veins. "It just so happens that I'm an expert at tracking at night. Truth be told, I saw a deer big enough to last you all winter around sundown."

Eliza clenched her jaw, her glare lingering upon him for a few more moments as she attempted to figure out if he was luring her into some sort of embarrassing trap. "Are you messing with me?" she asked.

"Would I do such a thing?" Pat scoffed, raising a hand to his chest, fawning offense before resuming his walk.

"If you are, I'll tell Claire," Eliza hissed the warning as she followed.

"I'm not afraid of many things," Pat replied softly as he

broke away from the forest trail, moving effortlessly through mounds of thick snow. "But I'm afraid of my wife."

Eliza gripped the freezing bark of trees as she worked to keep her balance, her eyes like daggers upon Pat's back. How could he move so easily? Maybe he's a Sorcerer after all, she mused.

After a while, Eliza began to realize that they were approaching uncharted territory. Her chest became tight as a cold sweat formed along her brow. None of the trees were marked, and if she were alone, she wasn't sure that she'd be able to find her way back. She'd been born and raised in Crane, but she'd never left its borders. And now, she was sure Pat had led her past them.

"Where are we going? I thought you said we were tracking a deer," Eliza asked, fighting to hide the fear quivering in her voice. She could feel her stomach beginning to twist into knots as she silently gave into the suspicion that he may have been lying after all.

"I just need to check something," Pat admitted. "Don't worry, I'll make sure you don't starve."

Eliza bit her lip hard enough to draw blood as she surveyed her surroundings. Rays of Moonlight seeped through the forest canopy, illuminating the snow around her. The beauty seemed surreal, as if it might be an illusion. She doubted she'd ever seen anything quite so alluring in all her life.

The sound of a baby's cry pierced through the silence, jolting Eliza where she stood. Her heart hammered against her rib cage as her gaze darted to Pat. He was already running, having abandoned her at speeds so impeccable that her eyes bulged.

Frozen in both fear and shock, Eliza stared for a moment at the spot he'd just been standing before she rushed after him. She wasn't able to run nearly as fast as he could, and the only clue as to which direction he'd gone in were his footprints in the snow. When she finally caught up to him, the sight set before her caused her to stop dead in her tracks. She swallowed against bile creeping up her throat, fearing she might wretch all over the sparkling white snow.

A newborn baby shivered in Pat's arms. Its flesh was pale and bore blue hue. She was shocked that it hadn't frozen to death in temperatures so frigid. "How?" Eliza heard herself ask, tears of both rage and devastation beginning to swarm her vision. "Who would leave a baby here?"

Pat's lips formed a hard as he remained silent. He sucked in a breath, appearing to know exactly what to do next. His jaw set, his demeanor grae as he unzipped his jacket and moved to unbutton his flannel shirt. As he brought the baby to his bare chest, tears began to stream from his eyes. "Come here," he told Eliza, trembling as he turned to face her.

Eliza didn't hesitate. She approached him, unsure of what to do. An intense shiver ran through her, rattling her bones as she pulled in a shaky breath. She fought to keep her emotions at bay, her mind still whirling from what they'd discovered. "I don't see any other footprints but ours," she said softly. "How did it get here?"

"Grab a hold of me," Pat ordered.

Wrinkling her brow, Eliza reached out and placed a gentle hand upon his shoulder. He stiffened beneath her touch, his eyes squinting shut as he cursed under his breath.

"Hold on tight, and tell no one of what we're about to do," Pat hissed. Eliza gripped the cloth of his jacket harder within her grasp.

Within a matter of seconds, Eliza found herself standing in the foyer of the Mcbride estate. A warm fire crackled nearby, causing her eyes to widen and her mouth to fall open. No words escaped her lips as she turned to stare at the man beside her.

"Tell no one," he repeated before rushing toward the fire. He dropped to his knees, continuing to hold the baby tightly to his chest as he rocked back and forth. She could hear him whispering. Praying perhaps.

Pat was painful to watch as he worked to warm the baby. The blue tint began to fade from it's complexion, and Eliza couldn't help but weep with joy once yet another loud cry escaped its lungs. And then another. And another. Before long, small footsteps could be heard coming down the stairs. Eliza looked over her shoulder, only to find Claire and Pat's eldest child staring back at her.

"Did mama have the baby?" Four-year old Quinn asked with wide cerulean eyes.

"No, lovely," Eliza explained softly. "Go back up to bed. Right now, your father and I need to take care of something."

It was abundantly clear that Quinn was too curious about what was happening to want to go back to bed, but even still, he obeyed. Sticking out his lower lip, Quinn lowered his chin to his chest and slouched his shoulders before turning his back on Eliza, beginning his climb back up the stairwell.

Eliza sighed as she turned her gaze back toward Pat, just in time to witness a note falling from the wool wrapped around the baby's small frame. She gasped, lifting her hands to cover her mouth. Her heart thrummed harder in her chest. "Pat!" she squealed, rushing to grab it as it grazed the fire. Her fingers wrapped around the parchment and she was quick to blow out the small flame blooming on the corner of the letter.

Pat's complexion paled, and the baby's cries faded into soft whimpers in his arms "What does it say?" he croaked, his eyes darting between Eliza and the baby.

Eliza gently opened the letter, praying that the fire hadn't burned away any of the script written upon it. She sighed as relief washed over her. The ink was untouched..

"To my darling, Ash," Eliza began, her heart breaking as she realized that this letter was from a mother to her infant daughter. A letter that explained everything. A lump formed in Eliza's throat as she prepared for the words she was about to read. Tears spilled from her eyes as she read the letter's contents, her heart breaking for the baby in Pat's arms and the late High Queen who had birthed her.

Eliza's hand trembled as the letter fell from her grasp, landing delicately on the floor beside her. She was sure she'd never be able to speak again. She looked toward Pat and found him staring down into the eyes of the baby, with tears welling up inside his own.

"S-she's a VanCamp," Eliza reasped. "We need to take her to the Elves.".

"No," Pat replied. "We can protect her. The Elves have never been trusted. How can we trust them now? Besides, she wasn't directed to go to the Elves. It wasn't what Meera wanted. Even so, if we were to bring her to Dracus, she'd live with a target on her back. That is no life for a child."

It was very clear to Eliza that Pat was struggling with the idea of how this baby would live if they were to turn her over. It led her to believe that it was possible he may have lived through a similar childhood. The idea of it sent a chill down her spine that caused her to shiver in front of the fire.

"We?" Eliza's stomach began to twist.

"You," Pat clarified. "You always wanted a baby, didn't you?"

"But they'll be looking for her."

"Yes, they will. But, they'll never find her here," Pat whispered, running one of his fingers along the VanCamp's soft, pink cheek. "And if they do, We'll make sure she's strong enough to face them all."

ABOUT THE AUTHOR

M.L Darlow was whisked away at the sparky age of seventeen and embarked on a magical journey called The Five Realm Chronicles which came to light seven years later in 2019. Since then, she has continued her mission and pursued A Wicked Fairytale along the way.

M. L Darlow plans to take The Five Realm Chronicles as far as she can, with no end in sight.

www.ingramcontent.com/pod-product-compliance
Lightning Source LLC
Chambersburg PA
CBHW070638310726
48982CB00001B/316

* 9 7 8 1 7 3 5 6 1 6 7 7 3 *